Celebrations
WITH
JAKE AND JOE

Celebrations
WITH
JAKE AND JOE

ROGER W. BUENGER

3RB ENTERPRISES, LLC

This book is a work of historical fiction. The characters, places, and events are the creations of the author's imagination. Any similarity to actual persons living or deceased is wholly coincidental. Furthermore, any and all references to real persons living or deceased, places, or actual events are done fictitiously.

Published by
3RB Enterprises, LLC
Florissant, MO 63034

Book design by Damonza.com

ISBN 978-0-9903080-5-8 (Paperback)
ISBN 978-0-9903080-6-5 (Hardcover)
ISBN 978-0-9903080-4-1 (Kindle)
ISBN 978-0-9903080-7-2 (ePub)

Printed in the United States of America

First Edition: January 2016

This book is dedicated to my family, fans, friends, and followers. In 2013, when I began writing Meetings with Jake and Joe, I had a story in my head, a life-long dream to become a successful published author, and no clue how to go about it. Thanks to your incredible support, I am not only achieving that goal but am now embarking on a new journey. Due to the overwhelmingly positive reception that my debut novel has received, I felt I had no choice but to answer my readers call for more to the story of Henry Engel. I am humbled and grateful for the outpouring of affection for these characters. Henry, Millie, and Joe are family to me. I am thrilled to find that they are important to you as well. This novel becomes the second book in what is now the Jake and Joe series. Who knows where it all goes from here? However, because of you, their story continues.

THANK YOU from the bottom of my heart for your incredible and generous support.

TABLE OF CONTENTS

CHAPTER 1

Finding Peace

"MY GOD, HENRY, are you serious? Of course I have a minute!" George exclaimed, stunned by the news. "So tell me, how did it go?"

"You know, it was really good. *Really good.*" Henry added extra emphasis on the repeated phrase as he recalled how it had felt to release feelings he had concealed deep inside himself for decades. He hadn't realized to what extent he had been affected by the years of suppressed hurt and anger but now understood that it had been like poison in his system. Henry's confession to Mary and the subsequent absolution he had received had lifted a terrible burden from him and given him a profound sense of peace.

"Honestly George, it was like *she was right there.* I could *feel* her. I know that doesn't make sense but... Does that seem crazy to you?"

"Absolutely not. I can feel Claire's presence all of the time," George answered without hesitation, attempting to comfort him. "When I walk into a room, when I smell something that reminds me of her, when I hear a song she liked... she's there. I swear to you, Henry, sometimes when I am lying in bed, I can feel her near me. Her touch, her breath. Heck, I talk to her all of the time. No, I don't think you're crazy at all." George's voice trailed off as the recollections of his wife briefly made him feel a bit melancholy. He quickly recovered.

"Henry, I'm really happy you did that. I truly am. I've been hoping that you'd go and clear the air with Mary and that it would be a really good thing for you," George offered with genuine joy in his voice. "I am eternally grateful that even though the good Lord took Claire, He gave me the chance to talk everything out with her. Nothing was left unsaid. Not one word, not an emotion. It has given me such a sense of peace about it all, and I wanted you to have that too."

"What can I say, George? You were right. I was kind of nervous this morning before I went, but I just knew that I needed to do it. After our talk yesterday, realizing what I'd done… It was a pretty tough night," Henry confessed.

"I'm sorry about that. I didn't mean to upset you. I just thought you needed to hear the truth. I know what kind of man you are, and I knew that if you…"

Henry interrupted before George could finish. "Don't apologize. You were exactly right to tell me, and I'm glad that you did. I wish I hadn't been so hard-headed all these years… Maybe things would have turned out differently. Anyway, that's certainly water under the bridge at this point. The bottom line is that I got the chance to make things right with you and Mary, and it feels terrific."

Joe sashayed into the room and gently rubbed her body against Henry's leg as she moved past him toward the fireplace. The contact diverted his attention from the conversation long enough to notice her, and it brought a smile to his face.

With so much ground gained in such a short time, George

couldn't resist the opportunity to ask about the remaining *elephant in the room.*

"So, my friend, where does all of this leave you with Bill?" he asked with mild reservation. The words had barely passed over his lips before he began to regret saying them. He was hoping he hadn't just ruined the moment by touching on a topic that he knew was a potential land mine.

"Funny you should ask," Henry replied with a light degree of sarcasm. "Got another letter right here from him," he said as he glanced over at the tri-folded single sheet of paper that was on the table beside him.

"No kidding? And?" George asked anxiously, intrigued by Henry's answer.

"Well, I finally decided to open this one, just to see what the hell he had to say."

George couldn't believe his ears. This was a major shift in policy for Henry, and he knew it. He was aware that Henry had been discarding these letters from Bill for years without ever having read one. He had often wondered why Bill seemed to be a special focal point of Henry's wrath but during the time following their own reconciliation had never pursued the subject with him. In light of recent events, it made little sense to him why Henry wouldn't settle things with his brother as well and move forward on all fronts. However, rather than interject something at this point and break Henry's momentum, he stayed mute and waited, hoping to learn the details of what the letter said.

"So… I read it. Oh sure, he feels bad all right. Wants to talk. Yeah, I bet he does. Well, I'm not interested." Henry's tone was firm and definite, as if he was dismissing an annoying intrusion from a telemarketer. Though he had made amends with George and Mary, his feelings toward Bill were hard and unmoved.

With the aforementioned two, *he* had been mistaken and had dealt with them harshly based on flawed decisions derived from imperfect and inaccurate information. In short, Henry had been totally wrong and had directly caused them both much pain. Worst of all, he knew it. As for Bill, his brother had betrayed him in a way unimaginable and to Henry that was an unforgivable offense. No matter how much he had changed, or indeed was still changing, he had not evolved enough to see that perhaps one man's sin was not necessarily worse than another's.

George could sense the resolve in Henry's voice and decided it was best to drop the matter completely. It was a great day and not one to be ruined by greed for more. They could cross that bridge at another time. The men shared a lengthy and enjoyable conversation as Henry explained in detail how the events of the morning had transpired while George listened intently. It was rewarding for him to witness the difference in his friend, and he felt abundant satisfaction for the part that he had played in it.

Joe silently observed things from her vantage on the cool stones along the base of the fireplace. She listened to Henry's voice rise and fall as she leisurely bathed and groomed herself with keen precision. She couldn't understand what he was saying, but she could tell that Henry was happy, and his presence pleased her. She gradually became disinterested with the proceedings and nestled her drowsy head onto her paws.

Just as Henry was completing his phone call with George, he heard the side door swing open. Millie had returned, and he rose from his seat to head for the kitchen to greet her.

"Well hey there," she said with a smile as they converged in the kitchen. "How was your nap?"

"Just what the doctor ordered," he answered, noting that he felt quite good and surprisingly rested.

4

Millie set a small grocery sack on the counter and walked past him toward the front door to put down her purse and hang up her jacket. Henry stopped near the kitchen table and watched as she removed the long gray overcoat that revealed an attractive royal blue dress beneath it. It was a sleeveless V-neck that was cut just at the knees. A pair of matching high heels completed the ensemble, and they complimented her toned legs. It was then that it occurred to Henry that she was a very attractive woman. He had always been aware of this on some level, but from this moment forward there would be no doubt about it ever again.

"Say, did you change clothes?" he asked, knowing full well that she had been wearing blue jeans earlier in the day.

"Why yes, I did," she replied with a giggle as she returned to the kitchen and walked past him toward the sink. This was her favorite dress, and she was fully aware that it flattered her curvy figure.

"Man, that's some dress!"

"You think so?" she asked with feigned humility.

"I sure do," he affirmed as he took his familiar seat at the island while still looking her over.

"Well thank you, kind sir. I figured as long as I was in town anyway I should swing by my place and change. You know it isn't every day a girl gets invited to dinner at Oak Forest." It was perhaps the understatement of the year as it had never occurred before, and they both smiled at the mention of it.

Millie removed a full-length apron from a drawer next to the sink and began to put it on.

"I'm going to start cooking. You gonna have an early meeting with Jake today?"

He was more than a little mesmerized by her appearance, but her words and actions snapped him out of it. *Cooking*? He had asked her to join him for a dinner that *she* had to prepare.

For the first time, he suddenly felt a little embarrassed about being her employer. It was one thing to have her tend to his daily needs but another to invite her to dinner in his home and then ask her to prepare it.

"Geez Millie, I didn't really think this thing through. You shouldn't have to cook your own dinner. We could just go get something or eat some leftovers."

"Nonsense! I love to cook, and it'll be fun to get to eat some of it with you," she responded, a tad surprised by his sensitivity. "Now, since you know darn good and well that it's killing me, how about you get a meeting with Jake going and tell me all about your big day!" she directed.

"I was wondering when you'd get around to that," he responded, perfectly aware that she was without a doubt quite curious about his meeting with Mary.

"Well, you brought me flowers, so I was pacing myself," she fired back with a wink. At that instant, she felt their warm furry friend at her feet. Joe had been roused from her slumber by their voices and was just now announcing her presence. As Millie looked down, Joe let out a distinct "meow" as a greeting.

"Oh my sweetie, did I forget about you?" she cooed as she knelt to pick up Joe. "Correction, that's a meeting with Jake and Joe, isn't it, baby?"

Joe's eyes were closed tight in delight as Millie gently massaged her ears.

Henry rose to arrange his meeting with Jake. "All right then, if I can't buy you dinner, I'll help you cook."

"Lord have mercy, I don't think my heart can take it. Are you sure you are *my* Henry Engel?" she needled as she put Joe down gently so she could get to work.

"It might surprise you, but I do know my way around a

kitchen. I've never missed a meal yet," he snapped back as he removed the whiskey bottle from the cabinet beneath the sink.

"Oh I see, so you just play dumb then with me," she teased.

Henry laughed. "Well, I didn't say I could cook as well as you, did I?" he conceded with false indignation.

"All right then, I accept, Chef Henry. You can peel the potatoes," she directed as she slipped into the pantry to retrieve the bag of russets that would soon be under Henry's knife.

"So, enough already. Spill the beans!" she implored from the other room.

"Hey, do you want to talk to Jake too?" he called back to her, trying to be hospitable as well as taking the opportunity to delay a bit and thereby antagonize her.

"No thanks, not right now," she answered as she re-entered the room. She put the bag of potatoes on the island and came back at him again. "Now, you quit your stalling and tell me!" She was perfectly aware of his diversionary tactics and wasn't about to let him delay any longer.

"OK. Well, you know George came over here yesterday, right?" he asked as he moved back to his seat and took a drink from his glass.

Millie nodded her head as she pulled bowls from a cabinet.

"So, he's been wanting to talk about things from the past for a while now. He's relentless. He'd bring it up, and I'd shoot him down. You know me; I can be a bit hard-headed once in a while."

Millie snickered a bit and then caught herself. "Oh, sorry," she said meekly as she realized that Henry wasn't making a joke this time.

Henry smiled. He wasn't offended by her honest reaction to his obvious shortcoming.

"So, we're looking at our coins and having a great time. We

were having a pretty good talk with Jake too and then George gives me this incredible George Washington book that once belonged to his grandpa! Well, you know how I like Washington, and it makes it extra special that this was his grandfather's. I really admired that man a lot. He was the one who gave me this silver dollar I always carry around." He pulled the 1921 Morgan Silver Dollar from his pocket and held it up for Millie to see.

She nodded as she was indeed aware of the coin. Over the years, it had occasionally found its way into the laundry by accident. By this point, she was fully engaged in his story. She deftly slid a paring knife through a juicy green apple time and again dividing it into equal slivers as she listened.

Henry placed the coin on the island in front of him. He then picked up a potato and a knife and began to work on his own assignment.

"You know, George still has his coin too. All these years, we've both been lugging them around. They are pretty worn out by now, kind of like the guys who carry them," he joked as he admired the well-worn piece that had lost much of its detail from years of handling. After pausing and pondering that statement for a moment, he turned his attention to the potato in his hand and resumed the story.

"By that point I was feeling terrific, and George could've asked me to go to the moon and I'd have gone. That's when the dirty dog is the most dangerous," he declared in a sarcastic voice with a smile. "I never even saw it coming. All of a sudden he says he needs to talk about '53; you know, all the stuff about Mary?"

Millie nodded. Now they were getting to the heart of the matter. She dared not speak for fear of missing a juicy detail.

"What could I say at that point?" he asked, recalling how George had set him up before letting out another small laugh at the memory of his friend's cunning. "You know, he's almost as sneaky as you are," he added.

"Ha!" Millie cackled. "That'll be the day!"

"Like I said, *almost.*"

"I'm gonna have to get to meet George one of these days. He sounds like my kind of guy," Millie quipped.

"Yeah, I don't know. The two of you together might be dangerous for me," Henry countered. "Anyway, that's when he finally told me his side of everything. The real story of what happened. The whole shebang." Henry's eyes dropped to his hands, and his mind drifted for just a moment as he engaged the memory of how it had felt to learn the truth.

"And?" Millie blurted out after it was clear that Henry had become distracted.

"Oh, sorry." Henry realized that he had left her hanging. "Well, let's just say I screwed things up royally. There was no affair. Ever."

"No-o-o!" Millie blurted out in shock. She couldn't contain her curiosity now. "Well, what was it then? What about the calls? What about the sneaking around? What about the hotel?" Her questions spewed forth like lava from an erupting volcano.

"Hold on, cannon ball!" Henry responded to the bombardment with a quick interruption. "If you let me talk, I'll tell you."

Millie had nearly come out of her shoes at the news but now was regaining her control. She did, however, decide that the heels should come off for the moment and slid her feet out of them. She nodded and allowed him to continue.

"Turns out it was all a huge series of misunderstandings. Mary was trying to get Bill and me back together. Some goofball psychic or preacher or something had told her that she was responsible for our falling out and that because of it God was punishing her. She thought it was because of that she wasn't able to have a baby."

Millie shook her head in disbelief. She hadn't anticipated this to be the story she was going to hear.

"Good Lord, that's a load," she mumbled. Henry nodded his head in agreement.

"OK, I've got lots of questions about all of that, but let's get to Mary. How'd that all come about?"

"Well, after George told me the way things really were, I was floored. My God, I ran out on my wife and divorced her, and she hadn't done anything. I quit my job, ditched my best friend, and left St. Louis. It's a helluva lot to digest, you know?"

"Yeah, it is. I can certainly understand how you felt. But you didn't know any of that back then, Henry. Anybody would've come to the same conclusions you did," she consoled him.

"George thought it best that I go clear the air with Mary. He was convinced that it would make me feel better and be good for both of us. I thought about it all night and this morning when I got up, I knew he was right. So I went."

"And George knew where Mary was? How you could find her?" she asked.

"Yep. Turns out he had stayed in contact with her after I left. She's in St. Louis. Got married again and had three kids."

"Oh my God, so she had children later?" Millie uttered from the sink where she was now working.

"Yeah, how about that? If the rest isn't enough, the topper is that it was *my* fault we couldn't have children. She blamed herself, but it was me." He looked down at a bowl now filled with neatly peeled potatoes sitting in front of him.

Henry gathered the pile of discarded peels and moved toward the waste can. Millie pondered all she had heard so far and felt for him. She knew what it was like to carry a burden, as she had one of her own. She was curious to learn how he had found his absolution and wondered if perhaps someday she might find hers as well. She was a little lost in her own thoughts as Henry returned to his seat and took another swallow from his nearly empty glass.

"That's why I drove to St. Louis this morning," he continued. Millie realized that the most important part of this story still lay ahead, and she returned to the present moment to hear it. She was nearly through mixing the ingredients for the crust and would soon begin rolling out the dough, but the pie was the last thing on her mind at that point.

"I was nervous, as you might imagine. Hell, I hadn't seen Mary in over 40 years. The last time we spoke in person was the morning of Christmas Eve in '53. After that, it was only lawyers and letters. I refused to even hear her voice. So now, I'm just going to show up? I sure didn't have a clue what to expect." He reflected for a few seconds and then noticed his sleeve and continued. "So, I put this on because it was her favorite color," he said, referring to the yellow shirt that he was wearing.

"That's a good color on you. I've always liked that shirt, too," Millie interjected as she placed the dough into the glass plate and began to assemble the pie.

"Why thank you, ma'am." Henry rose from his chair to make himself another drink.

"I thought flowers might be a nice ice-breaker, so I stopped on the way. She always liked flowers. I haven't been in a flower shop since I was married, and too damn rarely even then," he lamented gently. "The little girl who waited on me suggested a nice spring bouquet heavy on yellow daisies and what you see is everything but those," he said glancing at the kitchen table.

The remainder of the bouquet now stood prominently in a vase where Millie had placed it. "Like I said earlier, Mary thought you were long overdue for some flowers. I'd say she was right." He stepped back to his seat with a full glass and surveyed the countertops to assess what he might do next to help with dinner.

"You be sure and thank her for me too," Millie jumped in. "And thank you ever so much, Henry," she said as she reached across the island and touched his hand briefly. He was caught off guard by her expression of gratitude, but it pleased him. "They are so nice, and it was such a wonderful gesture. It really means a lot to me. More than you realize." He couldn't possibly have known that he had just given her the first bouquet of flowers she had ever received from a man in her entire life. It was a moment she would never forget.

Henry could hear the sincerity in her voice and feel it in her gentle touch, which despite its fleeting nature was warm and tender. Light smudges of flour from her fingerprints were left behind on the back of his right hand, and he admired them for a brief instant before wiping them away. Millie had a dear heart and a gentle soul, and he cared for her. It was becoming apparent to him that his feelings for Millie were perhaps deeper than he had been consciously aware of prior to this.

An awkward silence followed but soon passed as Henry asked what he could do next to assist in the dinner preparation. Knowing that he meant well but that trusting him with peeling the potatoes was as far as she was willing to go, Millie asked him to set the table. Henry correctly deduced that he had been bypassed for serious cooking duties but took it all in stride.

"All right then, so tell me about Mary. How'd that go when you saw her?" she asked, returning the conversation to Henry's all-important rendezvous.

"You know something? It was really, really good," he said, using the same words he had relayed to George earlier. "We had a nice long talk. I didn't know what to expect, or how I'd feel about it, but afterward I just felt so much better."

"Well, what did she say when you just showed up out of nowhere at her door? Has she changed much?" Millie asked.

It was just then that it dawned on Henry that he had left out one of, if not the most important details of the entire story—the fact that Mary had passed away in 1985. He thought about it for a moment as he placed forks next to their plates on the table and then decided it was time for some fun. After all, he was perfectly aware that she didn't trust him to help with the cooking, so this was a chance for a little payback.

"Oh, she didn't seem too surprised," he answered slyly.

"You mean to tell me her ex-husband pops over for a visit after all those years, and she wasn't shocked?"

"No, honestly, she didn't react one way or the other much," he replied.

"Wow, she must be one cool customer. I'd have knocked you on the head with my frying pan after putting me through all of that!" she joked as she stirred a pot at the stove.

Henry was starting to rethink his strategy about teasing Millie in light of the "frying pan" comment but being a brave man, he forged ahead shamelessly anyway.

"Oh yeah, she's definitely very cool. Didn't say a word. She's a lot better listener than I remembered from our married days. Just a very, very quiet lady. She let me talk and get my side of things out there without ever interrupting. She didn't have even one negative thing to say to me about it either."

"Huh, she sounds like quite a woman!" Millie declared. "So, do you think you all will be friends now? Did she forgive you?"

"She did. I didn't expect it, but I am sure that she does forgive me. She could've made it hard on me, but she let me off the hook. Believe me, I'm grateful for that," he said, now returning to his seat with the table fully set and ready for dinner.

"Has she changed much?" Millie asked innocently.

"Yes, very much so. But honestly in my mind she'll always look exactly the way I remember her from 1953."

"That's sweet," Millie said as she checked the clock and the progress of the food on the stove as well as the pie that was now baking in the oven.

"We're about forty-five minutes away here," she reported as she rinsed a couple of metal bowls in the sink.

"So, do you think you all will be going out to dinner or something? Might be nice to meet her husband. Maybe George could go too."

"No, I don't see that happening."

"Oh, don't want to get the new rooster together with the old one? Afraid a few feathers might fly?" she prodded playfully. "You never know, might be sparks there yet!"

"No, it's not that. It just wouldn't work."

"Well, how do you know if you don't even try?"

"Well Millie, it would be problematic because she's dead." Henry had dropped the bomb for effect. He had opted earlier to surprise her, but the *rooster comment* had motivated him to go all in.

"She *what?*" Millie exclaimed with shock as she spun around to face him. The bowl she was holding slipped out of her hands and created a messy splash of water on the counter as it hit the bottom of the sink. The look of pure satisfaction on Henry's face was confirmation that she had been had.

"Dead. Deceased. Not living," he answered in a matter-of-fact fashion.

"Well, you ornery son-of-a..." Her voice trailed off as anger swept over her face. She bent down and opened the cabinet in front of her and reached inside. Henry couldn't see what she was getting because by now his eyes had begun to fill with tears from the laughter that was gripping him. It was not often that he won the battle of wits with Millie these days, but when he did it was truly sweet, and he was relishing it.

Millie pulled the largest frying pan she could find from the cabinet and raised it with both hands over her head as she stepped around the island toward him.

"Hey!" Henry squealed in a combination of laughter and sudden fear as he gathered he was about to get the *frying pan treatment.*

"Gotcha!" Millie shouted with delight as she lowered the pan to a safer height. Henry exhaled a sigh of relief. Though he was relatively certain she had been joking, he wasn't totally convinced.

"I'm sorry, Millie. I just found out yesterday, and I didn't realize I hadn't told you until after I was through most of the story just now. By then, I figured I'd have a little fun with you, that's all."

"Ha... ha... ha! Mr. Funny Pants!" Millie groaned slowly in a deep male voice as she placed the frying pan on the stove. "You're just lucky I didn't have a heart attack! This has been some day. First, he invites me to dinner, then he goes to see Mary, then he brings me flowers, then he wants to help me cook dinner, then he tells me Mary is dead! That's a lot of dang surprises for one day!" she muttered under her breath to herself as she heated the pan in preparation to cook their chicken fried steaks.

Henry's joy at his ruse had rapidly melted away to regret, and he now felt a little guilty for teasing her.

"I'm sorry, Millie. It was uncalled for," he offered as an apology.

"Darn right, it wasn't! You can be as sorry as you want while you fix me a drink. I need to talk to Jake," she laughed as she let Henry know that she wasn't quite as traumatized by the day's events as she was putting on.

"That I can do," he said as he rushed over to the sink to comply with her request.

Things having settled down, she now pressed forward. "Ok, so, if Mary has passed, what happened? Did you actually go see her?" she asked in a calmer and more serious tone.

"Apparently she died from breast cancer in '85. I went to the cemetery today to pay my respects. She's buried in Black Jack where we used to live. There's a Lutheran church there she was fond of. Anyway, I swear to you I spoke to her the same as I am talking to you right now." There was not a hint of comedy now in Henry's voice. He had experienced something spiritual and was unashamed and unafraid of it. "I told her everything, and she forgives me."

"I sure am sorry to hear about Mary. I really am. And I believe you, Henry." Her words were not playful any longer either. "I'm so glad you went and talked to her. You'll be at peace about it now, and that's what counts." Millie was truly happy for Henry. She knew what it was like to live with regret, and the peace he had found was something she envied.

CHAPTER 2

Lost and Found

MILLIE FRIED THE steaks and finished the preparations for dinner with purpose and passion. She had cooked for Henry for years but had never prepared a meal for the two of them to share together. It felt both exciting and natural to her, and she wanted it to be perfect. For his part, Henry was equally enthusiastic. He turned on the radio in the family room and tuned it to a station with light music that danced through the air. He then retrieved a couple of long pale candles for the table and lit them. With Millie's flowers as the centerpiece, it was a charming setting. As for Joe, she had long ago taken up a comfortable position on the third stair of the staircase which provided an ideal perch from which to keep an eye on things. She dozed off and on, only occasionally showing mild interest in their movements.

Henry and Millie's first official dinner together was an unequivocal success. The food was as delicious as expected, and the conversation was lively and varied. Time passed quickly as they embraced the moment and began to see each other in a different light than perhaps they ever had previously. Before they knew it, they had finished their pie, and the candles were at dramatically lower levels. Henry was savoring the last swallow of his cup of coffee and reflecting on what had been quite a day for him. He also had something he wanted to ask Millie, and this seemed as opportune a time as any.

"Millie, I've been thinking about something for a while now that really is none of my business, but I want to throw it out there," he began.

"All right, Henry, what is it?" she asked, uncertain as to where he was going with this.

"Well, when we were taking Joe to the hospital after she was attacked, you told me that you had a son. I've been doing a lot of thinking about that."

Millie was taken aback by his words. They had covered many topics during their long conversations today, but this wasn't one she had expected to discuss or had much interest in pursuing.

"Honestly, Henry, I don't want to get into that right now," she said uneasily.

"I can understand that, but please just hear me out," he offered gently. After a pause, Millie nodded for him to continue.

"You said that giving him up for adoption and leaving him was unforgivable, and that it was too late to make it right."

Millie nodded in agreement as this was the burden that *she* carried with her every day of *her* life. Tears began to well in her eyes as she connected with the pain that the memories and thoughts brought her.

"Ok, well I am here to tell you that it is *never* too late. I just proved it this morning. Millie, I feel free. I am so glad that I went and found Mary. I want to give you that. I want to help you find your son Edward," he said as he reached across the table and took her hand.

It may have been his kindness, his words, or the thought of

reuniting with her son that brought them forth, but tears now streamed down her cheeks. She pulled her hand from his and used her napkin to dry her eyes.

"I don't know what to say, Henry. You're very generous and kind to offer, but I honestly just don't know what to say," she mumbled softly.

"If I'm sticking my nose where it doesn't belong, I sincerely apologize," he said.

"No, no of course not. That's not it," she said in a much stronger voice now. "It's just that I'm scared. I have no idea how to look for him or what I would say or do if I found him. What if he rejects me? What if he does me like I did him?" She paused for a few seconds and looked off into the distance. "It's just safer not to know."

"I understand how you feel, believe me, I do. But not knowing him for the rest of your life sure seems like a stiff price to pay for something that happened 35 years ago. Maybe today's Millie could find a way to forgive that Millie. Maybe Edward would like the chance to forgive her too."

Henry's words made a lot of sense to her, and she took them to heart. She knew in many ways that he was right and that running from her past was only giving it new life to torture her. She desperately wanted to see her son and to know him. She wanted the chance to explain things and make her own peace with him as Henry had done with George and Mary.

"For right now, can I just say 'thank you' and tell you I will think about it?" she asked softly.

"Of course you can. My offer doesn't have an expiration date. But if you decide that you want to do it, I'll spare no expense, and we'll find him." Henry's tone was firm and resolute.

Millie sat and stared at the flame of the candle in front of her as she meditated on everything he had just said. For once, she allowed her mind to imagine a happy outcome and it excited her. For all she knew, her son was married and had children too. *Grandchildren! Could it be?* A slight smile spread across her face as she contemplated the possibilities.

Henry was pleased when he saw the change in her demeanor. He hadn't wanted to upset her. He knew this was a very difficult topic for Millie, but he also knew exactly how she felt. His only goal was to relieve her of that regret and set her free from her past as George had done for him.

"You want some more coffee?" Millie asked, now having nearly fully recovered.

"No thank you, I think I'm good. Boy, as always, your cooking was superb. By the way, I thought the mashed potatoes were especially good too," he joked.

"It was the expert who peeled them that made all the difference, I'd say," she teased. She then let out a satisfied sigh as she surveyed the table and glanced outside into the darkness that had fallen some time ago. "I sure did enjoy this, Henry, but I'd better do these dishes and get myself on home."

"How about I help you?" Henry offered as they stood, and he blew out the candles.

"Ok then, sounds good. I'll wash and you dry."

They made short work of the dishes and before long all of the leftovers were put away as well. The only evidence of their meal that remained was Millie's bouquet of flowers on the table. She folded and hung a damp dish towel by the sink and then walked past the table on her way to collect her coat and purse. As she passed, she couldn't help but stop and lean over to take a final whiff of the fragrance that they provided.

"Aren't you going to take those along?" Henry asked.

"Nah, I'm going to leave them here. I'm here more than there anyway," she said with a smile as she moved toward the hall tree.

"Say, Millie, you know it is kind of late. Would you just want to stay?" Henry asked as he stepped toward the hall.

"Why Henry Engel, are you getting fresh with me?" Millie asked coyly with a faint hint of sass. "I know you've had a big day and all, but…"

"Oh, stop that," he interrupted, somewhat embarrassed. "You know what I mean. I just thought since it was getting late it might make more sense is all."

"Oh, I was just playing," she said as she returned to the kitchen with her coat on and purse in hand. "My car has perfectly good headlights, and I know the way just fine."

"Have it your way then. How about you give me a call when you get home so I know you made it ok?" he asked.

Millie looked at him and turned her head just a bit as she processed what he had said. In all their years together he had never asked her to do that, and it was a different but very nice gesture. For an instant, they looked at one another, unsure of how to part company. After all, they had never done this before either, and Henry found himself between her and the door she intended to exit through. Sensing the awkwardness, Henry moved out of her way and picked up Joe, who was standing at his feet. She had been awakened by their commotion and was now in the mood for a little attention of her own.

Millie gave Joe a light pet and her hand brushed gently against Henry's, which was also on Joe. She then shocked him by leaning up and giving him a light kiss on his left cheek. As she did, she whispered, "Thank you for a wonderful evening." With a smile, she retreated and headed for the door.

Henry's face instantly became flushed, and he was left speechless as he watched her leave the room.

"All right then, I'll see you again," she called out as if she was leaving on any other day. He listened as she pulled the door closed behind her.

Henry had always admired Millie for a myriad of reasons and held her in very high regard. However, on this special night he learned something new about her. He learned that in addition to all of her admirable qualities, Millie really knew how to make a memorable exit.

*

The following morning Henry headed downstairs feeling especially jovial. Joe was at his heels and seemed in high spirits as well. The kitchen was filled with the aroma of freshly brewed coffee, and Henry was eager to sample some of it. As he poured himself a cup, he reflected on the previous night's events. Yesterday had been an extraordinary day, and his dinner with Millie had been the perfect finale.

Meanwhile, Joe had seen this movie before. Yesterday Henry had neglected to give her the early morning saucer of milk she had grown accustomed to, so she decided that perhaps a reminder was in order. Before Henry could take a sip of his coffee, she rubbed against his legs and let out a loud cry just to remind him of his responsibilities.

"Are you worried I'm going to forget about you?" he asked his little companion. At that, he put down the cup and removed a saucer from the cabinet above him. Joe watched intently and decided to throw in a few more "meows" for good measure as Henry removed the milk container from the refrigerator and poured some into the saucer. Convinced now that he was indeed on his game, she sat on the floor beneath the sink in her usual spot and waited patiently like a patron in a five-star restaurant about to be served. *This is more like it,* she thought. Henry bent down and placed the dish before her, and she gently began to lap the cold, creamy milk daintily with her tongue. With his most important work now behind him, Henry replaced the milk carton and went back to his coffee.

He took a swallow from the cup and gazed out the kitchen window at the brilliant morning sunshine that was streaming through the leafless trees across the back yard. He loved spring. It was a time of renewal and growth. A time for hope, and right now he was feeling hopeful and excited about the future. Life was good and getting even better.

Once Joe had cleaned her saucer and Henry had filled his cup with a second round, he put on his jacket and headed out the side door with her in tow. On nice days, he liked to get outside and take walks around the place. It was a chance to look things over as well as stretch his legs. Joe, now apparently fully over her trauma from being attacked last year, seemed increasingly interested in going outside with him. She would trot ahead or lag behind but generally always stayed nearby. She too had plenty to investigate each day. Once Henry was satisfied that he had seen it all, or perhaps because his cup had emptied, he would call out to Joe and head for the house. Typically, she would come running and join him.

On this morning, however, he had become preoccupied with what appeared to be some loose shingles on the roof of the tool shed in back and had lost track of her location. When he called for her, she didn't come. He walked back toward the house and called to Joe a couple of more times, but each request was met with silence. Finally, as he stepped onto the porch, he let out a much more assertive and loud call for her. Still, she was nowhere to be seen. It was unusual, to be sure. However, he reasoned there was no need for alarm and went inside.

Henry's concern for Joe's whereabouts was soon interrupted by the arrival of Millie. She entered right on time and found him in his normal spot at the island in the chair nearest the kitchen table.

"Well, good morning," she greeted as she walked past him on her way to the hall tree at the front door. Noticing that he was studying the latest edition of the *Lewis Gazette*, she added, "Anything good in there?"

"Good morning to you too. No, not much," Henry complained as she passed. "Except Jenny Watson had her baby."

"No kidding? Ain't that the little gal that works over at the dry cleaners?" she asked as she returned to the kitchen no longer burdened by her coat and purse.

"Yeah," Henry confirmed. "She's a sweet girl. Already has two others according to this."

"Boy or girl?" she asked.

"Nine-pound four-ounce boy," Henry reported, reading from the article.

"Holy smokes, that's a big baby! Poor momma!" She laughed and shook her head as she poured herself a cup of coffee from the half-full pot.

"What'd they name him?"

"Emil. Emil Andrew Watson," Henry responded.

"Emil? Man, that's old school," she giggled. "Must be some sort of family name, huh?"

Henry chuckled in agreement.

"You want me to warm that up?" she asked as she glanced at his cup, which was nearly empty.

"Please," he answered, not looking up from the newspaper. He had been distracted a bit by the birth announcement he was viewing but now suddenly became more aware that there didn't seem to be any awkwardness at all between them. He had wondered what it would be like when he saw her this morning after last night's affair. It had been a magical evening, but he was hoping that there wouldn't be any lingering effects that would negatively impact their relationship. Fortunately, everything seemed to be normal, and he was relieved.

Millie moved over to the table and picked up a couple of petals that had fallen from the bouquet overnight. "These sure are pretty," she muttered to herself as she admired them.

Henry peeked over from his paper and admired the view of her from a different point of view than he ever had before. "I see you ditched the dress," he teased as he noted she was wearing her more typical attire of blue jeans this morning.

"Yeah, didn't want to get you worked up this early," she shot back, sensing his playfulness. "Gotta think about your heart. After all, you're no spring chicken."

"Ha!" Henry fired back. After a pause and a little reflection he mumbled, "Good call." It was a gentle confirmation that he had definitely approved of the dress, and it did indeed have an effect on him.

Millie smiled and took a sip of her coffee as she looked around the room gathering her thoughts about where to start for the day. Tuesday was her *light cleaning* day, and she intended to make the most of it. Suddenly, she realized that there was one very important party missing from the gathering.

"Say, where's Joe?" she asked with surprise. It was then that she noted that the little feline hadn't greeted her yet as was the norm when she first arrived each day.

"Good question," Henry replied as he looked up from the *Gazette*. He too now was reminded of his concern for her whereabouts. "We took a walk, and she headed off somewhere," he added. "Probably tracking down a mouse or something. I called to her a bunch of times, but she didn't come."

"Huh, that's kinda funny," Millie commented as she digested what Henry had just said. "That's not like her. She's usually right with you, ain't she?"

"Yeah, normally. I guess she's getting more confident again," he said, referencing Joe's former fear of the outdoors after her near-death experience the previous fall.

"Well, I guess that's a good thing," Millie said with a slight hint of concern. She scanned the backyard for Joe through the French doors, but she was nowhere to be seen.

"Oh, I'm sure she'll turn up soon. Probably just a little spring fever," Henry stated, attempting to disguise his own anxiety while alleviating hers.

Throughout the day, Henry and Millie took turns sneaking glances through the windows for Joe. Henry took several impromptu walks outside, and Millie had to go to her car on several occasions for items she needed or to look for something. Neither wanted to add to the other's uneasiness, but secretly they were both growing quite distressed that Joe had wandered away. It wasn't like her to do so, especially not for any length of time. The fact that she had not responded to either of their voices only increased their fears as it meant she was unwilling or possibly even unable to return for some reason.

The day seemed to drag along as the accumulating hours only emphasized that something was not right at Oak Forest. Finally, the clock indicated that it was time for Millie to head home. Even though she had delayed nearly thirty minutes past her typical departure time, there was still no sign of the little cat.

Henry had busied himself at his desk in the office and was reviewing some documents when Millie came in to say her farewell.

"All right Henry, your dinner is on the stove, and I guess I am going to go," she said in a slightly dejected tone. She preferred to stay until Joe had reappeared but felt obligated to stick with routine.

Henry knew exactly how she felt but didn't want to add to her angst. He smiled and said goodbye before returning his attention to his work. Once he was certain she had departed he intended to head outside and begin a comprehensive search for his pal.

Millie opened the side door to leave and was thrilled to see two icy blue eyes peering innocently up at her. Their missing family member had returned.

"Well, there you are!" she cried out as she knelt to gather up the little cat who didn't seem to understand what the fuss was about. "Where you been, girl? You've had us worried sick!" she gently scolded as she nuzzled Joe under her chin. Joe instantly erupted into a purring frenzy as she too was happy to be home. Millie immediately spun and headed back toward the kitchen with her surprise. She could not wait to tell Henry that all was ok. However, Henry had been anxious to get outside to begin his search and nearly plowed into the two of them as he entered the laundry room, not realizing Millie hadn't left yet.

"Whoa! Hey, she's back?" Henry exclaimed, startled by the near collision but elated at the sight of Joe safely in Millie's arms.

"Yep! How about that? Just opened the door and there she was looking up at me like nobody's business."

Henry took Joe from Millie and gave her a good once-over before deeming her unharmed and no worse for wear from her adventure outside. After concluding all was well, he released a deep sigh of relief and Millie continued on her way home equally relieved. It was time for Henry's meeting with Jake, and he was extremely thankful that Joe would be attending as well.

CHAPTER 3

Quite a Gal

OVER THE COURSE of the next several weeks, the regular routine of Oak Forest morphed into a *new normal*. Millie and Henry no longer ate meals alone or separately but instead regularly broke bread together at the kitchen table. In addition, Joe exhibited a far greater degree of independence than she had shown since her near-fatal encounter the previous fall. She now spent blocks of time outside patrolling the estate, exploring, or simply observing her world.

Henry felt good about both changes. He hadn't ever put any thought into why he and Millie ate separately from each other prior to this. However, he now realized that it had created a boundary between them, and he was comfortable removing it. His meals with Millie provided conversation and companionship that he had been unaware he was missing out on. As for Joe, Henry was pleased to see her feeling so confident. He perceived it as an indication that she was strong and well, and his worries about her safety had largely evaporated because of it. She sometimes disappeared for hours now but always returned in time to attend her daily meeting with Henry and Jake.

By early April, spring had swept away the last remnants of

winter and was fully in control at Oak Forest. Ample sunshine and regular showers were fueling an explosion of growth on the increasingly green landscape and in the forest canopy above. The light breeze was sweet and fresh, flavored with the scent of renewal.

Henry methodically pushed the sole of his right boot against the edge of the back of the spade and drove it into the soft earth. With each lunge, he twisted his wrists and overturned the soil to ready it for planting. This was just one of his many flower beds, which in addition to his vegetable garden, required such attention following the winter months. He paused for an instant to glance around the backyard and take in the sights, sounds, and smells before resuming his work.

It was Friday, and that meant Millie was engaged in her weekly ritual of *deep cleaning* the house. As a result, after having considered the weather forecast, Henry had astutely reasoned that it would be a good day for him to stay outdoors. He had put together a list of chores to accomplish and had spent the day crossing them off one by one.

The afternoon was waning, and Henry felt satisfied with all that he had achieved. He glanced at his watch and noted that it was nearing time for his meeting with Jake and Joe and so decided that enough was enough. Anything else that needed to be done could wait until another time.

Before long, he had put away his tools and Millie had gone for the weekend. She didn't get away though without a trip back into the house to retrieve her car keys, which always proved to be elusive. Henry had observed Millie's mental block about her keys first-hand many times and had often advised her about the advantages of placing them in one spot regularly in order to remember them. His best efforts had been for naught, and now he relished in the sport that teasing her provided. At every opportunity, he would move her keys from whichever random place she had left them to somewhere else just for fun. It had turned into a game of sorts for him, and he was amused by the fact that she had never caught on. However, the real mystery was that she had the same level of success in finding them whether he had moved them or not.

The air had become cooler now, so Henry decided to hold his meeting indoors and settled into his favorite leather recliner. His old friend Jake was in hand, and his newer friend Joe had nestled comfortably into her regular position between his right thigh and the arm of the chair. She liked it there because it was snug and warm, and it provided an opportunity for Henry to gently massage her ears, always a preferred delight. He was rather engrossed in a John Wayne movie that was on the television and nearing the end of his first drink when a knock on the front door disrupted the meeting.

"Now, who the heck could that be?" he asked Joe as he rose abruptly from the recliner. Joe wasn't sure what was happening, but she didn't like the interruption to the tender scratches she had been receiving. She jumped down from the chair with a mild cry of protest and watched with indignation as Henry exited the room.

Henry stepped through the kitchen and past the staircase toward the front entry. As he approached, he caught a glimpse of what appeared to be a younger woman through the sidelight to the left of the front door. *She must be lost,* he thought. A lone female stranger at Oak Forest on a Friday evening was a first in all the years he had been there.

He unlocked the door and pulled it open, revealing a smart-looking and attractive woman on the other side of the glass. She appeared to be in her late thirties and had sandy brown hair pulled back neatly into a ponytail with a few wispy bangs framing the left side of her slightly round face. Her emerald green eyes were stunning and sparkled as she smiled at him. An empty forest green Jeep Cherokee stood in the driveway, which confirmed in his mind what he had guessed, *Definitely alone and off-course.* He opened the storm door and greeted the wayward traveler.

"Hello there. Are you lost?" he asked.

"Well, I suppose that depends," she replied with a distinctly British accent. "Are you by chance Mr. Henry Engel?"

Henry was caught off guard by her question and her enunciation and stumbled on his own words just a bit. "Uh-um, yeah, I sure am. Can I help you somehow, miss?"

"I certainly hope so Mr. Engel. My name is Anne Francis Wagner, and I've come a long way just to see you," she said with a sigh of relief as she confidently extended her right hand toward him. Henry hadn't noticed the New York license plates on her vehicle at first but did so now as he reciprocated and shook hands somewhat timidly with her.

"I am so very sorry to be a bother, but might I trouble you for just a few moments of your time to have a word?"

Henry wasn't one for casual conversation with strangers. However, he could see that she represented no threat to him, and he was intrigued by her presence at his door. Therefore, he accommodated her request.

"Sure, I suppose so. Come on in," he said as he extended the storm door to its full reach allowing her to enter the home past him.

"Thank you ever so much! I beg your pardon for my uninvited presence here, and I do hope I haven't interrupted your dinner or anything. I promise I'll just be a bit," she apologized as she stepped inside.

"No, not at all, I was just having a meeting with my friends Jake and Joe when you pulled up," he said as he motioned for her to proceed down the hall to the kitchen.

"Oh dear me, I truly am sorry. I didn't know you had company."

Henry let out a small chuckle as Joe entered the kitchen from the family room at the same time as he and Anne were arriving. "It's not quite what you're thinking," he said as he pointed toward the little cat who was curiously surveying them. "That's Joe."

"My goodness! What a dear little cat," Anne exclaimed as she knelt near the table and extended her left hand toward Joe.

Henry walked past and into the other room for an instant to retrieve his glass. "And this is Jake," he said as he held the tumbler up for emphasis upon his return.

"Ahh!" she responded with a smile while Joe had moved close enough to her to sniff at her fingertips.

"So, how about you take a seat and tell me what this is all about," Henry directed as he headed past the pair toward the sink to replenish his drink.

Anne caught herself and realized she wasn't there to play with a cat. She rose quickly and took a seat at the end of the table nearest the front door.

"Well Mr. Engel, I am a writer," she began.

"Oh yeah? What kind of writer?"

"Books. Mainly novels but I've done a bit of non-fiction too," she explained.

"Are you any good?" he asked as he pulled the bottle of Jacob

Patrick Jasterson's Bourbon from its home in the cabinet beneath the sink.

Anne was watching him intently and duly noted that this was the "Jake" Henry had just referred to.

"Well, my publisher surely seems to think so," she answered slyly. "They've sold nearly *two million* copies of my books over the years." She had placed a little extra emphasis on the number hoping to catch his attention. Her ploy worked.

"No kidding?" Henry shot back with an impressed tone. "That's terrific! Should I know who you are?"

Anne laughed. "No, I wouldn't suppose so. You aren't exactly in my target demographic. No offense intended," she added with a light giggle.

"None taken." Henry smiled. He liked this woman already. There was something pleasant and comfortable about her demeanor. They had only met a moment ago, and yet there was a fascinating and familiar quality about her that he found very appealing.

"Say, I don't suppose you'd be interested in meeting Jake, would you?" he asked, holding up his full glass before he put the bottle away.

"You know, I've just been 10 hours in a car, and a spot of tea would be lovely, but I don't suppose you have that..."

"Sorry, I don't drink it," he confirmed while shaking his head.

"Well then, yes, by all means I'd love to meet your friend. Same as yours, please."

"Ok, you got it!" he proclaimed as he proceeded to retrieve a second glass from the cabinet.

Joe had now begun to rub against Anne's leg, which was concealed beneath a well-fitting pair of dark blue jeans. Anne noted the affection and reached down to pet her. As she did, she realized that she had yet to explain why she had just barged into Henry's world.

"So, as I said, I'm a writer. I look for stories that grab me. A few months ago I ran across one of those and decided I wanted to find out more about it to help me with something I am working on. So, I tracked you down."

Henry was approaching the table and smiled as he saw how Joe had taken to Anne. "I see you two are fast friends," he said as he handed her the glass he had just prepared and took a seat.

"So it would seem. Thank you very much," she acknowledged as she accepted the drink and took a sip from it. "Lovely," she exhaled after swallowing.

"I'm sorry, I don't follow. What does any of this have to do with me?"

"Well, I was in Natal recently, and I heard a story of a man named Engel, who is quite legendary there with some of the locals."

Henry's eyebrows rose as he listened intently and became even more intrigued now.

"Oh, really?" he said, quite surprised by this turn of events as he took a swallow from his glass. He had only been to Africa once in his life, and it had been a most memorable adventure.

"Yes, I met an elder tribesman there by the name of Jombo who told me of a white hunter named Henry Engel and a magnificent lion. Does that ring a bell?" she asked coyly.

Henry leaned back in his chair. "Wow! That was a lifetime ago. What on earth was so special about that to cause him to remember and then tell you about it?" he asked incredulously, remembering the safari he had gone on in 1967.

"Well, according to local legend that was the largest lion

anyone has ever seen there. After the 'great white hunter' referred to as 'Engel' refused to take him as a trophy, that lion took on a mythical status with the locals. He disappeared shortly after you left, only to be seen in shadows and glimpses on the savanna from time to time. The legend says the lion is a god-like spirit and that you could see that because you are a holy man of some sort with special powers. You didn't shoot it because it couldn't be killed. Jombo sure seemed to think so anyway. He spoke about you with reverent whispers." Anne was excited, and each of her words was expressed with great emphasis for effect.

"Really?" uttered Henry in disbelief as he digested what she had just told him. He recalled the hunt and Jombo's face like it was yesterday. The event had indeed been moving and almost spiritual. It was an experience that he would take to his grave. However, he felt that this version of it was quite far-fetched to say the least.

"Surely you didn't drive all the way out here from the East Coast to talk about that. A god-like spirit lion and a holy man who runs around disguised as a white hunter?" he quipped.

Anne laughed. She was impressed by Henry. He was witty and charming.

"East Coast, eh?"

"New York plates on your car."

She smiled. "No," she agreed, "I most certainly did not. I did, however, want to meet the man that walked away from what rumor has it might have been a world-record kill. A man who had gone on safari hunting for a prize lion and then when he had the ultimate trophy in his gun sight showed mercy. This is a most uncommon and extraordinary man. This is a man I wanted to meet. I smelled a good story. So, I tracked you down and here I am." She spoke with the matter-of-fact tone one would use to refer to a quick run to the corner market, not a cross-country journey.

Henry's mind drifted back to the waterhole, and he relived the moment his eyes first met the beast. He didn't often think of it, but each time he did, it still moved him. It was truly an extraordinary event in his life, but he was at a loss as to why it was worthy of her or anyone else's interest.

"Ms. Wagner, I can understand how a tale like that, told by a mysterious tribesman in an exotic location, could stir the interest of a renowned author," he said as he took a sip from his glass. "However, I regret to tell you that is all there is to it. It's just a tale. I'm just a man, and not an interesting one either. For someone who writes books, I suspect you were hoping to find more, but the man before you is all there is."

"Mr. Engel, with all due respect, I've been writing extremely successfully for over twenty years, and some say I'm quite good at it. I think I'm a pretty good judge of what is interesting and what is not. Besides, a man who has meetings with a cat and a glass of whiskey is *interesting* to say the least."

Henry smiled. "Well, I suppose you've got me there," he conceded. "So what exactly is it that you have in mind?"

"I'm working on a novel and the main character is a man that needs a bit of shaping up. When I heard the story of your hunt, I immediately wanted to use it in my book. It's unique and breathtaking. I want my guy to live that moment, but I need to know what it was like from your end of things. You know, to see it through your eyes so that it will be authentic, not just my guess at it. So, I was hoping I could persuade you to join me for lunch or something and tell me about it."

"Ms. Wagner..."

"Please call me Anne," she interrupted.

"All right then, Anne," he agreed. "I'm a pretty private person. I'm not one to have my life show up in a book."

"Mr. Engel, I can certainly respect that. Your story is your own, and I promise if you tell me, I'll change the names and places in such a fashion that no one would ever guess it was you. I just really want to know what you were thinking. You know, what it felt like to be there. That's all I am asking for."

Her words were succinct and had a sweet sincerity to them. Henry found her deportment and appearance to be both pleasing and persuasive, and he genuinely felt compelled to comply with her request. However, he had long been a very private person and though recent times had brought on a tremendous change in him, he still had reservations about sharing himself with others.

"By the way, how the heck did you track me down?" he inquired.

"Oh, I'm part bloodhound," Anne kidded.

"And you never thought to just pick up the phone?"

"What? And miss out on meeting Jake and Joe?" she responded deftly with a grin. "Actually, I needed to get out of New York for a bit and clear my head. I do my best writing when I get away so I thought perhaps a cross-country jaunt might do me some good. Besides, I'm a fan of little towns and Lewis sounded like my kind of place."

"Anne, I think I'm going to like you."

"Well, thank you, Mr. Engel, I think I'm going to like you too. Very much."

"It isn't that I am unwilling to help you, I just would like to think it over. I'm assuming you aren't driving back to New York tonight, right?"

"No, I'm pooped," she agreed. "I took a room in town. I plan on staying the weekend and doing a bit of exploring before heading back. Looks like a charming place."

"All right then, good. How about you join me for breakfast tomorrow and I'll sleep on things and let you know in the morning?" he asked.

"I say yes!" she replied with a broad smile. It was hard to determine which excited her more: the idea that he was entertaining her request or the prospect of sharing breakfast with him. They were suddenly equally appealing to her.

"You're going to be at the Western, I suspect," he asked.

"Smart man," she replied.

"Not so smart; it's the only motel in town," he teased with a wink. "Just down a few blocks on Hughes Avenue is a little diner where I eat breakfast on the weekends. It's called The Eager Beaver, and I'll be there by 8:45 if you want to meet up."

"The Eager Beaver? Yes, I saw it! It's the place with the very large and rather comical but dated neon beaver sign out front. Love the baseball cap, too. Fantastic. I'll be there with bells on!" she agreed as she rose from her chair sensing that was her cue to excuse herself from his company.

"That's the one!" Henry took the last swallow from his glass and replaced it on the table before rising as well.

"Good," he said cementing the appointment, "I'll look forward to it then."

"Me too," Anne concurred enthusiastically. "Thank you ever so much for inviting me into your home and for taking time out to talk with me. I do so appreciate it." She extended her hand again as she had upon entry and Henry accepted it more warmly this time.

"Honestly, I can tell you it's been an unexpected pleasure. You're the most famous author ever to set foot here," he teased.

"Now stop that," Anne fired right back with mock resentment, "you don't even know who I am."

"Ok then, the truth is you're the only author who's ever been here," he amended his statement with playful sarcasm.

"Now that's more like it!" Anne declared with a chuckle as she reached the front door.

After he had watched the Jeep pull past the mailbox and head up the road, Henry closed the front door and secured the locks. He was pondering the past half hour's events and contemplating all that had occurred. He had made a new acquaintance, and she was a quite young and attractive one to boot. She had proposed an interesting idea, and he was going to have to weigh the pros and cons before making his decision. It had been an unusual meeting with Jake and Joe to say the least. As he cleared their glasses from the table, he looked down at Joe, who was standing near the staircase looking up at him.

"You liked Anne, didn't you, kiddo," he said to her. "Yeah, I think I like her too. She's quite a gal."

CHAPTER 4
A Day to Remember

HENRY ENTERED THE Eager Beaver Diner at precisely 8:29 a.m. It had been a typical Saturday morning thus far. The drive to town and his regular weekly visit to the Lewis Bank & Trust had been smooth and uneventful. He was in excellent spirits, buoyed by both the warm sunny spring morning as well as his enthusiasm about his breakfast date with Anne Francis Wagner. Though he was planning to decline her request to share his story, he was excited to see her again and looking forward to continuing their conversation from the night before. It had been a long time since Henry had met someone as intriguing as Anne, and he was fascinated by her.

"Well, hey there Henry!" greeted Suzy Grainger, the owner of The Beaver. From her position behind the counter, she smiled broadly at him as she poured coffee for a patron.

"Hey there yourself, young lady!" Henry answered back. "How's the world treating you?"

"Oh, it just keeps on a spinning but it hasn't flung me off just yet," she crowed to the amusement of those within earshot.

In addition to the excellent food and good company to be found at The Beaver, one could always count on Suzy for a smile, a pleasant disposition, and some good old-fashioned country charm. They were hallmarks of the diner.

Henry slowly made his way toward his regular seat, which was the first booth past the counter along the back wall. As he proceeded, he exchanged greetings and handshakes with many of the patrons. As per usual, the diner was near full, and there wasn't a soul among them that Henry hadn't seen before.

By the time he had reached his booth, Suzy's daughter Jenny had already poured fresh black coffee into a cup and set a small pitcher of cool cream next to it for him. Alongside, the morning's editions of the *St. Louis Post-Dispatch* and the *Lewis Gazette* were stacked neatly and waiting.

"Good morning, Mr. Engel!" Jenny greeted as she moved past him on her way to retrieve his standard breakfast order.

"Hi, Jenny!" Henry responded. "Say, Jenny, can you hold my food back for a bit; I'm expecting someone."

"You are?" she asked with a look of genuine surprise on her face. From time to time, someone may join Henry for breakfast, but he had never waited for anyone before.

Henry smiled. He could read her mind and her reaction amused him. It was fair. He knew what a creature of habit he was, and deviance from his routine was cause for curiosity if not outright concern.

"Um ok, sure. No problem," Jenny added after recognizing it wasn't any of her business who he would be dining with. "I'll just check back in a bit then."

"Thank you, dear," he said as he settled into his seat. He figured that the town would soon be set on its ear when Anne arrived and joined him. In a place the size of Lewis, not much happened that didn't make the rounds. Having a stranger the likes of the English author in town was going to be gossip enough; that she would be seen with Henry might just make the newspaper.

Nearly on cue, Henry noticed a very attractive woman heading toward his table with more than a few pairs of eyes tracking her as she neared him. Glancing at his watch, he noted that she was early. *Always an impressive trait,* he thought as he stood and extended his hand to greet her.

"Good morning! Looks like you found me," he proclaimed as they shook hands.

"Good morning to you as well! Thanks so much for the invitation," she replied cheerfully.

Henry pointed for her to take a seat across from him and then retook his seat as well while everyone watched.

"This is a charming little place," she observed, taking in the sights and sounds of the diner.

"Yeah, you could say it's a bit of a local landmark in Lewis. Anybody within 50 miles has been here. It's a three-generation family business… And here comes the third generation now," he declared as Jenny approached and caught his attention

"Well, Mr. Engel you didn't tell me you were waiting on such a pretty lady. Hi there ma'am, I'm Jenny."

"Thank you, you're too kind. Nice to meet you, dear. I'm Anne."

"Oh, I just love your accent! You're English, aren't you?" Jenny asked excitedly.

"Guilty as charged. So, your family owns The Eager Beaver Diner?"

"Yes ma'am. My Granddaddy started The Beaver and then when he retired my Mom and I took it over. What part of England are you from?"

"I was born just outside of London, but I've lived in several places there and lots of other places in the world too. My father worked in the government and the private sector during his life, so we moved about a lot."

"And now you're here in Lewis," Jenny added with a huge grin, enthralled by the stranger.

"Yes, now I'm here in Lewis," the author grinned in response.

"Can I get you some coffee?" Jenny asked, now recovering from her trance and realizing that she needed to return to her duties.

"Honestly, I would die for a good cup of tea. Might you have any?"

"Tea? Of course. I'll be right back with that and a menu. Mr. Engel, did you want to see a menu too or are you sticking with the usual?"

"I'll have the usual but please hold it until she orders."

"You got it. Be right back."

"She's a lovely girl, isn't she?" Anne declared as Jenny walked away.

"Oh yeah," Henry agreed. "She's solid gold. Her mom and granddad are too. Just a real fine family all the way around. They're Lewis lifers."

"I like that. I've been on the move my whole life, so I envy people with deep roots."

"I can relate to that. I grew up here and then left but came back in '74 for good. I just couldn't shake the place off. Say, did you just say your dad worked for the British government?"

"Yes, he served for years in several capacities before he went into the private sector."

"Did he used to work for the Akron Corporation?"

"Well, yes. Right after he left the government he took a job with Akron. He was there for three years, heading up their Paris office."

"By any chance was his name Lawrence Wagner?"

"Why yes, it was! How could you possibly know that?"

"Well you see Ms. Wagner, as improbable as this may sound, I believe I knew your father! I dealt with him on several big deals in the late '60s."

"My God, you're kidding! That *is* incredible!" Anne exclaimed. "How terribly unlikely is that?"

"I'll say. You know, he used to mention his daughter, but I don't remember him telling me your name. He was a widower, too, as I recall."

"Yes, my mother died when I was seven."

"Cancer," Henry added.

"Yes... incredible," she whispered with a more solemn tone.

They sat and looked at one another in astonishment as they considered the bizarre truth that had just been revealed. Jenny brought a small pot of tea, a cup and saucer, and a menu for Anne while the pair just stared at one another in amazement. It was a strange and enchanting moment, and neither of them said a word until she had walked away.

"So, your dad is deceased?" Henry finally asked.

"Yes, he was killed nine years ago in an automobile accident in Germany."

"I'm very sorry to hear that. I hadn't seen or spoken to him in twenty years, but I knew him to be a good and generous man. A real man of integrity and honesty, too."

"Thank you for that, Mr. Engel, that is very kind of you to say," Anne responded as she poured herself a cup of tea. Henry could tell that she was affected by the memory of the loss of her parents. It had been unexpectedly thrust onto her, and he moved to diffuse her discomfort.

"Not at all, it's true. You know, I get it. I lost both of my parents *by the time I was seven.* My mother died trying to give birth to my sister, and my father was killed in an explosion at the factory where he worked. No matter how old you are, no matter how old you get, it never goes away, does it?"

"Never," she agreed, realizing Henry's losses in many ways matched and even exceeded her own.

"It looks like we have a lot more in common than I ever expected," Henry said as he lifted his cup to his lips.

"It does indeed," Anne confirmed as she gazed back at him.

With the revelation that they were connected via Anne's father, all attention swiftly turned to common ground they both could relate to. For the next hour and a half, as they ate breakfast, they shared stories from their past. They spoke of Lawrence Wagner and also of themes and events that only two souls who had endured the tragedy and achieved the success that they had could understand. They were both survivors and winners in the truest sense, and it created a chemistry between them that was both unique and palpable.

"You know, we never did get around to the subject I originally wanted to meet with you about," Anne declared as they exited the diner.

"I guess we didn't, did we?" Henry acknowledged while stopping beside her. His tone didn't reveal that he had previously decided against sharing his experiences from Africa with the author. That point seemed moot now that they had just conversed nonstop about themselves for the better part of the morning. However, he still had reservations about telling her intimate details of his life for the sole purpose that they would appear later in one of her novels.

"I'd really like to continue this at some point, if you're game. I've loved chatting with you so much, and I do truly want to hear your thoughts on that safari."

"What are you doing right now?" Henry asked abruptly.

Looking around before answering, Anne was puzzled but played along.

"Standing in a parking lot, I suppose?" she replied with a raised eyebrow.

Henry chuckled. "No, I don't mean literally at this moment, Ms. Author, I mean today, this afternoon, right now. How would you like the nickel tour of Lewis?"

"Would I!" she exclaimed, now understanding his meaning. "Where do I sign up?"

Henry motioned toward his SUV and began to walk away from her toward it.

"Jump in with me and I'll show you," he called back over his shoulder.

"Great! You're sure it's no trouble? I was planning to knock around on my own, but it would be grand to have an expert guide."

Henry never looked back. Anne wasn't one to look a gift horse in the mouth, so she quickly caught up with him, and they proceeded to his vehicle. Ever the gentleman, he first unlocked the passenger's side front door and removed his briefcase from the front seat before showing her inside. Once her door was secured, he rounded the back of the truck and opened the rear driver's side door where he deposited his briefcase on the seat before entering the front himself.

Anne was giddy with the prospects of being able to explore

Lewis with a savvy and knowledgeable host at the ready to give her the inside scoop on everything. She was especially thrilled that it was Henry who was going to show her around. Breakfast had flown by, and safari story or not, she was not eager to part company with him.

Henry eased the Explorer from its parking space and then slid it out onto Hughes Avenue as he began to explain the town's history to Anne. She absorbed every morsel of information he wished to dole out with great enthusiasm and asked questions at every opportunity. She was genuinely interested in Lewis and Henry liked that. He was proud of his home, and it was fun to see it through the eyes of someone new, especially someone as sophisticated and well-traveled as Anne.

Their tour of Lewis was leisurely and comprehensive. Henry had nothing of particular urgency to attend to for the rest of the day, so he made sure he showed her every corner of the quaint Midwest hamlet that he called home. For Anne's part, her purpose was to get to know Henry and to perhaps decompress a bit from the rigors of city life. Therefore, she was relaxed and enjoying every bit of their sightseeing excursion.

"What's that place there?" Anne asked, pointing out her window to the right of the vehicle. She was referring to a moderately sized two-story home with a "For Sale" sign in the front yard. Though it looked as if it had seen better days, it had the charm and style that often goes along with a vintage structure built a century earlier.

"That's the old Stewart place," Henry answered as he steered to a stop along the curb of State Street to allow her a better look. "Molly finally wore herself out. She was born in that house and lived there until just a few months ago. She had just turned 103 this past spring. Quite a lady. Used to teach at the grade school here in town."

"Fantastic! And you say she lived there her whole life?"

"Yes, ma'am. She never married. Her folks passed, and she kept the place. Was still living on her own right up to the last," Henry stated with a bit of tenderness that Anne picked up on.

"You knew her well?" she asked.

"She was my 7th and 8th-grade teacher," he explained with a smile. "I looked in on her from time to time. She was something special."

Anne gazed at the home and imagined the stories that it could tell. Stories of change and progress in the small community. Stories of hardship and the dedication of a teacher and her solitary life.

"Oh, how I do love places with character," she thought aloud. "I've been all over the world, lived in a lot of cities, but it's the *character* of a place that always gets to me."

Henry pondered her words. He had similarly gone out into the world and seen and done many things but returned to Lewis in 1974 and stayed for the same reason. It was yet another trait they shared. He pulled the vehicle away from the curb and proceeded forward down the street.

"So, you want to hear about Africa?" he reminded her.

"Oh yes, very much so!" Anne confirmed excitedly. She was enjoying their time together so much that she had forgotten why she was there in the first place.

"All right, I'll tell you." Henry's reservations about sharing his personal story had disintegrated as he became more and more comfortable with Anne and discovered that in many ways she was his mirror image.

"It was back in '67. I wasn't much older than you are now.

49

I had devoted myself to work and was doing extremely well. A couple of guys I did a lot of business with had been talking up a safari for at least a year and one day over lunch it came up again. We were sitting around and Harry, one of the fellows, says 'Say, Henry, why don't you come along?' I had always been an outdoorsman. I grew up on my uncle's farm, and I liked being outside. We hunted and fished and all that sort of thing, so it sounded pretty good to me. Besides, I hadn't taken any time off for nearly fourteen years, so I agreed to go. A couple weeks later, we're on a business trip and sitting around plotting out the details at a private club in Paris, and one of Harry's pals happened to be in there. Harry tried to get him in on the trip too, but he said he couldn't go. He had recently lost his wife and couldn't leave his daughter behind. I was awfully impressed by that. It showed real character and devotion to his family. That was the day I met your father."

"Daddy? That's incredible! 1967, yes, we were in Paris then. So *that's* how you met," she declared while nodding her head in amazement.

"How about that? Like I said earlier, I did some serious business with your dad. It made us both a lot of money. I knew from day one I could trust him." He continued driving, now heading on a course taking them back to The Eager Beaver. "Thought you might like to know that," he added with a slight grin. "Anyhow, we spent a week in Natal, and it was hotter than Hades. Just miserable. I was a farm kid, so I kinda rolled with it, but it was damned hot even for me. Harry and Ted just suffered and complained the whole time." He laughed recalling the misery of his two companions who were not accustomed to the outdoors or difficult living conditions. "Because of the extreme heat, game was scarcer than usual. We had only bagged a couple smaller animals and our time was almost up. As you already know, we had Jombo and Timbo these two locals who were twin brothers to guide us. We paid them well, and they were apologizing like crazy that we weren't having more luck getting something significant to bring home. Guess they were afraid we'd want our money back. So to make up for it, they kept telling us all week that we were going home with a lion. I really liked those two. Timbo kept getting the hiccups all week, and we were having a helluva good time teasing him about it. He was a joker and real outgoing. Liked American bubble gum. Harry had some, and you'd have thought Timbo had won the lottery." Henry laughed as he turned into the parking lot and brought his vehicle to a stop a few spaces down from Anne's jeep. She was so engrossed in Henry's telling of the story that she didn't realize that they had returned to the diner.

"I didn't meet him," Anne interrupted. "I wasn't aware Jombo had a brother."

"Yeah, like I said, a twin. It was hard to tell them apart at first glance, but their personalities were polar opposites. Timbo talked nonstop and loved to laugh and joke. Jombo was quiet and serious. Not unpleasant, just all business. I liked him too. So, we're getting down to the wire and around dinner we hatched a bet for fun that the guy who gets the lion is owed $500 by each of the others. Not exactly a fortune but not pennies back then either. I suggested that we split up to give us all a better chance to find a lion. I worked it that Jombo and I would head out the next morning one way, and those three would go the other. The truth was, I cared less about getting a lion and more about getting some peace." Henry chuckled. "I was getting pretty fed up with Harry and Ted's bitching about the bugs and the heat and

Timbo's yapping all the time was starting to wear me a little thin. Didn't hurt that I figured Jombo was the smarter brother either."

Anne smiled and giggled at Henry's cleverness as she imagined the scene.

"Early the next morning, Jombo and I set out. He had barely spoken all week, and he doesn't say a word until we get out of earshot of the others. Then out of nowhere he says, 'Gawd I missed dee quiet!!'" Henry imitated Jombo's voice for the quote, and she burst into laughter at his joke. After Anne had regained her composure, he continued.

"Within an hour he's picked up the trail of a pride of lions heading to the east. He tells me that he figures they usually eat at night or in the early morning so by now they are feeling 'fat and lazy.'" Again, he used Jombo's voice for effect. "He figures they will look for a good shady place to sleep it off out on the savanna. That would give us a chance to close the distance with them and bring them into rifle range for a shot. The next couple of hours we tromped along in silence through the dusty tall grasses and open spaces. Him out front, me behind. Not a word was spoken until, sure enough, early afternoon, he motions for me stop. Way out in the distance is this lone scraggly looking tree standing all by itself in an ocean of pale sun-bleached grass. I can't see anything, but he tells me there are lions sleeping beneath it. He says he doesn't like the setup. Too much open ground between us. He felt it was too chancy and too dangerous and that we should head over to a waterhole that was nearby and wait for them there."

Anne's mind had fully drifted away to the steamy African grasslands, and her curiosity was fully suspended as she didn't ask any questions but rather just enjoyed the adventure.

"When we got to the waterhole it was *perfect*. Jombo sure earned his keep on that one. There was a pair of rock formations on one end that were maybe ten to twelve feet high, and they overlooked all of the approaches. We climbed one of them and set up camp on top. It was a great place to shoot from and honestly it felt a bit safer up there too. The only real drawback was that as hot as it was on the ground, it was a damned oven amongst those boulders. No cover or shade at all, and all of that rock was just about too hot to touch. Anyway, we sat there for a long time and waited. Several hours later we had seen all sorts of exotic animals come in for a drink—zebras, impalas, even some elephants, but no lions. I enjoyed the show; it was like watching *Mutual of Omaha's Wild Kingdom* in person. Spectacular stuff to be that close to them out in the wild."

"Absolutely," agreed Anne breathlessly.

"I was really starting to wilt. I was about as hot and uncomfortable as I think I've ever been. But I was amazed at Jombo. He looked fairly comfortable and unfazed. I was just about to call it off and get out of there when he signaled with his hand for me to look off in the distance. I looked where he'd directed, and there was a pride of lions approaching, still about 50 yards away from us. After that, I don't remember the heat being an issue. I could see three females flanked by a pair of cubs. Off to their left, *I saw him. He was huge!* A truly majestic beast. I grabbed my rifle and got into a prone position. He was the perfect combination of power and beauty. His light golden mane was enormous, and his shoulders rippled with muscles. My God he was magnificent! Just flawless, you know? Like something from a movie, but he was right in front of me and coming toward my position. I could have shot right then, but my hands were shaking with excitement, and I decided to wait until he got to the edge of the waterhole, which was only about 20 yards from our perch. I was thinking about how envious Harry and Ted were gonna be and how much I was going to enjoy collecting their money. I guess I was caught up in the moment watching him because I remember Jombo gave me a poke and a look that told me it was time to shoot. I took a deep breath to calm myself and then drew a bead on him. He was right at the water's edge and was gently lapping when I prepared to pull the trigger. Right then, he looked up. I swear to you he looked directly at me the same as you are."

Anne's eyes widened as she waited to hear what may come next. She didn't speak a word but just listened with eager anticipation.

"He knew I was there. It felt like he looked into my soul and asked me what I wanted to do next. All I could think of were the words your dad had said to me at the club that day I met him. He said, 'What sport can there be in killing beauty?' As soon as I remembered that, I was done."

"Oh my God!" Anne exclaimed as chills ran down the back of her neck and shoulders.

"Yeah, what are the odds of that, huh?" he asked, now fully comprehending the bizarre turn of events that now placed Anne alongside him.

"I can't believe it... what did the lion do?" She was on the edge of her seat.

"He looked at me for a minute and then went back to drinking. I lowered my rifle and just stared at him. I think Jombo thought I had lost it in the heat, but he never said a word to me about it. I didn't really understand what it was to end or give life until that moment. Eventually, the others got their fill and one by one they started to walk off. He was the last. As he left, about ten yards out, he stopped and looked back right at me again. I've always kind of thought that was meaningful. It felt like he was saying, *You let me live, and now I will do the same for you.* I'll never know of course. Nevertheless, he headed off, and we never saw him again."

"Wow! That is quite the story, Mr. Engel, even better than I imagined it might be," she declared.

"How about you call me Henry?"

Anne's face beamed. "All right, I'd love that. Thank you, *Henry.*"

CHAPTER 5

The Inner Circle

A S HENRY DROVE home to Oak Forest that afternoon, his mind was occupied with thoughts of the unexpected events of the past twenty-four hours. Just one day earlier, he had never even heard of Anne Francis Wagner. Now, much to his surprise, he found that he slightly regretted that he didn't know when he might see or speak to her again. They had parted company with an exchange of telephone numbers and a promise to keep in touch but nothing concrete as to when, if ever, that might be.

He pulled into the driveway and stopped the vehicle to retrieve the day's delivery from the mailbox before heading up to the house. He loved his life at the estate, but it suddenly seemed to be less of an oasis than it had been for him in the past. More and more he found himself dissatisfied with his solitary life. However, upon entering the side door of the house, he was immediately greeted by a friendly face that changed his focus.

"Hi there babe, whatcha been up to?" he asked as he bent down to pick up Joe while juggling the mail. She purred and pressed lovingly against his chest as he snuggled her. "Aww, I missed you too, sweetheart," he said while massaging her ears as they entered the kitchen. The light on the answering machine was blinking in the distance, and it immediately caught his eye.

"Looks like we have a message we need to listen to," he declared.

He put Joe down and set the mail on the island before stepping over to the counter where the device was resting. Upon pushing the playback button, he was greeted by a familiar beep and then the customary robotic voice.

"You have one new message, received at 11:41 a.m. Saturday…" After a slight hesitation and another beep, the recording began to play.

"Hey Henry, it's George. Say, give me a call when you get a moment. I've got some information on that issue we've been looking into that I want to tell you about."

"Hmm, I guess I'll have to give him a call, huh?" Henry said aloud as he returned his attention to the stack of envelopes and publications on the island. Joe was less than interested in Henry's mail or his message. She had scampered to the side door and was loudly proclaiming that she preferred to head outside for a stroll. Upon hearing her cries, Henry walked into the laundry room to see what the excitement was.

"Now, what is this? What's all the fuss about?" he asked her. Joe was writhing around on the brown woven rug positioned in front of the door meowing and purring playfully. When she saw Henry, she immediately jumped up and began circling in front of his feet.

"Got a little cabin fever? All right, head on out, I'll be along in just a bit." With that, he opened the door and Joe shot outside and took off in the direction of the garage. Henry had noticed that she was more and more interested these days in spending time outdoors, but he chalked it up to the improving weather following the cold winter months. Henry and Joe shared this trait. They both preferred to get outside whenever given a choice.

Henry spent the rest of the afternoon attending to chores he wanted to address and puttering around the estate. He had gotten a late start and before long it was already time to head to his meeting with Jake and Joe. The only complication with that plan was that one of the participants was nowhere to be found. She had vanished, as was becoming a more frequent occurrence, and it appeared that Henry and Jake would have to proceed without her. Henry wasn't thrilled that she hadn't returned home yet but despite that he reluctantly called the meeting to order.

He prepared his signature drink and settled into his favorite recliner before dialing George's number on the telephone. After three rings and a swallow from his glass, he heard the familiar voice of his friend on the other end.

"Hello?"

"Hey, George!"

"Hello, Henry! You got my message?"

"Yeah buddy, I did. Sorry I didn't call you sooner, I wanted to take advantage of the daylight and get a few things done so I figured I'd catch you now."

"No problem. Judging by the clock I guess you're at a meeting with the gang, right?" George joked playfully.

"As a matter of fact, I am," Henry laughed. "Except I'm one short today."

"Oh, really? How come?" George inquired with a slight tone of concern.

"She's out and about again and hasn't come back yet."

"Huh, well that's been going on for a while now hasn't it?"

"Yeah, I guess it's a little bit of spring fever. She wants to get out and stretch her legs," Henry explained. "I certainly get that. Glad to be past winter. Anyway, what do you have for me?"

"Ok, that guy I know called this morning with an update for you." George was referring to a friend of his named Carl Johnston who was a retired former agent of the Federal Bureau of Investigation. Currently, Carl was putting his expertise to use as a private detective.

"Great, what did he find out?"

"Well, unfortunately, there isn't too much to report just yet. He's tracked down four possible candidates, but it's going to take some footwork to figure out if any of them is the guy we're looking for. He just wanted to let us know he was on it and said he hoped to get back to us within a week or two."

"All right, well, that's a decent start for now. Tell him to keep going; I'll cover the expenses. Let me know when you hear something, ok?"

"Yep, will do. Are you still sure you want to do this before getting the green light from Millie?" George asked.

"Yes. I'd rather see if we can find her son and check him out before pushing the issue with her. If he turns out to be some sort of bum, I'd rather spare her the heartache."

"You two haven't spoken any more about it?"

"Nope. Not a word since that night we had dinner. Right now, I plan to keep it that way until we find out who he is," Henry declared. He had offered to help Millie locate her son but upon reflection had become concerned about the ill-effects that may result from any number of possible negative discoveries. What if he was dead or in prison? What if he was a drug addict? Some sort of unsavory character? Henry knew that it was difficult for Millie to live with the regret of giving her son up for adoption. To find out that her decision had possibly played a part in some unhappy outcome for him might be a crushing blow. Above all, Henry wanted to protect Millie from pain, even if that meant allowing her to live with the lesser of two evils.

"I understand. Well, that's where things stand. I figured you'd still be in town when I called, but I wanted to let you know as soon as I heard from him."

The reference to Henry's trip to Lewis reminded him that he had some new and interesting information of his own to share. "Say, you won't believe what I have to tell you. I met a fascinating young gal last night and just spent the morning with her," announced Henry with a dash of false braggadocio.

"Oh yeah?" George's voice rose as he became intrigued with this juicy tidbit of information.

"Yeah, she's fairly easy on the eyes too," added Henry.

"Where'd you find her, out of a catalog?" joked George.

Henry laughed. "Not quite, but damned close. She just knocked on my door last night. She's some famous British author named Anne Francis Wagner."

"Are you kidding me? Really?" George exclaimed, now realizing that Henry was not misleading him.

Henry was caught off guard by George's level of enthusiasm at the news. "What? You don't think I can meet a girl?" he needled his friend.

"No, it's not that. Was it actually Anne Francis Wagner?" George asked excitedly.

"Well, yes, George, I just told you it was," Henry responded, further surprised at George's apparent glee.

"Holy cow Henry! She's one of the most successful authors in the world! What in the hell was she doing at Oak Forest?"

"Really? She told me she's sold a boat-load of books, but

I've never heard of her," Henry commented without addressing George's last question.

"Oh yeah, like *really, really* famous. Claire read a lot of her books. My daughters still do."

"No fooling?" Henry was the surprised party now.

"Absolutely. I've even read a couple of them. They're pretty darned good. So, what the heck is she doing in Lewis?"

Henry proceeded to relate the events of the day to George. Besides Millie, he was the only other person on earth with whom Henry would completely let his guard down. They enjoyed a lengthy conversation about all things related to Anne, and it felt good to Henry to share his thoughts and feelings with his friend.

In the midst of things, Henry got up to refresh his glass and decided to check again at the side door for his tardy friend. Much to his delight, just as dusk had settled in, he discovered that Joe was waiting for him to let her inside. Henry celebrated by extending his meeting with Jake to a third session, a move reserved for special occasions.

*

Henry awoke to find the following morning a stark contrast to the previous day. Bright sunshine and light warm breezes had been replaced by dark and turbulent skies touched with dashes of ash and charcoal. The air was becoming increasingly cooler, too. Intermittent gusts randomly ripped tender green leaves from the trees and scattered them across the yard, fostering a sense of unrest. Deep guttural thunder rumbled in the distance, further signaling that something ominous was brewing. In light of this, Henry decided that it was prudent to forgo his typical Sunday morning brunch in Lewis to batten down the hatches at Oak Forest instead. In short order, he turned on the radio hoping to learn more about what the severity of this storm was likely to be. He was disgusted to hear the same voice that just last evening had forecast "a fine spring day" now reporting that a tornado warning had been issued for the county and that residents should seek shelter. *Jackass,* he thought. He had never been a fan of the meteorological profession per se, but in his opinion this particular meteorologist frequently took ineptitude to an entirely new level. The ringing of the telephone spared the weather man any further analysis from Henry, and he grabbed the handset from the counter.

"Hello?"

"Hey there Henry, you guys doing ok?" called back Millie's familiar and concerned voice.

"Good morning Millie. Yeah we're just fine," answered Henry, a tad surprised by the unexpected call.

"I just thought I'd check, since they're saying there might be a tornado. Figured I'd rather know than sit here and worry. Besides, I know how much Joe hates all that thunder."

It was true. Joe had always displayed a real sense of fear and panic whenever there was thunder. They didn't know what caused this behavior, but it must have been due to something that had happened prior to her arrival at Oak Forest. True to form, with the first rumbles in the distance she had scooted to one of her preferred hiding places beneath the sofa in the family room. Henry shook his head in agreement as he acknowledged Millie's astute observation.

"Yep, she's holed up under the couch, safe and sound."

"Maybe you two ought to head down to the basement, Henry," Millie cautioned.

Henry knew that Joe wasn't the only one who suffered from storm anxiety. Millie had few chinks in her armor, but she had a genuine and sincere fear of severe storms. As a child, she had survived a tornado that had severely damaged her family's home, and it was not a memory she had forgotten. She once told Henry that *it was like a locomotive rolled right over us.* He knew that it was nothing to make light of.

"Will do, Millie. We'll head down. You doing ok?" he asked.

"Oh yeah, I'm fine, gonna head back downstairs myself just as soon as I hang up with you," she replied.

"Ok, well you get going and be safe, all right?"

"All right then, Henry. Take care now."

"You too; bye now," he said as he pushed the button to end the call. Henry had no intention whatsoever of heading to his basement, but he certainly wasn't going to let Millie know that and add to her worry. Before he could put the telephone down, it rang again. *My God, I swear she's psychic! How the hell does she know everything?* Henry was astounded by Millie's ability to read his thoughts.

"All right, Millie, all right. I promise we'll go downstairs," he proclaimed with amusement as he answered the phone.

"Umm, Henry? Is that you?" came a distinctly British voice from the other end.

Henry needed a few seconds to recover before realizing it was not Millie on the line but, in fact, his new friend Anne.

"Anne? Hi there! I'm sorry, I was just on the phone with Millie and thought you were her calling me again," he explained.

"No worries, Henry. Should I call back so you can call... Millie, was it?"

"Yes, it was Millie, she's my housekeeper and my... anyway, she gets frightened by storms, so she was checking on me."

"Oh, how lovely of her. Are you doing all right?"

"You bet, she's the one who gets scared, not me," Henry chuckled.

"Me either. I've been through two hurricanes and a typhoon. Takes a lot more than some noise and a bit of wind to send me to the bunker," she laughed.

Henry noted that yet again they were like-minded on another issue. He had never been one to be reckless with personal safety, but he had also never let Mother Nature intimidate him needlessly when the situation was uncertain.

"So, what's going on? I thought you were heading back for New York last night? Are you still in town?"

"Yes, I've had a slight change in plans. I'm heading out tomorrow now instead. I was wondering if perhaps later today I could pop out and see you for a bit?"

Henry was confused as to why she would still be in Lewis but welcomed the chance to visit with her again.

"Yeah, sure! Come out anytime. Might be best to let this heavy weather clear through first, but you do what you want; I'm here."

"That's smashing! I've got some errands to attend to. What would you say if I came out in time for a chat with Jake and Joe?" Henry was well aware that Anne knew from their dealings that his daily meeting was set for 5:00 p.m., and the suggestion appealed to him.

"All right, that sounds good to me. I'll see you then," he agreed.

"Looking forward to it. Now, you better get to your basement before Millie finds out," she teased sarcastically.

"You're more right than you know," he chuckled. "You don't know Millie."

Within an hour, it all proved to be much ado about nothing.

The skies began to brighten, and the winds subsided. Nary a drop of rain had fallen on Oak Forest and thankfully no hail or tornadoes had developed either. The storm had moved around Lewis, and potential trouble had been averted. Henry had observed it all from the comfort of his office as he forged through some overdue filing and did a bit of tidying up of his rather cluttered desk. Soon, blades of sunshine were cutting through the dissipating clouds above. Henry welcomed the change in the weather conditions as well as the news that Anne was still in town. He wondered what had prompted her to stay and why she wanted to see him but, regardless of the reasons, he was pleased by the opportunity to see her again.

With calm restored outside, Joe eventually emerged from her hiding place to assess the situation. However, she showed no signs of her recent obsession with getting outdoors. Instead, once she was satisfied that the coast was clear, she set up camp for the afternoon in the recliner. Except for an occasional glance in the direction of the office to check on Henry, she didn't move all afternoon. She didn't even react when he crunched sheet after sheet of junk mail into paper balls to be thrown away as he worked through the piles of correspondence on his desk. Typically, the hint that a game of fetch was available was a sure-fire way to arouse her, but today it wasn't even on her radar. Henry attributed her lethargic attitude to nothing more than fallout from her nervous morning and continued attending to his business.

Before Henry knew it, the clock indicated that it was ten minutes before five and nearly time for his meeting with Jake and Joe. He moved a final pair of file folders from his now neatly organized desk to a drawer and then excused himself. Choosing a route through the doorway nearest the front entry, he stopped and opened the front door in anticipation of Anne's arrival before moving on to the kitchen to fetch Jake.

He stepped to the sink and opened the door of the cabinet beneath it. Reaching inside, his right hand found the object it was looking for. The neck of the bottle felt cool and familiar to his touch as he grasped it and pulled it out.

"Hey buddy!" he greeted his old friend.

The 750 ml bottle of Jacob Patrick Jasterson's Bourbon was half empty due to previous engagements with Henry. He placed the bottle carefully on the counter before moving to the cabinet to retrieve a pair of glasses. Before he could proceed further, a knock on the front door announced the arrival of his guest.

"Come on in!" he called from the kitchen.

The click of the door handle and the light creak of the hinges indicated that the message had made its way to the intended recipient.

"Hello, Henry?" Anne called back.

"In here, kiddo. Perfect timing, I was just getting Jake ready for our get-together."

"Sounds wonderful to me," she responded as she set her purse and car keys on the kitchen table.

Henry turned with two expertly created concoctions to find Anne standing at the head of the table looking perfectly fetching. Her hair was pulled into a mussed-up ponytail, and her stunning emerald eyes were enhanced by an olive green sweatshirt that she had paired with faded blue jeans. Her broad smile conveyed that she was as happy to see Henry as he was to see her.

"Ahh yes, thank you!" she exclaimed as he handed her a glass.

"Happy Sunday," Henry toasted as he held out his tumbler.

"Happy Sunday indeed," Anne acknowledged as she tapped her glass against his before they both took a swallow.

"Still no tea around here, eh?" she quipped.

"Not a drop," Henry shot back.

"Pity, that," she lamented. "A dash of this in a cup of tea would be glorious."

"Oh yeah? Never thought to try it."

"Barbaric!" she jabbed again. Henry laughed.

"You know, Henry, Jake mingled with a spot of tea would make for a perfect English elixir."

"If you want tea you'd better bring your own. You'll play hell finding it around Oak Forest," he countered with a small chuckle. "This old German doesn't even own a teapot."

"Well, I will have to remedy that!" Anne teased back.

"Come on, let's sit down," he said as he motioned for Anne to take the lead before him. With a nod of her head, she spun and walked in the direction he had suggested.

Upon entering the family room, Henry scooted Joe to the side to make room for himself in the recliner. Anne followed his lead and took a seat on the sofa opposite him. Annoyed by the unexpected disturbance, Joe quickly jumped down and began a series of stretches while displaying a distinct air of agitation at having been awakened.

"Somebody sure is a sleepyhead," Anne observed as she viewed Joe's exaggerated antics.

"She's been out like a light all afternoon," Henry reported. They both smiled as they admired the little cat.

Diverting her attention to the surrounding décor, Anne felt compelled to express the compliment aloud that she was experiencing internally.

"Oh Henry, this room is simply marvelous. I just love your fireplace."

"Thanks," he answered proudly. "I've always really loved it in here too."

Joe had now shaken off the cobwebs and was becoming cognizant of Anne's presence. She immediately jumped onto her lap, nearly knocking the drink from her hands.

"Oh my goodness!" Anne exclaimed as she received Joe's affection.

"Well, how about that? Looks like she sure remembers you."

"So it would seem!" Anne concurred with a smile as she stroked Joe with her free hand. Joe purred and twisted with glee as she settled onto Anne's lap to receive the attention being lavishly offered.

"I have to admit it; I was glad that you called. However, I am curious why you wanted to see me."

"You were? That's awfully sweet! The truth of it is, I think I missed you. I know that sounds rather absurd considering we just met, but I've truly enjoyed our time together. It was so wonderful to talk about things and Daddy with you."

Henry was surprised and a tad embarrassed by her open display of affection for him. Before he could address what she had said, she continued.

"I also wanted to run something past you to get your idea of it."

Her last comment struck him. He was accustomed to being summoned for counsel on a wide variety of business issues, and he relished the opportunity to mentor anyone genuinely seeking his advice. It was a role that he had often assumed and performed with great passion and expertise. He quickly dismissed her compliments and turned his attention to learning what her predicament was.

"You bet, fire away!" he consented as he brought his glass again to his lips.

Anne was pleased by Henry's enthusiasm and leaned toward him to share her dilemma. As she shifted her weight, Joe became displeased by the lack of undivided attention and excused herself in favor of the more quiet confines of Henry's office.

"Oh, I'm sorry, dear," Anne apologized to the departing cat. She then returned her focus to Henry, who was dutifully waiting to continue the conversation.

"Well, I was planning to leave yesterday for home, as you know," she began.

Henry nodded.

"I had my bag in the Jeep and was all ready to go when something made me go and look up that little house we had stopped by."

"You mean the Stewart place?" Henry asked.

"Yes, that's right. Molly Stewart's home. I drove over there, and I just stared at it. It sounds crazy, but I just knew that I was supposed to buy it."

"You're kidding? You're gonna buy it?"

"Bought it," Anne corrected with a definitive tone. "I called the number on the sign and a very kind man named Ross offered to run right over and let me in." Henry knew that she was referring to one of Lewis' most notable citizens and the town's primary realtor, Mayor Richard Ross.

"He let me in, and I was a goner. Just love it. It's just so warm and engaging."

"Well, I'll be damned!" Henry exclaimed at the news. "So we're gonna be neighbors?"

"We are," she confirmed with an expansive grin.

"That sure as hell calls for round two!" he declared as he stood and collected her empty glass to add to his own. As he strolled to the sink to refill them, he pondered the possibilities and consequences of what he had just learned.

"Man, wait until George finds out," he thought aloud.

"George?" Anne asked from the other room.

Henry dumped the remnants from the first session into the sink before procuring fresh ice from the dispenser on the refrigerator door. "Yeah, George Schuetz. He's my best friend and apparently a big fan of yours."

Anne didn't quite understand Henry's partial joke but nonetheless moved forward with her request.

"In any event, I just agreed to buy a home in a town I know almost nothing about thousands of miles from where I currently reside, and where you are my only contact. Kind of nuts, wouldn't you say?"

"Well, it's not exactly something that you hear about every day," he agreed.

Anne patted her hands on her lap three times in succession as a means to refocus herself to the exact reason she had come to see Henry. "So... I am going to meet Mr. Ross tomorrow and then head back to New York. In a couple of weeks, I hope to return to start getting things in order. Here's the rub: Mr. Ross has informed me that the home needs more than a touch of work done to get it up to speed. Apparently, as dear Molly got on in years she neglected the maintenance, and so I am in desperate need of a handyman, but I wouldn't know who to trust or how to locate someone. Since you are my oldest and dearest friend in Lewis," she paused and laughed as Henry re-entered the room and handed her now full glass back to her, "I come to you for guidance."

Henry sat down and took a long slow sip from his glass before replying. When he spoke, he was resolute and matter-of-fact. "That's an easy one. Louis from Lewis is your man."

Anne's face contorted into a curious smile. "Louis from Lewis?" she repeated.

"He's a fireman named Louis Benhardt, but everyone calls him Louis from Lewis. He's a good family man. Has four kids and a real sweet little wife who teaches school in town. Honest guy and he does terrific work. He's the one I trust to help out around here and, believe me, with all of those mouths to feed he can use the money."

"Wow, with that recommendation how can I go wrong?" she laughed.

"You know, I've just got to ask you: *Why on earth are you buying a house here?*"

Anne sat back against the couch and took another swallow from her glass before answering. She stared out the window as she began to speak.

"Yes, I know, it's a little crazy, isn't it? But I've been thinking for a couple of years about getting out of the city. It's getting harder and harder to write there. Just so many distractions. Once I got here and got a taste of it, it just feels like I am supposed to be here. When you showed me the Stewart house, something inside me just said *Go for it, Anne.* I've been all over the world, but something here is very special. I want to see what happens next. I can see myself writing some very good books in that house."

Henry nodded. He got it. Oak Forest had snatched hold of him many decades ago and never turned him loose. Who's to say what determines where the heart goes? Henry had instantly fallen for the estate, as apparently Anne had for the Stewart house. Many people don't put faith into love at first sight, but Henry and Anne were true believers.

CHAPTER 6

Uncharted Waters

"HEY THERE," MILLIE warmly greeted Henry as she entered the kitchen.

"Good morning," he reciprocated, diverting his attention from the latest edition of the *Lewis Gazette* while she passed by behind him on her way to the front door.

She deposited her purse by the hall tree and hung her jacket. "And how was your weekend, sir?"

"Oh, pretty good I guess. Just the usual. How about you?" he replied as he began to once again skim the page in front of him.

"Not too shabby," she answered as she re-entered the kitchen pursuing a direct route toward the source of the delicious aroma that was permeating the air.

Millie first removed a cup from the cabinet and then grabbed the pot of hot coffee from the warmer on the counter. Before she poured for herself, she noted that Henry's cup had a scant amount left and asked if he was ready for a refill. Upon his affirmative nod, she filled his cup and then proceeded to pour her own.

"Well, that's good you had a nice weekend," she commented as she took a small sip from her cup. Henry didn't fully comprehend what she had said as he had immersed himself in an article about a proposed new boiler for the town's elementary school and the lack of funding to pursue it. He emitted a mild grunt of assent as he brought his own cup to his lips.

"I imagined you were kinda busy with that pretty young author and all," Millie stated with as much emotion as if she was reading off stock market prices from a ticker. Henry nearly gagged on his coffee as he fully comprehended her words.

"You ok, Henry?" Millie asked with genuine concern as Henry coughed up droplets of coffee that had found their way down the wrong pipe.

"Yeah, yeah I'm ok," he said as he gathered his wits and thought about how to answer her. The previous night after Anne had left it had occurred to Henry that at some point he would have to address the topic with Millie. However, upon arriving at the conclusion that his association with Anne was not only sudden and unexpected but also rather unusual, he had pushed it aside to deal with down the road. Unfortunately for him, Millie's knowledge of his activities seemingly eliminated the "delay tactic" as a viable option.

"Author?" he asked innocently.

"Yeah Henry, you know, Anne Francis Wagner?" She rattled off her name without a note of hesitation.

"Now, how in God's name could you know about her?" Henry asked both bewildered and impressed by Millie's never-ending clairvoyant skills.

"Front page," she declared with her left eyebrow raised and without even a note of humor.

Henry looked at her for a moment before realizing that she wasn't joking. He turned back to the front page of the newspaper and there it was. Approximately half-way down the page the headline read "Famous Author Buys Home in Lewis." Without saying another word, or even looking up at Millie, Henry dashed through the three-paragraph article to learn that the reporter was rather well-informed and detailed in his report. Henry had somehow missed the story on his first pass, but he now found his own name in black and white associated with the *tour guide* label. In addition, the details were remarkably accurate as to who Anne was and why she had just purchased a home in Lewis. Based on this information, the culprit who had ratted her out to the media could only be none other than Lewis' good mayor. In fairness to Richard, Henry reasoned, adding Anne to the town's rolls *was* good business and a real coup for Lewis so it wasn't totally absurd that he would try to publicize it. Henry understood that it was not a malicious act either by the mayor to reveal him to the media as the person who had taken Anne around town. However, he was not amused. *Isn't there a realtor-client privilege as exists for attorneys or doctors?* Henry was never a fan of his life or actions being available for public scrutiny. Also, for reasons he did not yet fully comprehend, Henry felt almost guilty about spending so much time with Anne without Millie's knowledge. It didn't make sense to him, but he was expecting that Millie would have something to say about it. Much to his surprise, she was incredibly subdued after it was all out in the open.

Because of that, Henry seized the opportunity that the mention of Anne had afforded him and explained the entire weekend to Millie in great detail. He told how she had shown up out of the blue at Oak Forest on Friday and then had breakfast with him on Saturday. He relayed the main highlights from their chat on Sunday as well. All the while, Millie nodded and listened as Henry spoke of how he and Anne had hit it off from the get-go. She took it all in as a mother might listen to a son's report of his school day without adding much to the conversation. Henry was relieved by her reaction and began to relax. His concern about how Millie would respond to his new relationship now seemed unfounded.

"So, that's basically it. She's going to move here this summer and in the meantime I'm going to help her get the house fixed up. No big deal." Henry picked his newspaper back up and returned to the last few lines of the article he had been reading.

Millie took a swallow from her cup and then sat it by the sink before turning toward the laundry room. Muttering under her breath, she released a barely audible comment that Henry couldn't quite hear. He wasn't certain, but thought it was something related to an affair she was planning to have with actor Eddie Murphy.

"Did you say something?" he asked, knowing full well she had but unsure if the words were entirely directed toward him.

"Nope!" Millie sharply shot back with a definite tone of agitation as she exited the room.

Any possible doubt was erased from his mind. Henry was certain now that she was irritated with him. He couldn't help but feel like a mouse with whom the cat had been toying. *Walked right into that one,* he thought. Sensing his opportunity to escape, he folded the newspaper and with coffee cup in hand retreated to his office. Besides his desire to avoid further conversation on the topic of Anne, he also had work to do.

A wide variety of rare coins housed in 2" x 2" flips were neatly organized by denomination into stacks on his desk awaiting his attention. The results of his meticulous review would determine which pieces would pass muster and be returned to their home in the safe. Others would be traveling with him to St. Louis for a possible upgrade later that week. The annual spring coin show held in the Gateway City was only a few days away, and he was earnestly preparing for it. The large and well-attended multi-day exhibition afforded him an excellent opportunity to inspect the inventories of many of the nation's leading coin dealers.

This year's event was particularly noteworthy for two reasons. First, due to a fire that had occurred in March at the original venue, the show had been moved to an alternate site and pushed back to the last week of the month. This was in stark contrast to previous years when it had always been held at the same hotel during the third week of April. More importantly, for the first time he and George would be attending the show together, and he relished the idea. Prior to this, his enjoyment of coin collecting had been a predominantly solitary exercise, but now it had added value. Their reconnection had enhanced his passion for his coins even further because it gave him a true confidant with whom he could collaborate and enjoy the hobby.

Henry nestled comfortably into his desk chair and sat his coffee cup off to the left. Just then, he noted a gentle rub against the side of his right leg. Immediately identifying the source he reached down and stroked Joe's back a couple of times, much to her delight.

"There's my girl," Henry affectionately acknowledged the little cat. She had been more lethargic and less playful of late, and Henry was glad to see her cozying up to him.

Joe purred and arched her back with glee as his hand ran across her spine several times. To her disappointment, the attention was short-lived as Henry's focus quickly diverted to the task before him. Sensing that the moment had passed, she contented herself with curling up into a comfortable ball at the base of the desk for a nap.

The next couple of hours were consumed by Henry's painstaking examination of each of the specimens in the several dozen coin lot. Noting the strengths and weaknesses of each, he agonized over whether an example was above average for its assigned grade or sub-par and in need of replacement. The exercise was both tedious and enjoyable in a way that only a true numismatist can understand.

However, as he studied the pieces, he was distracted by the nagging feeling that he needed to straighten things out with Millie. The house was filled with an uneasy silence, and he could sense the tension. Millie had busied herself with various chores but worked quietly without the typical banter or humming that he had grown used to hearing. It was uncomfortable, and he didn't like it.

Henry could not decide which troubled him more, Millie's obvious agitation about his dealings with Anne or the fact that *he cared* that Millie was upset. He was unaccustomed to answering for his actions to anyone, and yet he felt as though he owed her some further explanation. He pondered why Millie would be upset about Anne and also why it mattered to him that she was. It was then that Henry really understood for the first time the level of affection he felt for Millie. Deciding that he needed to address the matter, he rose from his desk and headed for the kitchen where she was mopping the floor.

As he entered the room, she glanced up from her work near the French doors to see his approach.

"Hold it right there, if you please," she directed. "The floor is wet. Gimme a few more minutes and I'll be done."

Henry stopped dead in his tracks just a few steps past the doorway from the family room.

"Oh right, sorry," he sheepishly responded as he retreated to the carpet's edge.

"I suspect you're looking for lunch," Millie mumbled with little expression as she glanced at the clock.

Henry was surprised by her statement and noticed that he had no clue as to the time of day. He had been quite lost in his thoughts all morning and was somewhat shocked to see that his watch indicated that it was nearly noon. His stomach clearly didn't know the time either because he wasn't hungry at all.

"Um, actually, no I wasn't thinking about lunch. I wanted to say something to you." Henry paused for a second as Millie sloshed the mop back and forth across the floor without looking up at him or stopping.

"I didn't handle things this morning very well, I know that. I'm sorry. This thing we are doing here, you and me... Sometimes it's hard for me to know how to handle it the right way. I don't guess I am much good at it, but I wanted to at least clear up some things about Anne anyway."

At the mention of Anne's name, Millie halted her mopping and looked up at him. Her expression was solemn and strained.

"Henry, you don't owe me any explanation," she offered quietly. "What you do is your business and none of my concern." She dropped her head and began to mop again.

Henry meditated on her words for a few seconds before pushing forward.

"Well Millie, I guess that's always kind of been the case around here with us, hasn't it? But just now, I guess I've realized that isn't the way I feel about it anymore. I don't exactly know what is happening here... with us, but I do know that there is *nothing* happening now or ever going to happen between Anne Francis Wagner and yours truly."

Millie stopped again and looked up at him. This time, her face reflected a clear sense of relief.

"Look, Anne's sweet and pretty and she seems like a really wonderful young gal. No doubt about it. You know, I think I liked her from the first I met her and that's real unusual for me."

Millie's left eyebrow rose slightly in protest. These were precisely the things that were troubling her and hearing about them wasn't helping. Henry could see the look in her eyes and continued.

"But that's it. I've never had a child, Millie; you know that. But I guess I kinda can see myself being like a father or an uncle or something to her as time goes on. Like I said earlier, turns out I knew her dad, and she and I really hit it off. We're just a lot alike, is all. I think I can understand a lot of who she is, and she seems to have a pretty good handle on me, too. I didn't mean for you to think it was anything else."

Millie stared back at him without saying anything. She was stunned by his candid comments but also relieved by their content that for once left her totally speechless. Her lack of response or expression suddenly made Henry feel a bit uncomfortable. He waited for another instant and then raised *his* eyebrows in an attempt to coax some sort of reaction from her. Failing to do so, he muttered, "All right then, I'm glad we cleared that up." Silently he spun and returned to his office while Millie still stood as if frozen in place.

Finally, after Henry was out of sight, she regained her senses. *Well, what do you know about that?* she thought as she started mopping again with decidedly more vigorous strokes this time. As she did, she began cheerfully humming a favorite hymn. Henry settled back into his chair and resumed reviewing the coins on his desk. From his office, he could hear the melody coming from the kitchen, and he delighted in the sound of Millie's voice. Despite her initial lack of reaction to his words, Henry knew that his message had been well-received, and it brought a smile to his face. It was a small step perhaps, but in expressing his feelings about Anne he had more openly revealed his deep regard for Millie and in turn he was confident that she felt the same way about him. Though they had been together for nearly 25 years, this new phase of their relationship was uncharted waters. The uncertainty of how best to navigate what lay ahead left Henry feeling a tad uneasy but excited as well.

CHAPTER 7

Quantity vs. Quality

ANY CONCERNS ABOUT the future and Millie were quickly pushed aside as the days leading up to Henry's sojourn to St. Louis seemingly evaporated. Before he knew it, Thursday morning arrived and it was time for him to head off to the Gateway City for his eagerly anticipated adventure. He and George had agreed to meet for brunch at the host hotel at 11:00 a.m. Following that, they planned to spend the afternoon searching the bourse floor for treasures.

Henry pulled the Lincoln Continental alongside the porch and parked it there for loading. As he did, he gave a quick glance in the direction of the vegetable garden, which, like the rest of Oak Forest, was beginning to burst with life. Briefly, he lamented that he wouldn't be able to tend to it or the surrounding grounds of the estate until after his return on Sunday afternoon. However, that feeling was hastily dispatched by the realization that great coin shows came along infrequently and yard work, even as much as he enjoyed it, was an ongoing daily reality.

Meanwhile, Millie was inside performing a final inspection of the contents of his suitcase at the island in the kitchen. As usual, she had ironed his clothes and packed all of the necessities that he required. This had been their standard practice for years. Whenever Henry traveled, Millie would ask what his itinerary was and then select the appropriate clothing for him as she saw fit. Henry preferred to leave such matters up to her and deferred to her completely on any wardrobe decisions that needed to be made.

"I think I've got you all set," she said as he entered the room.

"Good deal! I need to get on the road. It's nearly nine-thirty, and I don't want to make George wait on me."

"Well, you just take your time and be safe," she cautioned as she closed and fastened the bag.

"Yes mother," Henry replied with a sly grin as he tightened the lid on his thermos of coffee.

Millie smiled at his jest and turned to the counter near the sink to retrieve a brown paper lunch bag she had prepared for him.

"I've got some cookies in here," she said as she handed him the sack. "Figured you might need a little something to keep in your room for a quick snack if you get hungry."

"All right!" Henry grinned as he peeked into the bag to see the freshly baked chocolate chip cookies. "That's my girl!" he exclaimed with a subtle wink that wasn't lost on Millie.

"Say, where's my other girl?" he asked as he looked around for Joe, who typically was found near his feet on such an occasion.

"You know what? That's a darned good question. I haven't seen her all morning. She must be sleeping somewhere."

"Huh. That's strange. Man, she sure has seemed lethargic lately."

"You're sure right about that. She hasn't been eating too much lately either. I haven't had to add food to her bowl in three days," Millie said with growing concern as she stared off toward the family room.

"Huh, that doesn't seem right," Henry acknowledged as he did a final review of the contents of his briefcase that was on the kitchen table. "Maybe you ought to run her into Dr. Miller's and get her checked out."

"Good idea. I'll call and see if I can get her in there today or tomorrow."

Henry nodded in agreement as he gathered items to put in his car. Millie followed suit and between them they were able to carry everything out to the Lincoln in a single trip.

In short order, Henry was rolling down the highway on his way to meet George. His mind was filled with thoughts about the coins that he hoped to find at the show. Nothing matched the enthusiasm he felt for the hunt for new pieces for his collection, and he relished the chance to completely immerse himself in it. It was a pleasant diversion, and the trip passed quickly. He soon arrived right on time and as scheduled to meet George.

The two men enjoyed a delicious and robust brunch that was secondary only to the vibrant conversation they engaged in. Topics ranged from numismatics to British authors and kept their waitress entertained as she struggled to eavesdrop. Once their meal was finished, Henry checked into his room and dropped his bags there before the duo headed to the exhibition.

Thursday afternoons were typically slow on the bourse. Many of the collectors who would be attending the show were still of working age. Some might take a day off on a Friday to play some *numismatic hooky* but Thursday was, for most, too tall of an order. However, for the retired crowd, there were no such restrictions. The opening afternoon was a chance to get the first crack at the best coins ahead of the crowds that Friday and Saturday were sure to generate.

Henry and George were anxiously standing in line and ready to go as the show opened its doors at 1:00 p.m. The assembled crowd was somewhat bigger than they had anticipated but still far below the numbers that the weekend would produce. As this was a new venue for the event, Henry was unsure what to expect when they finally made their way inside. He was pleasantly surprised to find the trading floor much more spacious than the old location. Countless scores of eight-foot tables were organized into several long rows to accommodate the vast array of dealers who were there to buy, sell, and trade coins. The layout provided for generous aisles that would easily receive the attendees comfortably.

George and Henry agreed to go their separate ways initially and then reconvene later on to compare notes. That way, each man could browse at his own pace and seek out specific coins of interest without worry that he was delaying the other. George and most of the rest of the early birds moved en masse toward the dealer tables nearest the entrance. Seeing this, Henry opted to veer to the far side of the room where other dealers sat patiently waiting for customers to reach them. It was a typical move for Henry. Throughout his professional career, he was often one step ahead of the crowd. He could identify even the slightest advantage in any situation and regularly used this skill to gain an edge over the competition. On this day, it allowed him to acquire a unique and highly coveted piece for his collection before any of the others in attendance even got to see it.

The rest of the afternoon proved to be enjoyable and quite productive for Henry. In a handful of deals, he was able to land a few new coins and a rare medal as well as move several less-desirable old friends from his holdings along. The net result was that at the end of the day, he felt that he had upgraded the overall quality of his collection. Also, he had engaged in numerous conversations with other collectors and dealers alike, including a particularly plump fellow apparently known simply as *Blimpy*. This large and gregarious gentleman was particularly well-schooled about early American federal coins and also smelled oddly like bacon. The whole encounter left Henry feeling quite entertained by the experience and just a little bit hungry.

George's first day was slightly less successful than Henry's as he only located a pair of coins for purchase. Nevertheless, he had a good time perusing dealer inventories and also had the pleasure of talking with the aforementioned gentleman. Their conversation, however, had nothing at all to do with numismatics. Rather, it was entirely about a steakhouse named *The Ranch* located just down the street that Blimpy could not recommend strongly enough. Due to a lengthy discussion about charbroiled Angus beef steaks and the faint but distinct aroma of bacon in the air, George decided it was time to find something to eat. Henry was on board, and the two men opted to call it a day and head for dinner. They had a meeting with Jake at the hotel bar before venturing over to The Ranch to find out if Blimpy knew as much about steaks as he did about eighteenth century U.S. coins. It had been a very good day, and the chance for a terrific meal seemed the perfect way to cap it off.

By Saturday night, three things had been confirmed. The first was that Blimpy did indeed know as much or more about steakhouses as he did about coin collecting. The men had enjoyed an incredible dinner on Thursday featuring quite possibly the best porterhouse steak that Henry had ever tasted. The second was that attending the weekend coin show together was a brilliant move. Neither Henry nor George could recall the last time he had enjoyed himself at a show so much. The third and final truth was that Blimpy owned The Ranch and also regularly supervised operations in the kitchen. Following a ho-hum Italian meal on Friday night they chose to return to Blimpy's place for an encore performance of Thursday's magnificent dining tour de force.

"We've got to make this an annual event," proclaimed George as the two men waited for their steaks to be prepared.

"This place?" asked Henry from across the table as he sipped from his drink. "I can't wait a whole year to get back here."

"All of it, I mean this whole weekend," clarified George.

Henry shook his head. Now, he understood exactly what George meant.

"Oh yeah, I totally agree. Honestly George, I really can't remember having such a great time. It really flew by."

"Time has a way of doing that," George concurred.

"Well, it's not always about the quantity of time, but the quality, right?" Henry asked as he held up his glass for a toast. George followed his lead and the friends gently tapped their tumblers together.

"You know, I had that exact conversation with Claire right before she died."

"Oh, I'm sorry pal. I wasn't trying to bring that up," Henry apologized.

"No Henry, not at all. It doesn't upset me like that. Oh sure, I miss her like crazy every single day. Geez, she's the first thing I think of when I wake up and the last thing at night when I hit the pillow. But you know, I had a wife and best friend for nearly forty-four years. You can't feel sorry for yourself with a record like that. Sure it hurts, but no self-pity here," he declared as he eased back. "We did it all, left nothing to regret. It was the *best*. Just a real love affair. Of course, I'd kill for just one more minute together, but I never let myself think that way because God gave me such a wonderful life with her. You know how many guys have never had that?"

Henry listened intently to every word his friend said and nodded in complete agreement. He indeed understood exactly what George meant.

"Yep, I surely do."

George detected the solemnness of Henry's tone, and now it was his turn to beg pardon.

"I didn't mean it like that, buddy," George explained, referring to Henry and Mary and their failed marriage.

"Oh, I know that. But I have to tell you that sometimes I feel just a little bit jealous of you," Henry admitted.

"You do? Why?" George asked.

"You and Claire, your kids. Just all of it. George, I royally screwed up my chance at that. Now I'm just an old man with a cat." He laughed half-heartedly at himself as he gazed off into the distance in the direction of the kitchen.

"Hey, you've got Millie too," George reminded him.

The mention of her name caught Henry off guard, and he looked directly at George. "*What do you mean?*" he asked.

"Come on Henry, what's going on there? She's been with you for decades. You told me you guys get along real well. So what's the deal?"

Henry gulped the final swallow from his glass and placed it on the table in front of him. He considered George's question for a moment before responding. Then, finally, he decided it was time to break his silence on the topic.

"Well, I do have some feelings for her, sure. But I don't know what to do about that. She's been working for me for so long that it isn't like she's an employee anymore. Now, it's kind of like she's my family. Whatever the hell *that* is. I just don't know how to tell her that."

George smiled at his friend as he leaned toward him. "That's not a bad way to say it right there," he offered.

"Gentlemen, can I get you another round?" asked the waitress as she paused at the table.

"Yes ma'am, please," Henry replied as George finished his drink as well.

"Great! I'll be right back," she said as she headed off toward the bar.

"What if you asked her to dinner and brought her here?"

"You're kidding!" Henry scoffed.

"Why not? It's just dinner. She eats, right? Besides, you two had dinner after you saw Mary and you told me it was great."

Henry hesitated. He didn't have a valid objection.

"First off, I don't even know if she likes steak," he protested weakly.

"You're joking, right? Henry, she's worked for you for like what? Twenty-three or four years? How about you ask her?" George needled him. "Or take her someplace else with something she does like to eat," he added with a laugh.

"It's not quite that simple," Henry argued.

"The hell it's not. You're a man, and she's a woman. My friend, *that is how it works*."

"Yeah, I don't know," Henry mumbled as the waitress dropped off fresh drinks for the men and cleared away the empty glasses.

"Your steaks will be out shortly, fellas," she advised.

"Thank you, ma'am," Henry acknowledged.

"Henry, it's not my business, I know, but how long has it been since you've been with a woman?" George asked with a more hushed tone. Perhaps he was feeling his liquor, but it was a question that he had pondered before this.

Henry nearly spit his drink. "What the hell, George?" he fired back.

"Come on now Henry, we aren't kids. Seriously, how long?"

"George, I'm not interested in discussing this," Henry declared with a degree of agitation.

"Calm down, I'm not fishing for carnal details," he whispered. "I just think it might explain why you are hesitant to pursue Millie. You mean to tell me that in twenty-something years you never thought about being with her? You've never flirted with the idea, or her, for that matter?"

Not a moment too soon for Henry, the waitress approached their table with two large platters that were dwarfed by enormous steaks complete with baked potatoes on the side. "Here you go, gentlemen," she proclaimed. Clearly, she was completely oblivious to the fact that she had just interrupted George's interrogation at a critical juncture.

Though Henry gratefully viewed the arrival of their food as the end to the matter, George had other ideas. While he gave the appearance that he was now more interested in lathering sour cream on his potato than in pursuing the discussion of Henry's love life, nothing was further from the truth. To him, it was merely halftime of the game. He had successfully convinced a reluctant Henry to reconcile with Mary. Now, he was determined to continue his mission to help his friend fully return to the human race. Bill was going to be a tougher nut to crack, but with Millie, George could see definite light at the end of the tunnel.

*

Sunday's drive home from St. Louis was dramatically different for Henry than the trip he had taken to get there on Thursday. This time, rather than being blissfully consumed with thoughts of coins, he was meditating on what George had said the previous evening. Regardless of the fact that his friend had mercifully dropped the subject, Henry now could not seem to get entirely away from it.

Again and again, he rolled the words over in his head. George had touched on a nerve. Certainly, over the past forty years he had occasionally enjoyed the company of a woman. He was a handsome, rich, and powerful businessman who traveled the world. Such interludes were not beyond his grasp. However, none of those encounters could be characterized as anything approaching the status of an affair, much less a relationship. Rather they were more akin to business deals; emotionless and simply for self-gratification. He had never allowed anyone into his heart or permitted his feelings to become entangled with another. If someone tried to get too close, he moved on. The current state of affairs with Millie was rapidly drawing him into new territory, and he found himself unsteady and awkward. These feelings were foreign to him.

Henry had built his adult life on being confident, detached, and in control. Such qualities had always served him well and propelled him to high achievement in his business dealings. Along the way, he had found a certain sense of balance and happiness that now seemed like sand slipping through his fingers. He was nervous and unsure of how to proceed. At times, he now even felt lonely. These emotions were all new for him, and he didn't like them one bit.

Suddenly, he found himself exiting the highway and turning his car back toward St. Louis. George's questions may have been uncomfortable for him, but he was exactly right, yet again. As the Lincoln lunged back toward the city, Henry realized that only someone who had been in love and happily married could help him with his dilemma. He needed expert advice on how to proceed with Millie and move their relationship forward. He was through with being alone, both in his bed and in his heart.

CHAPTER 8

Transformation

HENRY EASED THE Lincoln to a halt and paused for a moment before exiting the car. His presence there was unplanned, and his intentions were certainly unannounced, but he hoped that he would be well-received. His anxiety and awkwardness about discussing his feelings for Millie were quickly overwhelmed by his need to get his affection for her out in the open with someone. In short order, he was out of the car and proceeding briskly on foot across the well-manicured cemetery lawn.

Clear blue skies and bright early afternoon sunshine brought warmth to the air. Henry noted that it wasn't nearly as cool as it had been on his previous visit to see Mary. As he neared the cottonwood tree that stood over her resting place, he regretted that he had not had the forethought to stop for flowers this time, but his mind had been elsewhere. Henry paused for a brief instant to pay his respects to Doc Winters and his wife before proceeding to the bench beside Mary's grave.

"Hello honey," he greeted her as he sat down. "I imagine you didn't expect to see me again so soon after not having been together for so long, huh?" he asked with a light chuckle, suddenly realizing his odd timing and reason for being there. As a way to procrastinate a bit and buy some time before explaining, he glanced around the cemetery grounds and noticed a navy blue sedan passing through the entrance. Beyond the arrival of that party, the place was completely deserted. Recognizing that he was stalling, he returned his attention to her and the matter at hand.

"Well... you see..." he stammered," I've got a problem... and I need your advice on how to handle it. I told you about Millie, my uh... housekeeper. Well, it seems things are a little different with her than I let on the last time I saw you." Henry was fumbling his words noticeably now because he felt abashed and embarrassed again about it all. In the midst of his ardor to get answers, he hadn't really thought through the wisdom of seeking counsel about his relationship with Millie from his now-deceased ex-wife.

Before he could go further, the sound of a car door nearby caught his attention. He looked over in the direction of the sound and saw the navy sedan now parked neatly beside his Lincoln. A young woman was approaching slowly. As she neared, he could see that she bore a striking resemblance to Mary. In fact, she looked nearly *exactly* like the image of Mary he held now only in his memory. Her large brown eyes and long flowing auburn hair were nearly identical to Mary's. In addition, she was surely in her early thirties, as Mary had been the last time Henry had been in her presence in 1953. In her hands, she carried a large bouquet of yellow daisies.

Henry was frozen as his breath was nearly taken away from him by the sight of her. Sensing something was slightly amiss, the woman took the opportunity to speak first as she arrived on the scene.

"Good afternoon, sir."

Henry couldn't believe it. She even *sounded* like Mary. It was is if he had been transported to some alternate universe.

"Hello," he weakly mumbled as he rose to his feet.

"Oh, please don't get up," she said gently as she motioned for him to keep his seat, which he did. His legs felt unsteady due to this strange turn of events. "I haven't seen you before. Did you know my grandparents and my mother?" she asked with a smile as she directed her eyes toward Mary's headstone.

Her grandparents and her mother. Of course! Henry instantly regained his wits as he comprehended what she had said and recalled that George had told him about Mary's children. She had given birth to two sons in addition to an attractive young daughter who was now standing before him.

I'll be damned, he thought in amazement.

"Yes, as a matter of fact, I knew them all, dear. I grew up in Lewis with her," he answered as he also turned toward Mary.

"Really? That's fantastic!" she exclaimed as she moved forward to place the flowers she held at the base of her mother's headstone.

"I should leave you alone with her," Henry stated as he again moved to stand.

"No, it's ok, please don't leave. I just wanted to stop and leave some flowers for her. She just loved yellow daisies," she declared as she stepped back.

"She sure did," he agreed. "She really liked things that were bright and cheery." The comment brought another smile to the woman's face.

"Yeah, she did. She was the happiest person I ever knew."

Now it was Henry's turn to smile. He was thrilled to hear that this was the legacy Mary had left behind. She truly had found happiness in the aftermath of the debacle their marriage became.

"Since you knew all of them, would it be rude and indelicate of me to ask who you are? I mean, I've never met you before is all."

Henry thought for a moment as he stood beside her before answering.

"Not at all. Well, let's just say I lost track of your mom a long time ago. Once, we were very close. Recently I found out that she was here, and I needed to come see her. I had some things I needed to talk about."

"I see," the woman replied and held out her hand. "I'm Elizabeth."

Henry turned toward Mary's daughter and recognized a familiar sparkle in her eyes and warmth in her touch as they shook hands.

"Hello Elizabeth, I'm Henry."

"It's a pleasure to meet you, Henry," she said as they returned to facing Mary.

"Did you get a chance to say what you wanted to Mom? I can leave you two alone," she asked sincerely.

"Actually, I was here a while back on a different day, and she and I took care of that business," he declared happily. "As usual, your mom was gracious and let me off the hook." Elizabeth smiled. "No, I came here today seeking advice on something else but after I got here, I realized it was a pretty silly idea."

"Really? How about you try me? Mom always told me I had her common sense," Elizabeth said as she moved over to the bench and sat down. "My friends are always hitting me up for help with their love lives and problems. Have a seat and tell me what's going on." She patted the open space on the bench beside her as Henry looked on, completely bewildered.

Sensing his trepidation, she quickly added, "Who better to talk to than a stranger? Especially if you've got woman trouble."

Henry immediately understood that Mary's daughter was extremely intuitive. Despite his typical aversion to such exchanges, he soon found himself sitting down next to her.

"All right then, what's the story?" she asked.

Henry looked at her with a funny expression. She was a very outgoing and comfortable sort, and he found himself oddly at ease with her. As she had said, who better to talk to than a stranger, right?

"Hmmm, what exactly would lead you to say 'especially if it's woman trouble'?"

"Well Henry, it's obvious. Why else does a man go to seek advice from a woman if it isn't about another woman?" she asked.

Her demeanor was confident, and her tone was matter-of-fact. Henry couldn't argue the point and broke into mild laughter.

"Point made."

"So, come on already. What did you want to talk to Mom about? I promise I'll do my best to tell you what I think she'd say."

As strange as the whole encounter was, Henry couldn't help but feel intrigued by her offer. It was just too good to pass up. Besides, to her he was just some strange man named Henry. He couldn't see any downside to opening up to her about Millie. In fact, it might just be the perfect scenario.

"All right... yes, it's a woman." Elizabeth smiled and nodded her head as Henry continued. "She's worked for me as my housekeeper for a very long time, closing in on 25 years. Her name is Millie, and we've never been anything but maid and boss until this last year. But now, I guess I've kind of figured out that I have some feelings for her. You know, more than that."

"I see," Elizabeth replied while seriously pondering his comments. "Does Millie know how you feel?"

"I don't know; I think so. At least I guess she has an idea anyway."

"An idea? Huh. Does she feel the same way about you?"

"I'm not sure. I get the feeling that she has some sort of affection for me; I just don't know how far it goes."

"During the time you guys have been together, have either of you ever been married?" she asked.

"Nope. I'm divorced. It happened a long time ago, and I've been alone ever since. Millie never married, never even had a boyfriend as far as I know in all the years I've known her."

"Henry, haven't you ever talked to her about how you feel about her? Or asked her how she feels about you?" Elizabeth inquired.

"No, we're not exactly at that stage yet. That's why I came to see your mom. I haven't dated much the past 30 years, so I don't know what to say when it comes to my feelings."

Elizabeth looked out over the grounds as she considered Henry's dilemma. *What would Mom tell him?* she wondered. They sat silently together, and both were lost in their thoughts for a spell before Elizabeth broke the silence.

"Henry, I've just met you, but I'd bet that Millie is in the same boat as you are. She's been with you all this time and never even has had a boyfriend? Is she ugly? Is she a rotten person?"

Henry chuckled. "No, as a matter of fact, she's quite pretty and a very lovely person. Extraordinary, to be exact."

Elizabeth smiled broadly. "You're in love with her, Henry."

Henry was taken aback by the word. *Love.* It was a big word for certain and not one he had often entertained in his life. However, upon reflection he couldn't argue the point. Placing his hands on his knees and looking at the ground between his feet, he surrendered to the idea.

"Yes, maybe. I don't know; I guess I am."

Elizabeth tapped her hand on his twice before retracting it. "That's wonderful!" she said, expressing the giddiness of a young girl.

"But how do I tell her? What if she cares for me, but as a brother or father?" he asked with the insecurity of a high school freshman.

Elizabeth was touched by his genuine sweetness. He displayed an innocence and sincerity that was more typical of a pre-teen than a man of his age and experience. She placed her hand on his once again, this time keeping it there. Her touch brought his eyes to hers.

"Henry, you are a very handsome and well-spoken man. I'm willing to bet that she *does not* think of you as her father or her brother. Ask her on a date."

"I can't do that."

"Sure you can; just ask her to go to dinner."

"Now you sound like George," Henry protested.

"Who's George?" Elizabeth asked.

"My best friend. He grew up with me and your mom; she knew him very well."

"Oh… *George.* Got it, sounds like a very smart man. Ok, well then, how about you invite her to join you on a picnic? Do you like picnics?" she pressed.

"I haven't been on a picnic in a *really long time.*" Henry's mind jumped backward to the last real picnic he had been on. It was with Elizabeth's mother, many decades ago.

"Well, then I'd say it's about time! Ask Millie to go on a picnic. Spend some time with her outside the house where she's always worked. You know, let her see you in a different light. Trust me; after that, the words will come."

Henry couldn't help but smile at the thought of what she had just said. It sounded like a brilliant plan. Elizabeth seemed to be a wonderful and sensitive young woman. *Truly her mother's daughter,* he thought. But before he could respond, she added a phrase that stunned him.

"Besides, Henry, you were good enough for my mom to marry, so I am quite sure you're good enough for Millie." As she delivered the clincher to her proposal, she winked and broke into a sly grin.

Henry was floored. *How the hell does she know about me?* His mind spun around, and his eyes glazed over for a moment as he absorbed her words. After Henry had regained his bearings, Elizabeth explained that her mother had told her all about him prior to her death. She further expanded that *Uncle George* had long been a favorite person of hers. George had conveniently neglected to mention that small detail to Henry, but in fairness to George, likely never expected them to meet. Henry was elated to learn that Mary spoke very well of him and held no ill feelings toward him despite their tumultuous divorce. Quite to the contrary, Mary had certainly come to understand all that had happened and made her peace with it.

"Mom told me during those last days, if I ever met you, to let you know that she was sorry about the way things ended and that she never stopped caring for you."

Henry was moved beyond words. It was as if Mary had once

again reached beyond the grave and orchestrated his heart's reclamation. He was well past tears. In fact, Elizabeth's words left him completely numb. By the time the pair parted ways, they had both become emotional and recovered. They exchanged contact information and agreed to keep in touch. It was cleansing and therapeutic for both of them, each in his or her own way.

Henry drove home both liberated and burdened by the meeting with Mary's daughter. He felt incredibly free of the past and yet somehow fully shackled by his current unfinished business. Elizabeth was right, and he knew it. It was up to him to move his relationship with Millie forward. The time had come, and it was squarely upon his shoulders to push ahead. If Millie didn't want him, if she didn't share his feelings, she would have to say so. However, Henry decided that being nervous and afraid of the future was a pathetically weak position that did not suit a man of his standing. As a result, along the miles of asphalt home, Henry Engel was transformed into yet another new version of himself. He resolved that he would lay his cards upon the table before Millie and accept his fate like a man, no matter the outcome.

*

As Henry entered the house with bags on both shoulders and his hands full, sunlight darted through the windows and sliced the afternoon shadows. Joe, thrilled at the sight of him, rubbed herself vociferously across his shins as he stood at the island putting his briefcase and luggage down.

"Hey, darling!" he called out to his furry pal. He was equally as happy to see her as she was to see him.

While he accepted her affection, Henry's eyes drifted to the answering machine, which displayed a blinking red light indicating that at least one message had been received since last it was checked. Next to the machine, a handwritten note on a scrap of paper also was waiting for him.

"It's all right, sweetheart," Henry mumbled while breaking away from Joe's homecoming to check the messages. As he approached the machine, he could clearly see Millie's handwriting on the accompanying note next to it. It read: "Please call asap – Millie". This was potentially cause for alarm because, in all of the years they had been together, Millie had not once ever left such a note for him. Before retrieving the other message from the machine, Henry grabbed the handset and dialed Millie's telephone number. Following a short delay and two loud clicks, the phone rang seven times before Henry gathered that she was not going to answer and depressed the button on the device to end the call. In case he had dialed in error, Henry tried the number once again before reaching the same result and ultimately abandoning the enterprise. He took a look at the clock and noted that the time was just past 4:00 p.m. *Maybe that's another message from Millie on the machine.* Henry moved to hit the playback button on the answering machine that was still blinking. However, rather than retrieving a message from Millie he was surprised to hear the voice of his new favorite British author. Anne had called to check-in and let Henry know that she had made arrangements with Louis to begin some work on the Stewart place. She informed Henry that Louis knew that he was to contact him should he have any issues and was unable to reach her directly. Also, she said that she hoped to be in town in a couple of weeks to begin setting up the home.

"Good deal," Henry said aloud in response to the news that Anne would be returning in the near future to Lewis. He was looking forward to seeing her again. Any concerns that Henry had about Millie's whereabouts were dismissed.

"Huh, I guess Millie's out and about somewhere. Oh well, if it was something big she'd be waiting for a call or would have left me a voice message. Hey, guess what? Anne is coming back soon. I'd say that warrants an early meeting with Jake, wouldn't you?" he asked Joe, who was looking up at him as he stepped toward the cabinet. Joe couldn't understand a word that he said, but Henry seemed happy enough about whatever it was. The sound of ice cubes hitting the bottom of his glass quickly revealed to her what was happening. Joe sat patiently as Henry prepared Jake for their meeting. She watched his every move with keen interest as she tried to determine if they would be going outside or to his recliner. The answer quickly came as he walked across the kitchen and into the family room. Henry was worn out from both a long weekend away as well as an emotional day, and the comfort of his favorite chair was calling.

Joe sauntered leisurely behind and waited for Henry to settle in before leaping up onto his lap. Once he had provided the requisite pets that she was accustomed to, she nestled herself alongside his leg and snuggled into her familiar spot. Henry was glad to see her feeling spry and like her old self again. She seemed very healthy and well and he wondered if maybe she had even gained just a touch of weight since Thursday.

"It's good to be home, baby," he told her as he leaned his head back and rested his right hand on her side. Joe enjoyed his touch and purred in assent. Henry closed his eyes and let his mind drift. His thoughts traveled to Millie and what his next move was going to be. Elizabeth had given him the advice and insight that he had sought. Now it was time to put that expertise into practice. *A picnic? Hmmm. Yes, that could be very nice.* He pondered how to approach her with the idea and ways to make it a most memorable day. Joe's purrs became softer as she slid into a deep slumber at his side. Henry's breathing eased and his eyes closed as he too gently dozed. All felt right at Oak Forest and the future, like the late afternoon sunshine, was bright.

CHAPTER 9

Breaking News

HENRY SAT AT his usual place at the island and sipped from his coffee cup while browsing through the Monday morning edition of the *Lewis Gazette*. His eyes were scanning the printed words before him, but he wasn't truly comprehending the stories that were found there. His mind was occupied elsewhere. It was nearly 9:00 a.m. and Millie would be arriving soon. Though he was quite anxious to see her, he was also feeling a little apprehensive too. Last evening, he had resolved to invite her to join him for a picnic, and he was not about to back down from it now. It was to be *a real* date and the thought of it was exciting as well as a tad unnerving. He hoped that his overture of romance would be well-received but was readying himself for all possible outcomes. *Plan for the best but be prepared for the worst* had long been a favorite saying of his Uncle Ed's, and it echoed in Henry's ears this morning. However, no matter the outcome, he was not going to let fear hold him back any longer. His heart had fully healed, and he was finally ready now to share it again with someone.

The sound of the side door opening announced that Millie had arrived. Hearing her, Joe rose from her resting place on the bottom step and raced to greet her. *All right, it's time to step up,* Henry thought to himself with firm resolve. As soon as she was settled in, he would ask her the all-important question. The door closed, and he could hear Millie greeting Joe affectionately in the next room.

"Well, hey there Henry!" she declared as she entered the kitchen. "How was your weekend?"

"Hello, there young lady! It was outstanding. We had one helluva good time," Henry replied warmly while readying himself to pivot the conversation to the topic that now dominated his thoughts.

"Oh, that's wonderful!" she remarked as she moved past and headed to the hall tree to put down her purse. "I was sure hoping you fellas were having a good time."

"Thanks! Yeah, we really did. The coin show was excellent, and we had a couple of top-notch steak dinners too," he declared recalling the fine meals he had enjoyed at The Ranch with George.

"That's sure good to hear! Say, did you see the note I left you? Man, do I have some crazy good news for you!" she proclaimed with glee as she passed by him on the way to the cabinet for a coffee cup.

"Yep, I got it. I tried to call a couple of times just after four, but no one answered. I guessed you were out. I planned on trying again later, but I dozed off in my chair. When I finally woke up it was nearly ten, and I figured maybe it was too late then and it could wait. You know, you really ought to get a machine." Henry was referring to Millie's lack of an answering machine. She had long held that no one of any importance ever called her anyway and, therefore, it was a luxury item that she didn't need. She loved to say that *if someone really needs to talk to me they'll call back.* Right on cue, Millie took the opportunity to play that same old song again.

"Nah, nobody ever calls my place anyway," she said as she poured herself a cup of hot coffee. "Besides, if someone really needs to talk to me, they'll call back." Her familiar refrain brought a slight smile to Henry's face.

"Yeah, well *this* nobody tried to call you," he protested playfully. "Tell me something, if you aren't there to answer the phone yourself and don't have a machine to leave a message on, then exactly how do you know that nobody ever calls you?"

Millie chuckled as she turned to the island with the coffee pot in hand. She raised her eyebrows to him, and he nodded affirmatively. After she had refilled his nearly empty cup, she returned the pot to the warmer.

"I'm sure sorry I missed your calls. I guess that was when I was at choir practice. We were…" Almost as if she had been abruptly given some sort of mild electrical shock, she looked up at him with a surprised look. "Oh my gosh!" she exclaimed. "I still haven't told you the big news!" Her last few words were excited and slightly exaggerated.

Henry was intrigued by her sudden shift in demeanor and curious to hear what had her so worked up. At the same time, he could not help but notice that she looked quite fetching this morning. He had seen her on thousands of mornings over the years, but now she somehow looked different to him. While hearing her news was certainly of interest, he was reminded that he had an awful lot that he was anxious to talk to her about too.

"Well, believe it or not, Mr. Engel, you are going to be a granddad!" she exclaimed. Henry heard the words, but they did not add up. Considering he didn't have any children, this seemed like some sort of far-fetched joke, and he couldn't see the humor in it.

"Huh? A what? What the heck are you talking about?"

"A granddaddy!" she repeated with a glowing grin. "Joe is going to be a momma!"

Henry looked at Millie as if she had just sprouted a second head. He didn't understand what could possibly be funny about such a preposterous statement but was attempting to discern why she was telling him this. For her part, Joe was completely unfazed by the announcement. She sat calmly by the French doors intently watching a small beetle that was traveling doggedly across the patio.

"What's the punch line, Millie? I just don't get it. Why is this funny?"

Millie was now becoming as confused as Henry seemed to be. "No, no Henry, I'm not joking. I took Joe into Doc Miller's on Thursday like we said, and she checked her out. Doc says she's just fine for a pregnant kitty." Henry's eyebrows jumped. "I know! I just about fell over too," she added noting Henry's obvious shock and disbelief at the news.

"But how?" Henry asked incredulously.

"Well, you see Henry, when a boy kitty loves a girl kitty then they..." she teased.

"No, not that!" he fired back. "I mean when? How? I don't understand how on earth that this could have happened?"

"Well, Doc Miller said that she must've found herself a boyfriend in the neighborhood."

"No fooling? I suppose that does explain why she was so anxious to get outside all of the time," he reasoned aloud. Millie nodded her head in agreement as she took a sip of coffee from her cup and allowed Henry to digest everything.

"I mean, I guess I never really even thought about whether or not she'd been fixed. I just figured if she was inside and around here all of the time it wasn't an issue. Hell, I've never even seen another cat around. Have you?" he asked.

"Nope. That part sure is a mystery. On the other hand, when a girl falls in love, I suppose she finds a way," she quipped as she looked over at Joe.

"Wow, kittens… What do you know about that? Well… Congratulations, Momma!" Henry declared as he too turned his eyes toward Joe, who was still single-mindedly locked in on the slow but persistent beetle.

"So, what now?" Henry asked returning his focus to Millie.

"Well, Doc Miller says she can feel them in there. She figures she's just about four weeks along right now based on how she's been acting and her size and all."

"But she's so tiny. How's *she* going to have babies?"

"She said she'll do just fine. Nature always seems to find a way. When it gets closer, she can take an x-ray if we want and see how many there are. She'll also decide if she's gonna need a C-section or not."

"Good Lord, five minutes ago I'm reading the morning paper and sipping on my coffee, and now I'm thinking about C-sections," Henry gasped.

"Aww, don't you worry none, Henry. I've got this." She put her cup down on the counter and walked over to Joe. As she knelt down and picked up the little cat, she continued: "It'll all work itself out. She's gonna be just fine. Besides, after it's all over we're gonna have us some baby kittens to play with!" Millie gently rubbed Joe's neck and ears as the feline quickly forgot all about the traveling insect that she had just been observing. Though Henry was still reeling a bit, Millie was unflappable.

She appeared gleeful and untroubled. Having given birth herself, she was at ease and excited about Joe's impending motherhood. It was a feeling that only a woman who has gone through it personally can comprehend. Her exuberance and confidence buoyed a previously unsteady Henry.

"Ok then, I guess *we're* going to be grandparents!" he declared. His inclusion of Millie in the statement and the fashion in which he did so were not lost on her.

"We sure are!" she beamed with a wink as she and Joe moved beside him at the island.

Henry reached over and patted Joe lightly a couple of times. She wasn't precisely certain what she had done to warrant such lavish attention, but she was sure that it was deserved in some way and relished their affection.

"All right then, what's next?" he asked.

"Well, let's see. Doc Miller said she is supposed to be eating kitten food from now on to get plenty of vitamins and nutrients for the babies. I stopped at the store on Friday and picked some up, so it's already switched out."

Henry nodded approvingly.

"She said that she expects that Joe ought to perk up now and start gaining some weight."

"I think she already seems better than she did last week," he offered.

"Yeah, I do too."

"Do we have any idea when all of these kittens will arrive?"

"Around 63-69 days out she'll be ready to have them, but Doc says Siamese cats sometimes can go a couple days longer. She's figuring they'll be here sometime in early June."

Henry considered the calendar while Joe purred vigorously and snuggled against Millie's chest.

"Doc Miller also said that she might be extra lovey-dovey these days. Guess she hit that one on the head, huh?"

Henry laughed. "Yeah, I'd say so."

He rose from his chair to take his customary morning stroll around the grounds. Sensing it was time for their daily inspection of things, Joe wiggled to get down from Millie's arms. Seeing what was happening, Millie was reminded of one further instruction that she had received regarding the expectant mother.

"Oh and by the way, she's gotta stay indoors from now on," Millie said as she lowered the cat to the floor.

"Oh, no kidding?" Henry complained. Joe meowed twice, seemingly in protest as well as if she too understood the doctor's orders.

"I'm sorry, kiddo," he apologized to the little cat as she looked wistfully up at him. He glanced out the kitchen window and could see dark clouds gathering, indicating that a spring rain shower was possible. "I don't expect I'll be outside too long though," he consoled her.

Before he could make a move for the door, the telephone rang, causing him to pause to see who was calling. Millie was nearest to the phone, and she picked it up and handed it to him.

"Hello," he said into the handset.

"Hi there, Henry," George greeted him.

"Hey partner, what's going on this morning?"

"I just got a call from our friend. Do you have a minute?" George asked, referring to the investigator Henry had hired to track down Millie's son.

"Yeah, sure, I've got that coin book," Henry answered without hesitation. "Let me get to my office and look that up for you." He immediately headed to the next room as Millie went about her business without suspicion. Realizing that he was no longer going outside, Joe decided to follow him and see what was going on.

"Gotcha, she's right there," George whispered in acknowledgment of Henry's meaning.

"Yeah, that's right, gimme a second," Henry directed as he passed through the family room.

Once he had reached his office, and Joe had scooted inside with him, Henry closed both doors and took a seat in his chair. He switched on the desk lamp as the growing darkness outside made the room too gloomy for his taste.

"Ok pal, sorry, she was right on top of me. What did Johnston have to say?"

"Well, he's got it honed down to two guys. Two guys named Edward James that are the right age, and both were adopted in Georgia. One was born in Atlanta and the other in Athens."

"Millie told me she was staying with her grandmother in Atlanta when she had the baby. That's gotta be him. Tell Carl to run him down and get me the full bio on the guy." Henry leaned back in his chair, quite pleased with himself. Though he had proceeded without her consent, he was certain that she would be happy to find her son and discover what kind of man he had become. After having witnessed her reaction to Joe's unexpected motherhood, he was certain that to finally be able to see her own child again would be a tremendous gift to give her. Now, the only concern was to find out if, in fact, Edward James fit the desired narrative. Either way, Henry felt confident about how he had played the cards. If Edward was anything but a model citizen, Henry would be able to shield Millie from it. There was no downside to this deal, as far as he could tell. However, though Henry had always been an astute businessman, he was less skilled and experienced in matters of the heart. He could not see the pitfall that potentially awaited him.

"Ok Henry, good deal. I'll call him back as soon as we hang up. Say, while I have you, *how is Millie doing today?*"

Henry was caught off guard by his friend's reference to Millie. It was clearly an attempt to reopen the conversation they had engaged in on Saturday night over dinner. It also reminded Henry that he had a bone to pick with George about Mary's daughter Elizabeth. George had conveniently neglected to tell him about the apparently close relationship he had maintained over the years with the Anderson family. However, rather than open that can of worms now and be forced to delve into a deep and drawn-out conversation, Henry opted to keep this hand close to his vest. News of his meeting with Elizabeth and the subsequent discussion he had with her about his love life could wait until another time.

"She's fine, George," he replied with disinterest. He was his best friend and his closest confidant, but for now, Henry preferred to pursue Millie privately without the added pressure of George's scrutiny. There would be ample time for that later.

Sensing that Henry was in no mood to be prodded today, George decided to simply let the matter drop. The two men spent the next half hour conversing about their weekend and rehashing favorite moments and coins. Suddenly, Henry recalled that he had breaking news to share.

"Hey, guess what? You won't believe this, but Joe is going to have kittens!" he proclaimed proudly. He was now past his anxiety about it and felt genuinely excited.

"No fooling?! How the heck did she manage that? Immaculate conception?"

"You got me; somehow she found a pal to play with."

"Maybe she could give you a few pointers," George jabbed.

"Ha! Very funny. Don't start that up again."

"Just teasing." Not wanting to antagonize Henry, George retreated as quickly as he had attacked. "So, where are you going with all of these kittens? Are you going to keep them all?"

Henry hadn't even had time to consider such things, and suddenly his initial trepidation was returning.

"You know, great question; I have no idea. No, surely not. I don't need a house full of cats over here."

"Well, there's plenty of time to figure it out. Hell, I might even be willing to take one off of your hands," George hinted.

"Seriously?"

"Yeah, I've been thinking about getting a dog or a cat or something. This house can get a little quiet sometimes," he explained.

"I get it. If you want one or all of them, George, you're first in line," Henry joked.

"How about you pencil me in for one for now, and we'll see how it goes?" George laughed. "You know, it'll be nice to have a little company around here. Besides, my grandkids will love it."

"Ok, I'll clear it with Millie but I'd say you're locked in."

Henry's words only reinforced to both of them just how intertwined he and Millie truly were. Realizing that he had an urgent matter of his own to attend to, Henry concluded his call with George and strolled back to the kitchen in search of a partner for a picnic.

CHAPTER 10
It's a Date!

UPON ENTERING THE kitchen, Henry was disappointed to discover that Millie was nowhere in sight. He quickly concluded that she must have gone to the second floor on a mission to collect dirty laundry or perhaps to inspect the cleanliness of his bathroom.

"Hey Millie!" he called upstairs as he lifted his right foot onto the bottom step.

"Yes Henry?" an immediate reply came from the laundry room to his left.

"Oh, you're in there?" he said as he turned in surprise.

"Yeah, did you need something?" Millie asked as she walked into the kitchen from the next room.

"Umm, well… as a matter of fact, I do need something."

"Ok," she acknowledged as she stepped toward him.

However, now that the critical moment was at hand, he was starting to feel just a little off-balance again. Joe was unfazed by the events transpiring before her and strolled casually from the family room to a comfortable spot on the second step of the staircase. There, she took up a post from which she could keep an eye on things while giving herself a meticulous bath.

"Umm, well... I'd like to know how you feel about picnics," he blurted out clumsily.

"Huh?" she answered without understanding his meaning.

"You know, picnics? Food and drink on a blanket under a tree somewhere."

The expression on Millie's face was a combination of confusion and surprise. Her jaw dropped, leaving her mouth slightly open while Henry's mind raced.

"Well, I'm sure you've been on a picnic before right? So, I just want to know if you want to go on one... with me. A real one, you know, on a date."

It was all out in the open now. The word *date* had been uttered and the official invitation extended. There was no turning back from here.

Millie was completely caught off guard by the request and could only muster a barely discernible grunt. Her eyes seemed to glaze over as if she had just been hypnotized. Sensing her stupor, Henry seized the opportunity to attempt to explain himself and hopefully seal the deal.

"Well, you do eat, right?" The rhetorical question brought only a weak nod from Millie.

"All right then, well so do I. How about we eat together on a blanket somewhere? You know, on a picnic."

Millie continued to stare at him in utter silence with a blank expression on her face. She was flabbergasted and still reeling from the unexpected invitation. Finally, after she'd taken a deep breath, she managed to mutter weakly, "But it's raining."

"What?" Henry asked not understanding the strange response. He looked out the kitchen window to see that the skies had opened, and a deluge was pouring down on Oak Forest. It seemed that his plans, for now at least, had been derailed. Not one to go down without a fight, he quickly adjusted accordingly.

"Oh ok, right. Well, then how about tomorrow or the next day?"

Millie had now started to regain her wits and finally was figuring out what Henry had in mind. She immediately saw it as an opportunity to have some fun with him.

"So tell me, would I have to fix the food for this shindig, or would it be your treat?"

Henry had been so consumed with the idea of asking Millie on a date that he hadn't given the actual meal any thought prior to this. Nevertheless, it was an important detail, and he thought that she had a valid point. The night of their first dinner together Millie had prepared the meal despite Henry's protestations. Now, for what would be truly their first official "date," he felt a repeat of the same was unacceptable.

"No, no, it will be my treat, of course," he assured her.

"Are we talking a sub sandwich from the deli or something more?" she asked with the tone of a cold hard negotiator holding out for the best offer. Henry was unsure what to say to this since he had no clue what he was doing with regard to picnic menu planning. However, he was an expert at negotiating and had made his fortune by striking tough deals when others could not.

"I have a little something better in mind than that," he answered coyly.

"Will there be barbecue pork sandwiches and coleslaw on this picnic?"

"Huh? I don't know. Yeah, I guess so."

"What about potato chips? You know the real thick, crunchy kind?"

"Ok, sure." As he answered her, it occurred to him that he

hadn't previously understood what a key selling point the menu apparently was when proposing a picnic date to someone.

"How 'bout root beer? You gonna have root beer?"

Now Henry was starting to wise up to what she was doing.

"You mean cold root beer, right out of a glass bottle?"

Millie smiled. "It's just not a picnic without root beer," she added.

"Of course. It's not a picnic without root beer," he agreed.

Deciding that she had tortured him enough, she opted to give in.

"How can a girl say no to all of that? Why sure, Henry, I'd love to!"

"All right then, it's a date!" Henry declared with a sly grin as if he was the cat who had just swallowed the canary.

"Yes sir, it sure is. It's a *date*." Millie repeated his words with a wink as she brushed his left arm briefly with her right hand before turning to go back to her chores.

"You sure you don't want some pie with that too?" he called out with mock indignation at her demands.

"Surprise me," she tossed back playfully over her shoulder without turning around.

Henry laughed at her sassy remark. *Hot damn, that went pretty well!* he thought with delight as he watched her step away.

"About time; I thought you'd never ask," Millie whispered aloud with a giggle after she had passed through the doorway and out of Henry's earshot.

Feeling thoroughly happy about how things had played out, Henry gathered Joe in his arms and retreated to his office. Once there, he occasionally looked out to see the rain falling outside his window as he considered how to make their picnic a day that Millie would never forget.

In the afternoon, a knock at the front door and a look at his watch combined to tell Henry that the day's mail had arrived. It was 2:01 p.m., and Lucy Dawson was on time as always. His mail carrier knew that he liked to peruse the day's mail as soon as possible. On days when the weather did not cooperate to allow for his walk to the street, she drove up to the front door and brought it to him. Such was the character of the man that he commanded her respect. Such was the character of the woman that she gave it to him.

Henry opened the front door to find Lucy's bright smile waiting on the other side of the glass. In her hands, she held a small stack of envelopes and periodicals along with a large package.

"Hi, kiddo!"

"Hiya Henry!" she answered back enthusiastically as he opened the storm door.

"Thanks a lot for running it up. It's raining cats and dogs out here today," he said, making note of the mini-tsunami that had now settled over Oak Forest.

"No problem. I had to come up either way to bring you this package." As she spoke, she handed over the mail and the box.

"Do I need to sign for it?" he asked as he accepted the day's haul.

"Nope, you're all set. Gotta run, don't want to lose time with the rain."

Henry knew that she was referring to the impaired driving conditions and her obsession with delivering her mail on time to each of her appointed stops.

"Tell Millie and Joe I say hello!" Lucy hollered to him as she stepped into her still-running truck.

"Will do! Be safe, see you again," he called back to her.

Following an exchange of waves, Lucy was off down the

driveway and on to her next destination. *After they made Lucy, they sure broke the mold*, Henry thought as he closed the door.

He flipped through the assorted envelopes and magazines on the way to the kitchen but found nothing of urgency there. However, as he entered the room, the strange and unexpected package had captured his attention. He had nothing to speak of on order as far as he could recall and, therefore, no way to explain what was in his hands. Furthermore, only his name and address had been scrawled onto the brown paper that covered the box, so there was no indication who had sent it either.

"Whatcha got there?" Millie asked as she glanced up at him from a bowl of carrots she was in the middle of dicing up for a stew she was working on.

"You know, I have no idea," Henry answered as he studied the box intently. The thought had crossed his mind that it might be some ill-conceived contact from his brother Bill, but the method and handwriting didn't point to that. For a few seconds, Henry just stared at the box without action or commentary.

"Ain't you gonna open it up? It's not a bomb," Millie prodded.

"You never know," Henry countered in jest, now broken loose from his trance. He reached into his trousers and retrieved a small brown pocketknife that typically resided next to his silver dollar.

Millie turned to the sink to rinse her vegetables as Henry proceeded to cut open the box. As he opened the flaps, he was as surprised as a child on Christmas morning by what was inside.

"Well, I'll be damned!" he exclaimed with a huge smile.

Hearing the joy in his voice, Millie turned away from her work to see what the cause was.

"So what's in there?"

Henry separated the packing paper inside the box and pulled a most charming antique English teakettle from it.

"Well, I'll be damned too!" Millie declared at the sight of it. "Is that from your author friend?"

"I'm guessing so; I can't imagine who else would send it. Here's a note underneath," he answered as he sat the teakettle down and reached back into the box. Upon retrieving the slip of paper he unfolded it and read it aloud to Millie and Joe, who by now had entered the room to investigate what the commotion was all about.

"Dearest Henry, Any fine gentleman such as yourself needs one of these. Besides, I decided that it was high time that Jake be introduced to a cup of tea. I look forward to our next chat and hope to see you very soon. Thank you ever so much for all of your kindness. Your friend, Anne."

"Well, what do you know about that?" Henry declared as he admired the fine copper kettle and tested the carved wood handle for strength.

"Yep, that's a dandy, all right," Millie agreed as she returned to her meal preparations.

"It sure is," Henry beamed.

"Don't know why we need that; nobody around here drinks tea," Millie grumbled from the stove.

"What? What's that?" Henry asked having not been able to clearly hear what she had said.

"Oh nothing," Millie responded with slight annoyance with her back still to him.

Henry was too consumed with the surprise to detect her agitation. He gathered the mail and walked from the room with the teakettle in hand. Noting that he had left for his office, Millie turned to see the box and packing paper still littering the island behind her.

"You want me to keep this box from your *daughter* too,

or you want me to throw it out?" she mumbled quietly for no one in particular to hear while shaking her head. All the while, Joe looked on with curiosity. She could sense the tension in the room but didn't understand what was happening. Unsure whether Henry or Millie offered the most entertainment at this point, she opted to stay put and wait things out.

Millie had no legitimate reason to doubt Henry's sincerity about his feelings for Anne or his appraisal of his new-found relationship with her. If he saw this young woman as a possible daughter figure or some sort of protégé, then so be it. Rather, her jealousy stemmed from the possibility that the British author might not share the same view of things. In her estimation, it was entirely possible that Anne was consumed with him. Henry was a dashing and accomplished man. He could be both gentle and formidable. He was affluent and powerful. *What is there not to like?* Though there was a significant age gap between the two, Millie was well aware that many women of Anne's generation would be fascinated by such a man. A famous and wealthy British author seemed a likely candidate to be enthralled by a great man like Henry. Millie had dedicated the better part of her adult life to him and his care. She had waited a long time for him to make a romantic move in her direction, and she was not about to give ground now to Anne Francis Wagner or anyone else.

As she sloshed a wood spoon gently through the contents of the stewpot before her, she contemplated the state of things and considered what her response, if any, ought to be. She briefly glanced out the window over the sink to her left to see that that the raindrops had all but ceased, and the skies were starting to brighten. At that moment, she knew what she was going to do.

I think I'm going to have to have a chat of my own with this author and set her straight. She started to hum melodic notes from one of her favorite hymns as a small smile began to overtake her face. The discord that had been introduced into her day by the unexpected package was soon replaced by thoughts of Henry's romantic overture, and her mood was lifted.

She turned and picked up the box with the intent to move it outside to the "burn barrel." This was the name Henry had given to an old 55-gallon drum that stood permanently out back near the garage. From time to time, he would use it to incinerate cardboard and paper refuse that had accumulated in the house or to dispose of stray fallen sticks and branches that appeared around the yard.

However, as she did this, she noted that Joe had taken an interest in the box. The little cat had moved from her perch on the staircase to a position at the base of the kitchen table. From there, she was keenly observing Millie's actions.

"Say, girl, would you like to play in here?" she asked while tilting it forward. Joe's eyes were locked onto her and followed every movement. Millie stepped forward and put the box on the floor beside her. Joe was elated and immediately jumped over the side, past the flaps, and hid beneath the packing paper. By the time she had completely nestled into a good spot, all Millie could see were her eyes and nose.

"I guess that answers that!" Millie announced with a chuckle.

Meanwhile, Henry sat in his office chair scratching down notes on a small yellow pad of paper. His newest prize and the day's mail were off to the side, as yet unopened. There would be plenty of time to go through the envelopes, to attend to bills, and to think of tea. At the moment, he was brainstorming and consumed by thoughts about planning a picnic.

CHAPTER 11

An Up and Down Morning

HENRY CAME DOWN the staircase with light and jovial steps as Joe skipped along beside him. It was early on Thursday morning and just hours prior to his much-anticipated outing with Millie. For three days in a row, the spring weather had foiled his plans, but now the skies were clear and bright and for once it seemed that the weatherman had indeed nailed his forecast. The prediction had been for a warm and pleasant day with a high-temperature landing in the mid-70s, and by all indications it was headed for just that.

Joe sprang from the last step in pursuit of Henry as he crossed the kitchen with purpose. The rich aroma of the freshly brewed coffee filled the air, and he was anxious to partake of the first cup of the day. It was to be a busy morning with errands to run and last-minute preparations and he was eager to get to it.

While he briskly glanced through the day's edition of the *Lewis Gazette* and guzzled from his second cup, the telephone rang. The unusually early call surprised him, and he looked over at the clock to see that it was just past 7:30 a.m. The ringing also startled Joe, who had moved into her cardboard box following the completion of a saucer of milk. The box, since its arrival on Monday with the teakettle from Anne, had instantly become a favorite resting place for her. Noting this, Henry and Millie had decided that it could stay in the corner on the far side of the breakfast room, at least for now. Millie had rightly pointed out that Joe would be in need of a place to deliver her kittens some-day, and Henry had agreed with her wisdom.

Since he rarely received any phone calls this early, Henry moved with urgency to answer in anticipation that perhaps something was wrong.

"Hello?"

"Hi Henry," greeted George from the other end.

"Hey pal, everything ok?"

"Oh sure. Sorry about calling so early, but I knew you'd be up and wanted to catch you before Millie got there." George was well-acquainted with Henry's habits and knew that by now he'd typically be on his second or third cup of coffee.

"Oh yeah, you know me. Couldn't sleep in if you paid me. It's no problem; you just caught me off guard. What gives?"

"Well, I just hung up with our man Carl. He called me with news on Millie's son, and I wanted to get it to you right away."

"He's another early bird, huh?" Henry quipped, noting that their fellow retiree was apparently cut from the same cloth as they were.

George laughed. "Yeah, for sure. Anyway Henry, it's not good at all," he said with a sigh.

Henry's face dropped, and he leaned back against the kitchen sink where he was standing. He took a slow deep breath and pondered what he was about to learn and what the effects of it would mean for Millie.

"Ok, I hear you. Go ahead, what do we know?"

"The worst of it is that he's dead," George stated solemnly.

"Oh no..." Henry lamented softly.

"Yeah, Carl says he was incarcerated in a prison in Alabama, and some other inmate stabbed him to death. It was a couple of years ago."

"Oh Good Lord, I sure wasn't prepared for that kind of news," Henry said with regret.

"Boy, no kidding," George agreed. "I was hoping we were going to find out something a lot better."

"What was he in for?" Henry asked knowing that it did not make much difference at this point.

"He stole some cars and was doing ten years. According to Carl, he had quite a rap sheet and had been in and out of trouble *a lot.* The people that adopted him split up when he was eight. He ended up living with his mother, but she had to work all of the time to try to support him. So, it sounds like without her around he got mixed in with the wrong crowd and dropped out of school. I think Carl said this was like the third time he'd been locked up."

Henry just shook his head slowly with his eyes closed. This was a "worst-case scenario" and he knew it. If he delivered this news to Millie, she would be devastated. She would blame herself for giving him up for adoption and for the subsequent consequences of that decision that ultimately led to his imprisonment and death. This was not the way the story was supposed to go. This was not a burden that Henry could or would allow her to bear.

"All right my friend, thanks for quarterbacking all of this," he said sadly. "Can you give Carl my address and have him forward me a bill for his time? Once I get it, I'll shoot a check off to him."

"Already did that. He's going to send you a complete report with all of the nitty-gritty and documentation he collected on it. I sure am sorry about this, Henry. What are you going to do?" George asked.

"Well, I sure as hell can't tell her *this* if that's what you mean."

"No, I don't guess you can," George concurred with a sigh of his own. "How are you going to handle it with her if it comes up?"

"She hasn't mentioned it again since that night we had dinner so I'll just let it go and hope that it dies quietly. If it ever does come up, I'll just have to figure out a good excuse for why we can't find him… or something. I don't really know what else I *can* do at this point."

There was silence between them for a moment as they both considered the information that had been learned and the repercussions of it. Suddenly, Henry broke from his trance and remembered that he needed to get on the move.

"Oh hey, George, I've gotta run. I've got a couple of errands in town and need to get out of here so I better let you go. Thanks again for tracking down Carl for me and handling all of this; it was a real favor."

"No problem, buddy. Give me a call this weekend if you get bored."

"Will do, take care now." With that, Henry hung up the phone and looked at his watch.

"Ugh," he grumbled. He was irritated that he was falling behind his predetermined schedule for the day. In truth, his agitation was far more about the bad news he had just gotten than it was about a few minutes lost to a phone call. There was ample time to run to town and make a few stops. If anything, it was still too early to arrive at most places. A much greater issue was how to put this tragic turn of events out of his mind. He was not typically one for dishonesty and the thought that he knew horrible and tragic information about Millie's son that, as of yet, she did not, felt deceitful to him. Furthermore, he knew that he might someday be faced with either concealing this information from her or revealing it and hurting her deeply, and this troubled him. For now, he consoled himself with the fact that she had not made any mention of his offer to look for her son. Therefore, it could be reasonably assumed that she had dismissed the matter. In any event, it was time now to turn his attention to the immediate future and his desire to make their first date as memorable as possible.

After placing his cup in the sink, Henry wrote a brief note to Millie and placed it next to the coffee pot. He then bid Joe farewell, grabbed his car keys, and headed out the side door. He was off to Lewis to procure the necessary components of a fantastic picnic complete with the finest cold root beer that money could buy.

*

Millie stepped into the kitchen just after 9:00 a.m. She was in a jubilant mood and excited about the day ahead.

"Hey Henry, it's just me," she called out as she strolled past the island toward the front door to put down her purse.

Upon hearing no reply she called out a second time, but it was again to no avail. She noted that Joe hadn't greeted her either and walked over to the box in the corner to investigate.

"There you are, Momma," she cooed to the sleepy little cat. Joe could barely open her eyes to see Millie standing above her, but she acknowledged her pets with immediate and affectionate purring.

"Well, this explains where you are. Now, where is your

daddy?" she asked. The smell of the coffee pot beckoned her, and she broke off from her affection toward Joe to fetch a cup for herself. Stepping to the counter, she immediately saw the note that Henry had left, and a smile spread across her face.

"Millie, I ran into town for a few things but will be back to pick you up at 10:30. See you then, Henry."

He's going to pick me up! Just those words alone were cause for exhilaration. She could not recall the last time a man had "picked her up." The mere thought of it made her giggle. Certainly there had been suitors over the years seeking her affection, but she had never accepted their advances or been moved to action. Each time that someone had approached her on a social level, she had found cause to resist the overture.

Perhaps this preference for solitude was because of her past and the guilt she carried with her. She had never forgiven herself for putting her son up for adoption or for the behavior that led to the pregnancy in the first place. Possibly her lack of interest in romance had been due to the responsibility she had accepted in caring for her ill aunt and the time constraints and demands of that care. These were both valid reasons that each had merit and could partly explain why she had never dated or married after her arrival in Lewis.

Primarily though, her lack of a love-life could be attributed to a deep connection she felt with Henry and the world that she had created around him. His care and well-being had been her main focus for more than two decades, and she found self-worth and security for herself there. Romance had never been part of the bargain between them. Until now, it had been enough for her to be what he needed her to be. She had shared in the parts of his life that he was willing or able to allow her to, and she had been satisfied. It was safe and comfortable, and an alteration of any kind in the balance of things posed too great a risk.

However, the new world that was now emerging brought excitement and possibility with it. There was now a dream of something more. After Joe's arrival at Oak Forest, the chemistry of things began to change. Henry had softened and was evolving into something very different and attractive to her. He was warmer and more forthcoming now. His shift in demeanor had sparked a change in her as well. The result was that they were growing closer and becoming more playful. They were seeing one another in a different light and discovering feelings that, though they seemed new to the two of them, really had been developing beneath the surface all along.

The clock seemed to be standing still as Millie checked it with great frequency. She noticed a light tingling behind her knees and an odd emptiness in her stomach. She wondered if perhaps she might be coming down with something but after noting that her palms were moist too, realized that she was just excited. Millie was reminded of being a little girl and how nervous and anxious she had been the first time she had ridden a Ferris wheel. Her father and mother had taken her to Atlanta to attend a large fair, and it was the first time she had ever seen such a colossus in person. It was scary and thrilling and a day she would never forget. Now, a lifetime later, she could feel the same sensations in her body. To calm herself, she attended to small chores to help pass the time but it felt as though 10:30 a.m. would never arrive.

The *Lewis Gazette* that Henry had left behind that morning was lying on the island, and she passed by it several times before finally deciding that some reading might be just what the doctor ordered to soothe her nerves. Millie settled into a seat at the island and began to scan the articles for something of interest to occupy her mind. Her thoughts drifted, and she wondered if perhaps it would be prudent to make a couple of sandwiches or a snack to take along with them. However, she quickly squashed that idea when she remembered that Henry had been adamant when he had said, "I've got everything covered. You just show up in some comfortable clothes and leave the rest to me." Looking down at her jeans and favorite sneakers, she was satisfied that she had followed his instructions and was ready to go.

Soon, Millie was deeply engrossed in an article about a dispute relating to a proposed new cell phone tower. The structure was to be erected in the heart of Lewis near its most famous landmark, The Eager Beaver Diner. The mayor was touting it as a major step forward that offered modernization and mobile phone service to the residents. He proclaimed it to be just the type of progress that would bring growth and prosperity to the town. A local man named John Everett was the key driving force behind the project and owned the land where the tower was to be constructed. In spite of this, many of the locals were predictably vociferous in their opposition. The old guard didn't see the need for cell phones and claimed that it would be an eyesore that would damage the small town charm that residents and visitors held so dear. Millie noted the name of John Everett and knew that Henry despised him, though she had no idea why.

"Are you ready?" came a voice as a hand touched her right shoulder.

"Oh, my dear Lord!" Mille shouted as she threw the newspaper up into the air and whirled around in the chair to find Henry standing behind her. She looked as if she had just seen a ghost and her reaction ignited a series of belly laughs from him that brought tears to his eyes.

"What on earth?" Millie exclaimed as she put her hands over her face and tried to restart her heart.

"I'm sorry, Millie, I thought you heard me come in," Henry apologized as he moved toward the kitchen sink to wash his hands.

Millie took a small series of breaths and looked at the clock. It was 10:35 a.m. She realized that she had become so lost in the article that she hadn't heard Henry come inside the house.

"You like to kill me. A body can't take that kinda shock you know. I'm no little girl. One of these days you're going to knock the life right outta me!" she gasped as he chuckled.

"What were you reading that had you so caught up in it?" he asked.

Millie collected the sheets of the newspaper which were now strewn across the island and also onto the floor next to her.

"I was reading about that new phone tower that the mayor wants to build," she explained.

"Oh yeah? I didn't read that yet. Well, it's about time Lewis got cell phones I guess. Lots of other places have them. What's the big deal?" he asked while drying his hands with a yellow and white checkerboard towel left next to the sink for just such a purpose.

"Well, that man John Everett that you don't like has a piece of land off behind The Beaver and wants to build it there, and people are mighty angry."

"Next to The Eager Beaver? You've got to be kidding? And Everett is in on this? Well, we'll just see about that," Henry snarled as he walked over to the phone on the counter and lifted the handset. "If that jerk is for it, it's good for him and not so much for Lewis. You can bet your life on that," he scowled as he dialed the number of the mayor's office while Millie looked on. She had seen Henry angry on many occasions and knew that he meant business. Instantly, his countenance softened, and his voice became bright and friendly.

"Good morning Shirley! This is Henry Engel. How are you today?" His voice was kind and pleasant as he greeted the mayor's secretary. "Great! Glad to hear it. Say, is Dick around? I'd like to have a quick word with him if he is in."

There was a brief pause, and Henry took the opportunity to look at Millie, who was standing beside the refrigerator watching him. He gave her a wink and a nod to indicate that this would be only a minor delay before they would be heading out. She understood his meaning and stepped into the bathroom to make final preparations before their adventure.

"Henry?" greeted Richard Ross from the other end.

"Hi Dick, how are you?"

"I'm terrific, thanks," he replied. "How are you this morning?"

"I'm excellent, just getting ready to head out for a picnic as a matter of fact."

"No kidding? Well, good for you, Henry! It's sure a fine day for a picnic. So, what's on your mind?" he asked, knowing that Lewis' most influential resident did not normally waste phone calls to check on the well-being of the town's leadership.

"I was just running through the *Gazette* and noticed a story on that cell phone tower."

"Oh yeah? How about that? Could really be big for us, I think. Sure has some folks worked up, though. I'm guessing if you're calling then you're in opposition to it too?" the mayor asked while bracing himself for Henry's barrage.

"Nope, I think it's a good idea. Cell phones are the wave of the future. It's only going to get bigger from here, so we better get in on it. I agree that it's time Lewis moved forward," Henry asserted, much to the mayor's relief. "I do have a couple of concerns about the details though and would like to talk to you about them before this thing moves any further. Would you have time for lunch tomorrow to discuss it?"

"Of course, Henry. You know me, I always welcome your input. I'd love to hear your thoughts on it. If you've got a better idea, I want to know about it." Richard Ross was not just grandstanding. He was well aware that Henry had been a staunch backer of his and had always come through when the town was in need. The most recent example of this had been the previous summer when Henry had footed the bill for a new roof for the town's community center. It was a large expense, and Henry had stepped up to assume all of it.

"Ok, terrific. How about we meet over at The Beaver at 11:30?"

"Works just fine for me, Henry; I'll be there. I'm looking forward to it."

"Great! I'll see you then, Dick. Goodbye now," he said as he hung up the phone. Henry was quite satisfied with the conversation. He liked Richard and believed that he was a good mayor who put the town's best interests first when making decisions. He had always treated Henry with the utmost respect and been an honest, straight shooter. All of these were key qualities that Henry held dear and, in turn, they earned Richard Ross his unwavering support. With that matter now handled for the moment, Henry's attention returned to the immediate future. It was the dawn of a new day at Oak Forest, and he was eager to explore it.

CHAPTER 12

A Beautiful Spring Day

"AREN'T YOU READY yet?" Henry called to Millie through the closed bathroom door.

"Oh, stop all your fussing, I'm almost done. Don't want me looking like an old washwoman, do you?" she fired back.

"Can't imagine what you're doing," Henry muttered quietly to himself as he paced around the kitchen slowly while looking out the window at the bright sunshine on the other side.

"Already nagging at me like a husband and we haven't even gone out yet," Millie teased as the bathroom door opened. Henry stopped on the far side of the kitchen table. He smiled at the humor and watched as she stepped into the room to see how her final preparations had turned out. Millie entered with a slight grin as she too was relishing the joke just made and the connotations of it.

"Wow, you look just beautiful!" he declared with true sincerity. Millie's face glowed. These were words that Henry had never said to her before, and they felt wonderful to hear.

"Aww thank you, Henry! You're too sweet," she responded as she passed by him on the way to collect her purse. Henry watched as she walked to the door and returned, enjoying the complete view of her.

"No, I really do mean it, Millie. I sure like that color on you," he proclaimed referring to the light orange knit top she was wearing.

"I'm sure glad you do," she said as she paused at the corner of the island by the refrigerator and looked back at him.

"Here I am. You ready to go?"

Henry had been mesmerized momentarily but her question snapped him out of it.

"Hold on, stay right there," he instructed as he stepped past her and out the side door. In an instant, Millie could hear the door opening announcing his return.

"Close your eyes," he called out from the laundry room.

"All right, they're closed," Millie smiled and shut her eyes as he had asked.

Henry stepped through the doorway and placed something on the island in front of Millie. The minute he entered the room she could immediately smell the object of the secrecy. The smile on her face broadened.

"Ok, you can open them up now," Henry told her.

When Millie opened her eyes, the largest and most beautiful bouquet of yellow daisies she had ever seen was in front of her.

"Oh my, Henry! They're so lovely!" she exclaimed.

"Well, last time we were a little short on yellow as I recall." Henry was referring to the day he had brought home flowers for Millie after his visit with Mary.

Millie bent forward putting her face just above the bouquet and deeply inhaled the rich fragrance. Her eyes closed as she enjoyed the delightful smell. After a brief spell, she stood up and turned to Henry, who was standing next to her. She placed her hands in his, and her touch made his fingers tingle slightly.

"They're just wonderful, Henry! And so are you." With that, she moved to her tip-toes to reach his left cheek and gave him a soft kiss. Henry could feel the blood rushing to his face, and he became slightly warm all over. He hadn't expected her reaction to be this affectionate, but he welcomed it.

"I'm sorry it took me so long to do things like this."

"Well we're here now, ain't we?" Millie asked with a squeeze of his hands. Before releasing them, she added, "And that's enough for me."

Henry smiled and nodded. He understood her point perfectly and was in complete agreement. There was no gain to be had by looking backward. It was time to enjoy the present and look to the future.

"I'm going to leave these right over here," she said as she moved the vase onto the kitchen table. Before moving away from them, she leaned in their direction and took another sample of their glorious scent. After that, she walked over and gave Joe a few small strokes as she slept in her box. "We'll be back, sweetie," Millie whispered to her.

"Well ma'am, are you ready to go?" Henry asked as she moved back across the room toward him.

"Yes, sir!" she answered as she picked up her purse and stepped past.

As Millie opened the side door, she was shocked to see Henry's 1930 Ford Model A pickup truck sitting just outside waiting for them.

"Holy cow! Your Uncle Ed's truck?!" she exclaimed as she darted over to it.

"I thought maybe the old girl might like to join us," he

143

declared proudly as he followed Millie outside. The late morning sunshine reflected brightly off of the truck's glossy black paint as Millie ran her hand across the smooth front fender.

"She's so beautiful!"

"Yeah, I polished her up yesterday back in the garage," he explained.

"So that's what you were doing all afternoon back there? I was wondering what you were up to."

Henry smiled as he stepped past her and opened the passenger's door.

"Here you go," he said as he beckoned her to get into the vehicle.

"Why thank you, sir," she replied playfully as she stepped up onto the running board and slid onto the seat. Henry closed the door as she put her purse on the floor behind her feet. She looked around at the small and simple interior of the cab and felt like a child at an amusement park anticipating the start to a great ride. It was charming and surreal to say the least. As Henry opened the driver's door, Millie was nearly bursting with excitement.

"You know, I've never even *sat* in this truck?!"

"Really? Never?" Henry asked in disbelief as he slid inside and closed the door.

"Nope, never! I've seen it over the years on 4th of July or when you'd wash it or take it out but never been in it myself until now."

"Well, what do you think of her?"

"Are you kidding me? *She's fantastic!*"

The compliment brought a huge smile to Henry's face as he started the motor. The antique vehicle was his greatest family heirloom and being able to share it with her made him happy. The old truck came to life and Millie giggled with joy.

"Kid, you ain't seen nothing yet," he said impishly as he moved the gear shift and released the clutch and the brake. Suddenly the old truck eased forward, and they were on their way around the island and headed down the hill.

"You might want to crack your window a bit; no air conditioning in this old lady," Henry suggested as they passed the pond and began the climb toward the mailbox. Millie heeded his advice and turned the hand crank on the door with her right hand until the window had dropped a couple of inches.

Henry brought the truck to a halt at the top of the driveway to make sure that no other vehicles were approaching.

"So tell me, Mr. Engel, where are you taking me?" Millie asked with a hint of intrigue.

"*You'll see,*" Henry replied slyly in a comical high-pitched voice. Millie laughed at his clowning.

After confirming that the coast was clear, he pulled the Model A out onto County Road 27 and headed it down the pavement. Millie was shocked by the action because instead of pulling out to the left toward Lewis, he had turned to the right and was traveling *away* from town. In her entire life, she had never proceeded past his driveway and had no idea what lay ahead.

"So where in the world *are* we going?" Millie asked again, now extremely curious about what he had in mind.

"*You'll see,*" he repeated with the same silly intonation as before. Millie laughed again as she slapped his right shoulder lightly with feigned aggression.

"You're mean!" she protested.

"Oh, quit your squawking and just try to enjoy the ride," he commanded cheerfully with a grin. Millie reluctantly surrendered and decided that he was right. She didn't care where she was going; she was simply glad that it was with Henry.

The road snaked along through rolling hills lined by dense forest. The trees created a wall of green, which was intermittently broken by meadows and farm fields. The sky was blue and clear, and bright yellow sunshine washed over the landscape. The hum of the motor and the sound of the tires rolling on the warm asphalt combined to play a soothing song as they rode along.

"You know, I learned how to drive in *this very truck*," Henry said with pride out of nowhere.

"You did?" Millie knew that the Ford had previously belonged to Henry's uncle and that Henry loved the classic truck, but she hadn't heard this story before.

"Yep. My Uncle Ed taught George and me both back on the farm when we were just a couple of snot-nosed teenagers. George picked it up right away, but I needed a little more practice than he did," Henry confessed with a chuckle. He was recalling the day he had misjudged a turn and found a large fence post. The net result was a broken fence in need of repair, a healthy dent in the front fender of the truck, a sore neck for Uncle Ed, and a bruised ego for Henry. Time heals the wounds of men, fences can be mended, and the damage to the Ford had long ago been repaired when the truck was restored. However, the details and pictures of that day were etched into Henry's memory forever. As he related the events leading up to and after the accident, Millie listened intently and gasped and then laughed as she imagined the scene. She enjoyed hearing about Henry's family and his past. Though they had been together for decades, there was still much they did not know about one another, and it was fun to explore that territory now.

As they rounded the next curve, Henry slowed the truck in anticipation of making a turn. Millie watched with keen interest as a discreet opening in the forest appeared on the left in the distance. As they neared it, she could see that it revealed a lane that led back into the countryside. Henry eased the truck to nearly a complete stop before coaxing it into the entrance and slowly proceeding along the gravel drive. It had the look of an old farm road that had long ago become grown over and was now seemingly interspersed with as many weeds as there were rocks.

"Do I dare ask? Are we getting closer?" Millie quizzed Henry, who responded with a smile.

"Yeah, we're close. Just ahead there's a nice little place I wanted you to see."

Further up the lane, Henry could see a rise. He knew that just on the other side of it there was a clearing that gave way to a large meadow. Once upon a time this had been a farm field but the man who had tended it was put in the earth long ago leaving only debt behind him. The current owner of the property was the Lewis Bank & Trust. The bank's president, Tom Donaldson, had made arrangements with a local farmer to sharecrop the place and it was now covered in clover. Tom was an avid hunter, and he and his friends used the place for turkey hunting in the spring and deer hunting in the fall. Henry knew this, and he also knew about a beautiful spring on the property just below the field that Uncle Ed had taken him to as a boy. On Monday, he had called Tom to investigate if the access to the spring was still tenable and if he could have Tom's permission to come here. He had received a thumbs up on both accounts.

Henry guided the Ford up the road and over the hill before bringing it to a halt along the edge of the field where the gravel ran out. The lush green meadow provided for an inviting setting, but Millie couldn't quite understand what was unique about it yet. In her estimation, it was certainly no more special than the pasture below Henry's house at Oak Forest. She surveyed the surroundings while Henry exited the cab.

"Everybody out," he joked as he closed the door and moved around to the rear of the vehicle. "From here, we walk."

Millie opened her door and stepped out as Henry pulled back a large gray tarp that he had draped over the bed of the pickup. In all of her excitement, she hadn't even noticed that he had something concealed in the rear. It suddenly occurred to her that this was to be a picnic so of course there must be some sort of lunch, or at least she hoped so as she was starting to get hungry.

"Here you go, take this," Henry called out as she closed her door and walked behind the truck toward him. He was pointing to a small blue and white plastic cooler. Henry already had a large wicker basket by the handle, which was covered by a red and white checkered cloth. With his left hand, he reached into the truck bed and retrieved a thick old tan quilt that Millie recognized as being one of his spares from the upstairs closet.

"Isn't this nice! Thank you for doing all of this, Henry."

"All right, follow me," he said without acknowledging her last statement. "We've got just a short walk, and we'll be there."

Millie grabbed the small cooler, which jingled with ice and glass bottles, and followed behind him. Her eyes were trained onto the field to her left in an attempt to discern where he might be going. Henry, however, marched forward along the tree line and down a gentle slope away from the meadow and toward more forest.

"Down below there, just inside the woods there's a natural spring I used to come to with my Uncle Ed when I was a kid. It's a top-notch spot for a picnic," he explained. "Or at least it used to be," he added with caution.

148

"Oh ok, I gotcha. That sounds real nice!" she agreed with growing anticipation.

As they neared the edge of the forest, a well-designed stone path appeared out of nowhere. Henry's eyes lit up when he saw it.

"Yes! It's still here, just like I remember!" he proclaimed excitedly. Millie could see that the path led down at a somewhat sharp angle into a little glen. A small creek was flowing below, fed by water emanating from a pool at the base of a rock formation. The ripples of the water glistened like diamonds in the sunlight.

"Oh my goodness! It's breathtaking, Henry!"

"Isn't it? Now, come on, follow me. Just watch your step in case any of these stones are loose." With that, he went ahead of her and tested the way but there was no cause for concern. Clearly Tom and the hunters had made sure that the access to the spring was indeed safe and well-maintained. As they reached the bottom of the trail, Millie could see that someone had erected a half-circle-shaped wall of red bricks at the base of the rocks. The structure was mortared to the natural stone and stood roughly three feet high while extending out approximately six feet. In the end, the man-made portion combined with nature to create a catch where the spring water that was falling along the stones above would pool before running over the bricks and into the creek bed. It was an ingenious and simple way to capture the water before it flowed away.

"Wow!" Millie exclaimed breathlessly. *"This is amazing!"*

"I'm glad that you think so," he said with satisfaction at her reaction as he put the basket and quilt down. He walked over to the edge of the collecting pool and reached his hand down into it. The water was very cool and crystal clear. He scooped a small portion into his hands and brought it up to his lips. It tasted fresh and sweet, exactly as he remembered.

"Now that's *real* spring water!" he declared. "Come here, you've got to try it."

Millie raised her eyebrows with a look of mild skepticism. She had drunk lots of water over the years but never any directly out of the ground. She preferred hers from a faucet or from a bottle that said it had been "purified."

"Oh, come on," he scoffed, noting her trepidation. "I promise it's a lot better than that stuff they're pawning off on you at the store in the bottle. Where do you think they get all of that *spring water*? Trust me, this won't kill you," he assured her with a light chuckle.

She stepped beside him and reached down with her free hand to gather a sample. The temperature of the water surprised her. "Why, it's cold!" she reported.

"Sure is; comes right up out of the earth. It's like that year round. This was the best place to cool off in the summer when I was a kid."

Now emboldened, she brought her hand to her lips and tasted it.

"It's kinda sweet too, ain't it?" she said with astonishment as she reached back to get a little more.

"Yeah, I guess it has something to do with the minerals around here."

"Well, isn't that just something?" she muttered as he turned to find a suitable location for their picnic.

Henry noticed a level grassy spot just off to the left with light shade and a perfect view of the spring, and he moved to it. "I'm going to spread the blanket over here; it looks like a good place."

"Sure does! Hold on, let me help you," she said as she put

the cooler down and walked over to assist him. They each took opposite corners of the quilt and soon had it spread neatly on the ground providing a perfect place to sit and eat lunch.

"There!" Henry declared as he moved the picnic basket to the middle of the thick blanket and sat down. Millie followed suit and soon she and the cooler were seated beside him.

"Oh Henry, this is such a gorgeous place! How on earth did you ever find it?"

"My Uncle knew the farmer that lived here. They were friends. He'd bring Bill and me over to visit, and we always took time out to come down here," he said while looking around.

Millie was surprised by the mention of Henry's brother Bill but let it pass without pressing for more details. She was well aware that this was a topic that normally was off-limits. The mood was far too joyous and the day far too nice to risk introducing a discordant note.

"That's a nice memory," she commented as she stared off at the flowing water.

"Yeah, the old man was a guy named Jim Briscoe and we'd come over every now and then to see him. His wife had passed, and he didn't have any other family, so he was always happy to have us stop by. Now that I think of it, it seems like he always had a bunch of cats around too. Anyway, there's a house just over there where he lived with a bigger entrance to the road. That's where the majority of the tillable ground is," he said, pointing off to the east through the woods. "This over here is a secondary field that he had, and he used to keep it in corn or wheat or beans."

Millie imagined what things might have looked like back in the day. She pictured Henry as a young boy racing down the stone path with his brother and uncle in tow to see the spring. It was a touching scene, and it made her feel close to him to share in it.

"Was that farmer the man that put all those bricks down here?"

"Yeah, he was a really sharp old guy. He and my uncle built that," Henry answered with pride. "Pretty damned ingenious, huh?"

"I'll say. I think it's just beautiful!"

Henry paused to enjoy her praise and to think back to his youth. He could see his uncle and brother standing there as if it were yesterday. He remembered Jim and Uncle Ed sipping on cool bottles of beer on the banks of the creek while he and Bill played in the water on a hot summer day. The pictures in his mind were clear and vivid. He was briefly completely lost in his thoughts before snapping himself out of it and returning to the present moment.

"Anyway, are you getting hungry?" he asked as he turned his attention to the basket he had brought along.

"I sure am," she answered enthusiastically.

"All right then, let's see what we have." Henry's eyes sparkled as he peeled back the checkered cloth from atop the basket to reveal its contents. Inside were an assortment of wrapped items and containers and Millie eagerly tried to peek to see what he had brought for them to eat.

"With a little help from our old pal Jake, I think I might have some goodies in here you're going to like," he announced. The reference was not to Henry's liquid friend but rather to Jake Le Detour, who was the proprietor of the town's most renowned barbecue restaurant. It also just happened to be Millie's favorite eatery.

"I was hoping you took the hint!" she laughed aloud recalling their conversation about picnic menus from Monday.

"Hint? It was more like blackmail, I'd say!" he teased.

"Oh, you go on with yourself!" she responded in mock defense.

Henry pulled out two white china plates, some silverware, and a pile of snow-white napkins and handed them to her. Millie smiled as she accepted the items and arranged two place settings between them while Henry fumbled among the remaining contents inside the basket.

"Ok, I believe you ordered the pulled pork," he said as his hands emerged with a large sandwich wrapped in foil and handed it to her. Her eyes lit up as she pulled the aluminum open and released the aroma of the smoked meat.

"I also think you asked for coleslaw," he said as he removed the lid from a carton of the salad and placed it in front of her. Millie sat and watched with a wide smile as Henry unveiled the smorgasbord.

"Hmm… we also have some baked beans and as requested, *real thick, crunchy* potato chips," he added with a note of sarcasm trying to do his best impression of her.

Millie giggled at his wit.

"Of course, no picnic is complete without ice-cold root beer out of a glass bottle. Therefore, if you'd do the honors…" he said as he motioned for her to open the cooler that was next to her and just beyond his reach. True to his word, when Millie opened the lid of the cooler she discovered four bottles of the soft drink nestled in a bed of ice. As Millie retrieved a pair, Henry dove back into the basket for a bottle opener and popped the tops.

"And if you're still hungry after all of that, I've got a couple of dandy pieces of apple pie here to finish things off."

"Well Mr. Engel, you have truly outdone yourself. I'm totally speechless," Millie proclaimed as her eyes beamed.

"Well, that's gotta be a first!" he joked as she flashed him an overly melodramatic frown. "Nah, I'm just fooling. I'm very happy that you think so." Henry held his bottle up and made a motion for Millie to do likewise. "I want this to be the start of a new chapter for both of us. I guess by now you've figured out that I have feelings for you. I truly care for you, and I regret it took me this long to realize it. I don't know exactly where it all goes from here, but I know what I want now and I... I really want to find out. To the future!" he declared with confidence and excitement.

Millie's eyes moistened at his sincere expression of his affection for her. She understood how hard it was for Henry to cross the chasm that had long separated them, and it was deeply moving to her. She also knew what she hoped the future might hold, and it was surreal to now see it beginning to unfold.

"I feel just the same way, Henry," she tenderly said as she tapped her bottle against his. "To *our* future!" Her words made his heart soar and their eyes locked for a few seconds as the emotion between them was palpable. Henry had wondered how or when they would share their first kiss and right then seemed the ideal moment for it. However, they were seated opposite one another with lots of obstacles between them including various containers of food. Had he been in his twenties, he might have smoothly dashed around to her in an epic romantic gesture and taken her into his arms for a kiss worthy of the silver screen. However, since he was now in his seventies, he imagined it might take a bit more effort and be a bit more awkward than the situation called for. Regretfully, he reasoned that this opportunity would have to be squandered. Sensing that it was time to move forward to their meal, they each took a drink from their bottles and savored the exchange they had just had. For now, the first kiss would have to wait.

The picnic lunch that Jake had prepared especially early that morning as a favor to Henry was exquisite. Time flew by as they laughed and shared the meal along with lighthearted conversation about topics ranging from Joe's impending motherhood to events in and around Lewis. Millie and Henry delighted in each other's company in a way they had never before in the quarter century they had known each other. Soon, the food and drink had been consumed, and the sun was moving lazily across the mid-afternoon sky as they returned the dishes and containers to the basket.

"You're sure you don't want pie?" Henry asked.

"No thanks, not right now. I'll take a rain check. I'm stuffed."

"Ok, me too, so we'll save it for another time," he agreed as he placed the cloth back across the top of the basket and moved it aside. Millie was sitting a couple of feet away but now with nothing between them, took advantage of the chance and scooted to be near him. Likewise, Henry adjusted his positioning and settled into a spot next to her so that they were seated side by side and facing the creek. Suddenly, they both started to feel slightly strange. It was a bit awkward for them to now act in ways that for so long were completely foreign to their relationship. Millie giggled nervously.

"This is kinda weird, right?" Henry asked, fully cognizant of what she was experiencing because he was feeling the same way.

"Uh-huh," she confirmed. "Just a little. So, it's not just me?"

"No, of course not, it's hard to know how to act after all these years of being something else," he said reassuringly. The words hung in the cool spring air as the sound of trickling water and birds singing in the trees above echoed around them.

They sat and pondered their next moves for a bit before Millie broke the silence between them. "Maybe we just need to follow our hearts and just let things happen naturally as they come. You know, don't think it over too much. It's kinda like cooking. Sometimes it might get a little messy but in the end it usually all works out."

Henry smiled at her wisdom. He knew that what she said made a lot of sense. It didn't matter if things were clumsy at times; they would just have to figure it out. What mattered most was that, in the end, they had each other. He reached with his right hand and took Millie's left into a soft embrace. His touch was gentle and warm, and she smiled as she leaned her head over onto his shoulder. It reminded him of how he once felt about another woman.

"This is a very special place," he thought aloud.

"It sure is," Millie agreed softly.

"In my whole life, I've only ever brought one other girl here before today."

Millie knew that he could only be referring to Mary, and she was both surprised and touched.

"Is that true? Just Mary?" she asked as she lifted her head and looked at him.

"Yep, just her. A long time ago, this was kind of one of *our places* to go."

Millie sat up and looked at him more directly. "Oh Henry, I'm so sorry. You shouldn't have brought me here then," she said without a hint of jealousy. "This place and its memories are for you two, not us. You could have taken me any old place, and I'd be happy."

Henry grinned. Millie's selflessness and sincerity were two of the qualities he cherished most. It was for precisely that reason that he wanted to share his life, and this place, with her.

"You don't understand," he said as he moved his hand to her cheek. "I was lucky enough to find *two women* in one lifetime that I wanted to share this with."

Millie gazed upward into his eyes as he lowered his lips to hers. Their first kiss was slow, passionate, and magical, leaving her lightheaded and giddy. She felt as if she couldn't catch her breath, but she dared not pull away from him. She had waited far too long, and the reality was far more sensational than any imagination of the moment could have been. Henry moved to take her into his arms, and they slowly fell backward onto the blanket. With each ensuing kiss, they drifted further from their minds and deeper into their hearts. Henry's much deliberated and highly anticipated first kiss of Millie was anything but awkward. Instead, it was a classic Hollywood moment that would have made Cary Grant proud.

CHAPTER 13

Carefully Chosen Words

THE AFTERNOON HAD been unlike any other Millie and Henry had ever spent together. They were exuberant as they drove back to Oak Forest and agreed to call a meeting with Jake and Joe to celebrate the new status of their relationship. Millie gazed out the window of the truck while Henry guided the Ford home.

"I don't think I've ever had a nicer day," Millie purred as she looked through the glass at the scenery flowing by.

"Me either," Henry agreed as he reached with his right hand and patted her leg softly. Millie moved her hand atop his, and he rested it there, enjoying her touch.

"If I had known you could kiss like that, I would have taken you for a picnic years ago!" he teased, punctuated by a little squeeze of her thigh.

"Oh now, you stop that," she shot back, slightly embarrassed. In truth, she wasn't actually offended but merely portraying a perceived role that she was supposed to be "hard to get." *If I'd have known you could kiss like that, I'd have gone with you years ago too!* she thought with a sly smile remembering their passionate interlude at the spring.

"I'm just kidding with you," Henry said as he attempted to soften his statement. "I just want you to know how much I liked kissing you. I liked it… *a lot.*"

Millie looked away so that Henry couldn't see how those words made her smile, but she squeezed his hand in subtle confirmation that she felt the same way. It may have been a long time coming, but it had been well worth the wait.

Once they had returned to Oak Forest, Henry dropped Millie and the picnic supplies off at the house before taking the truck back to the garage. After he had wiped it down completely, he pulled it into its usual spot inside the building and slid a custom-made cover over it. He took a slow walk around the perimeter of the Ford and upon deciding that he was satisfied that everything met his expectations, he slid the garage door closed. The antique vehicle was much more than just a prized possession. It was a connection to his family and his past, and he cherished it. Yet again, it had played a key role in one of the most important days in his life. Now outside, he looked at his watch and realized that time had gotten away from him. Henry eagerly headed for the house with the gait of a man half his age. It was nearly thirty minutes past his traditional meeting time, and he hoped that Millie and Joe were not upset by his tardiness.

Henry's concern, however, was all for naught. He found the girls patiently waiting for him in the family room. Millie was seated on the couch with her shoes off, and Joe was lounging peacefully on top of her. She was engrossed in administering an intense massage session for the little cat, and Joe was enthralled by the lavish attention. Neither of them had any inkling what time it was or any care about it.

"Hey, I'm sorry I got lost out there," Henry apologized as he entered the room.

"It's no problem; we girls understand about you men and your trucks," she said with not even the slightest note of agitation. Joe certainly didn't seem fazed either as she never lifted her head from Millie's lap to acknowledge his entry. Henry liked that Millie was so accepting and understanding of his ways, and he stepped over to her. While reaching down to give Joe a few light scratches on her neck, he also leaned and gave Millie a peck on the lips. The romantic move surprised her, but also made her smile.

"Mmmm, I could get used to that," she said flirtatiously.

"I hope you do," he replied as he moved in and gave her a second light follow-up kiss. "Do you still have time for a talk with Jake?"

"You kidding? *I'm all yours, Mr. Engel.*"

Henry winked at her as he pulled away and headed to fetch Jake for their meeting. In short order, he returned with two expertly crafted cocktails and after delivering one of the glasses to Millie, settled into his favorite chair.

"What a day!" he proclaimed and took a sip from his glass.

"You can say that again," Millie chimed in.

Henry leaned his head back against the recliner and let his mind wander to the afternoon at the spring. It had all gone by too quickly, but now he had another chance to relive the events of the date, and he was enjoying the experience. That was, until things took an unexpected turn.

"I've been thinking, Henry. Do you remember the night we had dinner?"

"Of course I remember," Henry answered without knowing where this was leading.

"Well, that night you offered to help me look for my son. I

told you that I needed time to think about it, and I have. I want to find him. Is that offer still good?"

Henry's heart nearly stopped. His mind had been a million miles away, and he was completely caught off guard by Millie's request. As she was speaking, he was in the process of taking a swallow and somewhere between the glass and his stomach things took a wrong turn. Suddenly he lurched forward and began to gag and cough as his reflexes attempted to clear his airway.

"Oh my goodness, Henry! Are you all right?" Millie asked excitedly as she sat up and put her glass down on the coffee table in front of her. In her excitement, she inadvertently knocked Joe to the floor. Before she could stand and come over to him, Henry motioned with his hand that he was going to be all right and that she should stay where she was. In seconds, he was up and out of his chair.

"Damn, I swallowed wrong," he gasped as he headed to the kitchen. "I'm just going to grab a towel, be right back."

"You sure you're ok? I can do that," she called.

"Nah, I got it," he replied. In truth, he needed a chance to collect himself and figure out how to handle things.

"You had me worried there for a second; I didn't know what was happening," she said with concern.

"I'm fine. It just went down the wrong pipe," he explained as he knelt and wiped up the small amount of liquid that had spattered across the floor by the chair. Satisfied that Henry would survive the incident, Millie picked up her glass and leaned back on the couch. Joe decided that she had seen enough and retreated to the cool and quiet of the office for an early evening nap.

"Sorry about that. You were saying?" Henry asked after

dropping the towel next to his chair and returning to his seat. He knew perfectly well what Millie had said, but he was buying time as his mind raced to find an appropriate response. Having just learned that morning of the unfortunate circumstances of her son's life and his untimely demise, he already knew that a search for Millie's son would result in heartbreak.

"I was saying that if you were still willing to help me, I would like to find my son. I don't want your money; I've got plenty of that. I just need help in figuring out how to go about it. I don't even know where to start."

Henry listened intently. He was deathly opposed to lies and valued honesty above nearly all else. The last thing he wanted to do was to start their new life together off with untruths and secrets. He knew how dangerous and costly dishonesty could be. It was a painful lesson learned from his relationship with Mary and one he had never forgotten. However, he knew how terribly devastated Millie would be by the truth, and he wanted to spare her that pain at all costs. One thing that Henry had become an expert at during his years in business was the art of deflection and diversion. It was a way to not say something you would later regret without having to lie. He could make a statement that another would believe implied something when, in fact, he did not actually commit to it. In a world of deals, contracts, and legalities this skill had often been invaluable to him. Now, in order to buy time and protect Millie's feelings, he employed the tactic masterfully.

"Millie, I'd do most anything for you. Of course, I am always ready to help you any way I can," he answered sincerely, carefully choosing each of his words. Her face glowed as he spoke. "But what's this about you don't need my money?" He was pivoting the conversation away from the hot topic to be sure, but also was curious about *her* choice of words. Millie laughed.

"Well, it's not like I'm some pauper. You know you've paid me very well for lots of years, Henry. I don't spend too much; you never know when a rainy day might come along. So, the bank is pretty near getting full up with my money," she declared proudly.

Henry was impressed by her confidence and common sense. He was anything but a moneygrubbing miser and lived quite well, to be sure. Be that as it may, he also did not throw money around and believed strongly in accumulating wealth. He was pleased to discover that Millie shared in this belief.

"Well, since we are dating now maybe I could pay you a little less then," he teased mischievously.

"That's not gonna happen," she zipped back. "If anything, now that I'm seeing the boss, I'm in line for a raise. That's what those women on TV do!" she joked. Her jabs were flirtatious, and they made Henry chuckle.

"I guess we'll have to see how good you are and then decide about the money."

"I was pretty darned good today!" she fired again without missing a beat.

Henry nearly spit his drink as he had earlier but this time it wasn't from choking. He was completely enthralled by Millie's sassy side and felt like a young man again when he was with her.

"I certainly can't argue with that!" he agreed.

Their meeting continued for another hour as they shared a second round of drinks, and the conversation turned to less scintillating topics. Finally, at last, Millie left after a long and exhilarating day and headed for home with the taste of Henry's good night kiss still fresh on her lips. Henry watched as she pulled out of the driveway and reflected on the fact that both of them would now be alone until she returned the next morning. *We'll have to do something about that,* he thought.

*

The following morning, Henry was already seated at his favorite table at The Eager Beaver when the town mayor walked in just before 11:30 a.m. Both men were notorious for their punctuality, and Richard Ross was disappointed that Henry had bested him.

"I was hoping to beat you here," the mayor said in jest.

"Come on now, Dick, you know better than that," Henry joked as he rose to shake hands with him.

"You're right, I do," Richard happily conceded as the men sat down.

"How've you been, Henry?" he asked.

"I'm great! How's life as the most powerful man in Lewis?" Henry inquired.

"I wouldn't know. Suppose *you* tell *me*," Richard stated with obvious deference to the elder man's status within the community. Henry smiled. Richard was a clever man and a savvy politician. He fully understood that Henry Engel had been the anonymous driving force behind the majority of the town's most important projects over the years. It was the very reason that he had dropped everything and agreed to meet with Henry on this day.

"Hi, Mr. Engel! Hey, Mayor!" greeted Jenny with enthusiasm as she approached and placed two menus on the table. "This is a nice surprise seeing both of you. Can I get you fellas something to drink?"

"Good morning Jenny, I'll take a glass of iced tea," Henry replied.

"Make that two please," Richard added.

"All righty then, I'll be right back to get your order," she said sweetly as she spun and headed off to retrieve their drinks.

"So, Henry, what concerns you about the proposed cell phone tower?" the mayor asked cutting to the heart of the matter.

"Well, I'll tell you, Dick, I'm certainly in favor of bringing cell service to Lewis. It makes all the sense in the world as far as I'm concerned." Richard nodded as Henry continued. "The questions I have are more related to why here and why this outfit?" Henry was referring to the proposal to erect the large tower on a lot situated just behind the Landmark Center where the diner was located.

"Honestly, Henry, it's the first and only proposal that's ever come into my office. It's really no more complicated than that."

"How did it come about?"

"John Everett brought it to me. He said the phone company approached him, and he stands to make a good payday if he leases them the land. He's got the whole deal already in place, just needs approval to go ahead. The town gets cell phone service out of the bargain, so it seemed like a reasonable win-win to me. That is, anyway, until word got out, and folks started squawking about *eyesores* and *blight* on the town's skyline. I've even heard they want to hold a rally out front against it."

Henry nodded his head, understanding the uproar that had been generated. The Eager Beaver was one of the most recognizable landmarks around Lewis, and it was revered by many. It was a place that both in appearance and attitude oozed small-town charm. In many ways, it was also an iconic symbol of the old-fashioned family values typical of rural Middle America, and many residents would resist any attempt by the modern world to spoil that.

"Yeah, I guess folks get cranky when progress rears its ugly head," Henry commented.

"Hell, Henry, we've got a giant sign out front with a grinning beaver on it. Just as many folks call me every year screaming that we need to get it down and get something more modern around here."

Henry laughed, and Richard broke into a mild smile at the irony. Such are the dilemmas of a small-town mayor caught between the future and the past.

Jenny returned and placed two tall glasses of freshly brewed iced tea complete with lemon wedges in front of them.

"Are you gentlemen ready?" she asked.

"We're going to be back in just a few minutes; can you come back in a bit?" Henry asked her.

"Of course, no problem. I'll watch for you."

"Thanks, Jenny. Dick, you feel like stretching your legs?" Henry asked.

"Sure," Richard agreed without knowing where Henry wanted him to go.

"Let's take a walk around back and look at the lot," Henry suggested with a twitch of his eyebrows. They rose and exited the diner after a few obligatory handshakes with patrons and an assurance to Suzy Grainger, the proprietor, that they would be right back. Once outside, their conversation continued.

"What's up, Henry?" Richard asked as they walked around toward the back of the building.

"I want you to see something. Besides, too many ears in there," Henry said, referring to his desire to keep the remainder of their conversation confidential.

"Gotcha. So what am I looking for?"

"Ok, that's the lot that Everett owns right there," Henry

stated, pointing to a small parcel of mostly weeds directly behind the strip plaza.

"Yep," the mayor concurred.

"We both know what he wants. He's looking to get paid *and* get his rear end kissed for bringing cell service to town. Probably plans to put his name on the tower too."

The mayor chuckled, knowing that Henry was spot-on with his assessment.

"Ok, now look just through those trees about fifty yards over and tell me what you see," Henry directed, now pointing to the far side of the proposed site.

"The old fire house?"

"Right! And who owns that building *and* the adjoining piece of ground?"

Mayor Ross broke into a huge grin and shook his head as he now knew where Henry was going.

"Why, the town of Lewis owns that fine piece of property," he announced.

"I think the town would benefit from leasing that unused ground to a cell phone company for a brand spanking new tower, don't you?" Henry asked the mayor facetiously.

"I sure do!"

"Over there, you're off the main drag and out of sight but still in close enough proximity to get the coverage they want. Your constituents will be tickled pink and on top of it, Lewis gets the payday instead of Everett."

Richard laughed and slapped Henry on the shoulder. He wondered why he was the mayor and not Henry Engel.

"Can I ask you a personal question that's always intrigued me?"

"Sure, go ahead. I don't promise you an answer, though," Henry replied with a twinkle in his eye.

"What the heck is the deal with you and John Everett? On the outside nobody can really tell, not much is ever said. But since I've been on the inside on a few things with you over the years, I know how much you like to stick it to him. What's *that* all about?"

Henry stared off in silence for a moment at the lot and considered his answer. Then, he spoke slowly and chose his words carefully.

"Let's just say he crossed the line with me a long, long time ago, and I figured out what he is all about. Now, anytime I see his name attached to something, I know that it's good for him and not as good for everyone else. If I can knock that blow-hard down a peg or two and do right by everyone else, it suits me. Unlike him, I'm not one for airing my affairs in public. So, just like always, keep me out of this cell tower deal."

"Sure Henry, of course, I completely understand."

"If my name comes up, it'll just piss him off. Everett would love to meet me at noon on Main Street for a gunfight and put on a big show anyway, not that he'd ever draw. I don't roll around with the pigs, Richard; once you're done you're both dirty, and no one can tell who's who. I'm more than satisfied just to be the fly in his ointment once in a while."

"Good deal, Henry, I'm grateful for your help on this one. It gets me out of a jam and will really help the town," the mayor said as he shook Henry's hand.

"Believe me, Dick, it's my pleasure. Let's go eat!" With that, they went back inside and enjoyed a robust lunch. The meeting left both men changed. Mayor Ross left that day with an even greater respect for Henry Engel. He appreciated his devotion to the town and his candor. He knew that whatever grudge Henry held against John Everett, it must be well-deserved, and he respected the manner in which Henry dealt with it. He also left with a brilliant plan that would benefit the town of Lewis greatly and aid in his reelection.

As for Henry, his evolution as a man was continuing. He was learning to share his feelings and let his guard down in ways that would have been impossible for him a year before. His expressions of genuine affection for Millie had sparked a change inside of him. He was beginning to see that he could trust people other than just a chosen few who were included in his *inner circle*. The world was now beginning to open up, and it included more than Jake, Joe, Millie, and George. A year before, he would have never answered the mayor's question. However, now he could see that Richard was not just an honorable man, but also a friend. Helping him solve a problem while improving the quality of life for the residents of Lewis made Henry very happy. The added bonus of sticking it to John Everett and depriving him of his bragging rights and bag of cash was merely icing on the cake.

CHAPTER 14

Girl Talk

MILLIE PEEKED OUT the front window for any signs of Henry's return, but as of yet, he was nowhere in sight. She knew that his lunch meeting with Mayor Ross would likely take a while, and her interest wasn't due to concern about his well-being. It was simply that she missed him and was anxious for him to come back home. Nevertheless, since it was Friday, which had long been designated as her *deep cleaning* day, there were plenty of chores to keep her busy while he was gone.

"No sign of him yet, baby," she reported to Joe as she walked past. The sleepy cat was taking an afternoon snooze on the bottom step of the staircase and cracked open her eyes at the sound of Millie's voice. However, she quickly determined that there was no cause for movement on her part and resumed her slumber.

Millie picked up a damp sponge and began scrubbing the counter surrounding the kitchen sink. As she did, her thoughts drifted back to her date with Henry and she happily hummed a soft melody. However, her pleasant song was abruptly interrupted by a sudden knock on the front door. The sound of it startled her and caused Joe's head to pop up with alarm.

"Now who on earth could that be?" Millie said aloud as she

dropped the sponge in the sink and looked over at the clock. It was a tad before 1:00 p.m. and certainly too early for Lucy Dawson, the extremely punctual mail carrier, to be dropping off a package. She turned on the faucet and rinsed her hands quickly before grabbing a nearby towel and drying them in haste. Since Henry hadn't forewarned her to expect anyone, she reasoned that it must be some sort of delivery and stepped toward the door.

"Hold on, I'm coming!" she called ahead as she made her way down the hallway. She looked through the panes of glass on either side of the door but couldn't see a delivery person or any type of truck for that matter. *Good Lord, couldn't even wait a minute while I washed my hands?* she wondered with agitation. As Millie pulled open the large door, she was growing perturbed by the thought that whoever had been knocking had been rudely impatient and already left. Much to her surprise, there wasn't a uniformed package-toting person on the other side. Instead, she was greeted by an attractive younger woman who was peacefully waiting for someone to answer the door. Millie thought that she looked tired as if she had been on a long journey. She also immediately noted that this young lady had the most sensational green eyes she had ever seen. The expression on the visitor's face indicated that she was just as surprised to see Millie.

"Hello there miss, can I help you?" Millie asked as she opened the storm door.

"Hello, I'm looking for Henry Engel. Is he home by chance?" the woman asked politely.

The British accent was unmistakable. Millie instantly guessed that the person standing on the porch was none other than the famous author that she had heard so much about from Henry. *He said she was pretty; never said she was a knockout,* she thought with a degree of jealousy. Off to the left, Millie noticed a dark green Jeep Cherokee that looked to be packed to the gills.

"Why hello, Ms. Wagner! I've heard plenty about you. Mr. Engel isn't here right now, but he ought to be home directly. Would you like to come in and wait for him?" Millie's hospitality was genuine and typical. She treated everyone she encountered with great respect and would give the shirt off of her back to a stranger in need. However, in this case, her invitation was also slightly self-serving. The opportunity to size up her competition and possibly speak privately with Anne was too good to pass up. She felt better about Henry's mindset after the events of the past twenty-four hours, but she was uncertain what Anne's intentions might be. If need be, she was determined to set the Englishwoman straight about a few things related to her relationship with Henry.

"That would be simply lovely! I'd so appreciate it, if you don't mind. I drove all night and just hit town, and I'm pooped," she said with a fatigued laugh as she stepped through the doorway.

"Well come on in, and take a seat," Millie beckoned as she led the way toward the kitchen.

Anne followed closely behind and felt glad to be back at Oak Forest. The estate had a discernible warmth, and she was drawn to it.

"Oh, hello Joe!" she exclaimed as she caught sight of the little Siamese cat on the staircase. "How have you been, darling?"

Joe immediately stood and cried out at the sight of her, causing the weary author to kneel and shower her with lavish affection.

"Looks like somebody sure remembers you," Millie observed, a little irked by the cat's vociferous reaction to their visitor. Joe was generally friendly toward guests, but clearly she was particularly thrilled to see Anne.

"I'll say! We hit it off right from the first, didn't we baby?" Anne declared happily as she scratched the feline's neck and ears. Suddenly, it occurred to her that she had not formally introduced herself.

"Goodness sakes, now look at me. Where are my manners? Here I've intruded on you and disrupted your afternoon and not even introduced myself properly," Anne apologized as she stood and stepped toward Millie with her hand extended. "It seems you already know who I am, and you are Henry's housekeeper I suppose? Millie is it?"

"Yes ma'am, Ms. Wagner, I'm Millie all right. I'm Henry's *housekeeper*." For the first time, the title stuck in her throat like a dry bite of a sandwich.

"I've heard about you too," she said with a smile as they shook hands politely. "Please do call me Anne; all of my friends do, and I so hope that we can get to be friends in time."

Millie smiled. *We'll have to see about that Ms. Wagner*, she thought.

"I hope so too," she replied courteously. "Would you like something to drink?"

"That would be delightful. I could really go for a spot of tea. I don't suppose Henry ever got any?"

Henry? She calls him Henry? Millie didn't like where this was headed. She shook her head with a forced smile.

"Sorry, no tea. He's got a fine-looking teakettle, though," she said referring to Anne's recent gift.

"Oh lovely! Did he like it?"

"Put it right on his desk where it's been ever since," Millie jabbed, softly downplaying his interest in the present.

"Ugh, he's such an American man!" Anne moaned in jest.

"He is certainly all of that and a handful more. How about a glass of lemonade instead?"

"That would be wonderful, Millie, thank you."

"All right. You rest your legs, and I'll get us some."

Anne pulled a chair from the table and sat down as Millie stepped to the cabinet. She retrieved glasses and then moved on to the refrigerator for the pitcher, which held two quarts of the freshly made refreshment. As she filled each glass with ice from the dispenser on the fridge door, she could understand why a man would be attracted to Anne. *She's young, gorgeous, and sweet. What's not to like?* After she had poured lemonade into the glasses, she picked them up and moved to the kitchen table.

"Thank you so much!" Anne said as she accepted her drink and took a long sip from it. "My, that is good!" she announced as she savored the flavor.

"Hard to beat on a spring day," Millie pleasantly agreed as she sat down and took a sip as well.

"Indeed."

"So, I hear we're going to be neighbors. Henry told me that you bought the old Stewart place," Millie stated, attempting to make conversation.

"Yes, that's right. You know the home?" Anne asked innocently.

"Oh yeah, it's just a couple blocks over from where I live. My place is on Maple."

"That's grand!" Anne declared excitedly, not truly knowing yet where that street was but guessing that it was close to her new home. "I do hope you'll come by and visit once I get settled."

"I look forward to it!" Millie was impressed by Anne's

friendly demeanor. She was having a hard time not liking the engaging British author.

"I've contracted with a nice man from town to fix things up. You might know him, he's called *Louis from Lewis*?" Millie smiled and nodded her head affirmatively at the mention of his name. He had been a fixture around Oak Forest for years when a problem arose, and Millie knew him to be a fine father and excellent handyman.

"I was originally planning to hold off on moving until summer, but I couldn't wait. Henry is such a dear; he's been keeping an eye on things for me, but I decided to go ahead and come out here now and oversee the renovation in person. I may have to rough it for a bit, but I confess I'm excited to make a go of it," she added with a giggle.

The mention of *dear Henry* reminded Millie that Anne may, in fact, be a wolf in sheep's clothing. She realized that all of Anne's *girl talk* may be no more than a device to get into Millie's good graces and get her even closer to Henry. Things had gone too far, and her heart was too taken by Henry to sit idly by and watch as anything or anyone attempted to wedge in between them. Therefore, she sensed an opportunity to feel the Brit out a bit about the nature of her interest in him.

"Yeah, Henry is a very special man for sure. He and I have been together for near twenty-five years now." The mention of the tenure of their relationship was deliberate and intended to make the point that Anne was treading on Millie's well-established turf. "He's been awful good to me. He's one of those rare people that is just awful good to everybody, you know? I couldn't have found a better man... To work for, that is." Millie caught herself and added that last phrase as she realized that her heart was overflowing with affection for him these days. She had wanted to feel Anne out, not confess her own love for the man. It was a slip that wasn't lost on the astute younger woman.

Anne smiled. She had become a renowned and accomplished author in large part because she understood people and was able to convey their genuine human emotions in her books. It now occurred to her that her presence in Lewis might be seen as a threat and she rapidly moved to quell any concerns that might exist. In just those few moments shared together, she already had a strong desire to befriend Millie and make her an ally, not an enemy. She had an idea for a bestseller, but she knew that it might take Millie's help to make it happen.

"Yes, I concur completely. Henry is a rare and special man to be sure. From the very first time I met him, he was different than what I expected. I came here looking for a story; you know, something I could use in a book I am working on. *Instead, I found someone that so reminds me of my father.* I lost him tragically some years back, and it left a huge hole in my heart. In some weird way, Henry fits there, and I'm just drawn to him. It's a large part of the reason I bought Molly Stewart's house and decided to move here. I suppose that sounds a little daft, right?" she asked, mildly embarrassed by her own confession of her feelings.

"Not at all, *Anne.* Are you hungry, can I make you a sandwich?" Millie's face broke into an enormous smile as she reached her hand across the table and patted Anne's forearm. Her reservations and jealousy about the author's budding relationship with Henry had been entirely misplaced. She fully understood precisely how Anne felt and shared the sentiment. It was exactly the same reason, just from a different angle, that had drawn her to him all those years ago. Henry Engel was an extraordinary man and knowing him made you feel better about yourself.

Now that Millie knew that she could let her guard down, she could see that Anne might be wonderful for Henry. He had never had any children of his own, except for Joe, and it was something that she knew he regretted. Perhaps Anne was just the piece he needed to complete that section of his puzzle. It was something that Millie could relate all too well to, and it was also the reason that she was now highly motivated to find her own son and reconnect with him.

Anne was famished and gratefully accepted the offer. Millie cheerfully prepared a fine lunch for them both featuring ham sandwiches, potato salad, and sweet peaches. While they ate, they chatted and laughed and got to know one another. They also spent a good deal of time talking about Henry. Anne was very curious to learn more about him and asked lots of questions that Millie happily answered. By the time Henry arrived back at Oak Forest, the women had been talking for nearly two hours and were beginning to feel like old friends.

"Uh-oh, this can't be good," Henry protested in jest as he entered the kitchen.

"Hello, Henry!" Anne cried out as she popped up from her seat.

"Hi, kiddo! What in the world are you doing here? You didn't say anything last time we talked about coming out here yet. I was shocked just now when I saw your Jeep out front."

"Bad surprise?" Anne inquired with a playful twist of her head.

"Just the opposite," Henry reassured her with a smile as she reached up and kissed him on the cheek. "Good to see you again!"

"You too! I've just been having the nicest afternoon with Millie!" she said as she turned to the table.

"So I see," Henry noted cautiously. "And what have you two been talking about?"

"You of course!" Millie chimed in without missing a beat as Anne laughed.

"Wonderful," he declared sarcastically, pretending that he was upset by their meeting. In fact, nothing could have been further from the truth. Seeing them enjoying each other's company made him very happy. It also made him hope that Millie would now be able to move past her worry about his interactions with Anne. He couldn't possibly know at this point that Millie had accidentally found an ally in a much greater plan, and he was the object of it.

"I've learned all kinds of interesting things about you," Anne teased as she sat back down in her chair.

"I just gave away all your secrets, Henry. She's got you figured out now," Millie piled on.

"Yes, my book just got a lot more intriguing."

Book? The jokes had just gotten a whole lot less funny as far as Henry was concerned.

"Yeah, I don't think so," he said as he walked past them and circled to the far side of the table to take a seat of his own.

"I'm just joshing, of course! Your secrets are safe with me, Henry Engel," Anne promised with a chuckle.

"So, what brings you back already? Did you drive straight through?" he asked. Before Anne could answer him, Millie made a move to get up.

"If you two will excuse me, I've got lots to finish that I let go this afternoon. I'm going to get some chores done and let you two visit," Millie said as she stood and left the table. Henry smiled. He knew that Millie was not just conscientious about her cleaning but also very considerate. She understood that Anne had come to Oak Forest to see Henry and was giving them their privacy. Before she headed upstairs to attend to his bathroom, however, she paused momentarily.

"Say, Henry, how'd your lunch go with Mayor Ross? Seems like it ran kinda long. Did everything work out the way you hoped?" Millie asked.

"It went perfect; everything played out just the right way. I ran a couple of errands afterward, and that's why I didn't get back until now."

Millie smiled and nodded in approval as she continued up the stairs. She could see that Henry was happy, and that was all that mattered to her.

"You had lunch with the mayor today?" Anne asked.

"Yeah, we had some things to talk over."

"He seems to be a fine man. Very professional, too; I thought he did a smashing job for me." Anne was referring to the mayor's dual role as a realtor and the manner in which he had helped to facilitate her purchase of the Stewart place.

"No doubt about that; he's a top-notch guy for sure," Henry said as Joe rubbed her body against his right calf to greet him. "Hello, sweetheart! I missed you," he said sweetly as he bent to pick her up.

Joe held still as Henry scooped her up and snuggled her against his chest.

"Were you happy to see Anne again?" he asked the little cat.

"Was she ever!" Anne answered on Joe's behalf. "She made me feel very, very welcome, that's for sure."

"Good! I'm glad to hear it! What did you think about the big news?" he asked not knowing that Millie had neglected to tell Anne about Joe's upcoming motherhood.

"News? I'm sorry, what news is that?" Anne asked with no clue as to what he was referring to.

"You mean Millie didn't tell you? Joe is going to be a mother!" Henry proclaimed proudly like a father speaking about his cherished daughter.

"Really? That's fantastic!" Anne declared jubilantly. "I had no idea. I thought that perhaps she might have gained a wee bit of weight since I saw her last, but I didn't put two and two together on it."

"Yeah, how about that?" he crowed as he nuzzled Joe's face against his chin.

"When is she due?"

"Should be sometime in early June, according to the vet."

"Aww Henry, that's wonderful news! Have you decided yet what you plan to do with all of the kittens?"

"No, not really. My pal George is already penciled in for one, but I don't have a clue yet about the rest. Depending on how many she has, I'd guess we might keep one. After that, I honestly don't know yet. Do you know anyone that might be in the market for a kitten?"

"You're looking at her!" Anne trumpeted with enthusiasm. "I'd be honored to adopt one of Joe's babies if the opportunity presents itself."

"No kidding? Did you hear that, Joe?" Henry asked the expectant mother. Just then Millie came down the steps to get a bottle of window cleaner. Henry couldn't resist the chance to needle her. He knew that Millie loved to be the one to deliver the latest scoop when she knew something others did not.

"You didn't tell Anne about Joe's big news? Man, you're slipping," he marveled.

"Oh my gosh! I sure forgot. How did I miss telling you that?

I guess we were so caught up in talking about everything else, it somehow slipped my mind," Millie explained to Anne with a wink. The truth of the matter was that when the author appeared at the front door, Millie had an agenda to pursue, and kittens weren't a part of it. Then, once she realized that Anne was not her enemy but, in fact, a potential confederate, Millie pivoted to a different and even more important matter. Amid all of her strategic movements, the news of Joe's motherhood had been inadvertently pushed aside.

"Anne says she'd like a kitten. What do you think about that?" Henry asked, seeking her approval.

A broad smile spread across Millie's face. "Really? You want a kitten, Anne?"

"Oh yes, very much so."

"I think that would be wonderful! See now, Henry, I told you everything would work out. They aren't even here yet, and we've already got two sold," she teased as she went back about her business. Henry and Anne laughed and resumed their conversation.

"All right then, so what gives? How come you're here?" he asked like a concerned parent addressing a college student who had just come home unannounced.

"Just couldn't wait to get started is all. I found myself day-dreaming about my new home more and more and decided to load up some things and head west," she laughed. "My agent is going to handle things on the backside so that I can get going here."

"And so you just jumped in your truck and drove all night from New York?"

"Daddy always said I had an impulsive side," she joked impishly. "Besides, who better than me to oversee the renovation. You were a dear to be willing to look after things, but that wasn't fair of me to ask. I'm going to write books and renovate the house all at the same time."

Henry couldn't help but admire her fortitude. It was yet another quality that the two shared.

"Well all right! Have you been by there? Louis hasn't called me on anything yet, so I really don't know what the situation is inside," he advised.

"No, I haven't been there yet. I came here first for fun, hoping to surprise you. I did speak with him on Wednesday though, and he said that the power and the plumbing both work so I'm off and running. I've got a sleeping bag and my checkbook so I'm certain I can make a go of it."

"Are you kidding? Is there even any furniture in there? How about you stay here in the guest room until you get the place livable?"

Anne was quite touched by his caring concern. "Thank you ever so much for the dear offer, Henry, but I could never impose on you like that. Besides, I am sure I can find suitable accommodations at the Western if things are too out of sorts." Anne was referring to the town's lone motel, which had served as her lodging on her last trip to Lewis.

"But..." he protested.

"Now Henry, I'm a tough girl. I've traveled the world and spent nights sleeping on the sands of Cairo and in the deepest jungles of Peru. I'm quite positive I can survive the perils of Molly Stewart's house," she assured him with a chuckle and a smile.

The exchange sounded like something her own father might have said to her and it warmed her heart. Realizing that she was not a child that needed his guidance and seeing that she clearly had her mind made up, Henry let the matter drop. The pair continued to talk for a time about a variety of topics as Millie occasionally passed through while finishing her cleaning. Soon, the afternoon was waning, and the effects of Anne's marathon journey were finally beginning to show.

"Do you want some more lemonade?" Henry asked, noting that her glass was nearly empty. "Or something else maybe?" He knew that it was almost time for his meeting with Jake and Joe, and he was more than open to her and Millie joining him in the festivities.

"I was originally hoping for a cup of tea. I heard a rumor that the proprietor of this establishment has a glorious antique teakettle. However, I learned that he thinks it's an ornament for his desk and not an indispensable part of a civilized gentle-man's kitchen," she lamented and shook her head in disapproval. Henry's face blushed modestly as he recognized that he had neglected to thank her for the gift. Misunderstanding his reaction and thinking that her playful reprimand had embarrassed him, she immediately moved to diffuse the situation. She didn't comprehend that Henry had no interest whatsoever in tea. He was simply mortified that he had allowed her kindness to go unrewarded. It was against his nature to do so.

"Not to worry, I'll just have to teach you how to use it next time I'm here."

"Oh, I don't care about the tea. I feel rotten that I forgot to thank you for the gift, even though I don't want it and didn't ask for it," he jabbed, to Anne's delight.

"Damned Yankee!" she remarked dramatically as if she had been insulted to the very core of her being. Their witty repartee made them both laugh.

"My, I truly do hate to break this up, but I think I best be on my way before I get too bleary-eyed to make it home," Anne said with a light yawn. She had been awake for over thirty hours but she still caught herself referring to her new house as *home* and it made her happy to think of it. She had been transient for a good deal of her life, and the idea of now sinking roots in Lewis was compelling. It was made even more so by her burgeoning friendships with Henry and Millie.

"You know, since you're getting tired I can drive you into town if you like. We can come back and get your truck tomorrow," he offered.

"You're very sweet Henry, but that's not necessary, I'll be fine," she responded as she stood up. "It's not very far."

Millie was in the laundry room and could overhear their conversation. She noted that it was getting near her usual time to head home as well. She wondered how to handle that now since her relationship with Henry had suddenly changed so drastically. Normally, she would leave on Friday by 5:00 p.m. and then wouldn't see him again until Monday morning. Now, the thought of such a prolonged absence from him seemed unthinkable. She wondered how he felt about it. They hadn't had an opportunity to discuss such things due to Anne's surprise visit, and she was uncertain of what to do next. However, she soon learned that Henry had given things a bit more thought.

"If you want, you can follow me home. I'm leaving soon," Millie called to Anne as she entered the room, causing the author to turn in her direction.

"Really? All right, Millie, I would like that." Anne cheerfully accepted the offer as Henry's face contorted into a forlorn grimace behind her. He looked as if he had just been shot. Because Anne's back was to him, she couldn't see his dismay but Millie delighted in his reaction because it indicated he had indeed preferred that she stay. It took all of Millie's self-control not to react as he silently mouthed a pathetic looking "n-o-o-o-o" to her before Anne turned back to him. As soon as Anne had diverted her attention again his way, Henry instantly regained his composure to conceal his emotions. Millie's face exploded into a wide smirk, and she silently mouthed "Sorry!" so that only he could see.

Anne bid Henry and Joe a fond farewell and headed to her vehicle to wait for Millie to gather her things and lead the way. As soon as Henry closed the door and he was sure that Anne couldn't hear, he complained aloud about Millie's gesture.

"Why did you offer to let her follow you?" he grumbled like a lovesick teenager.

"I'm sorry, I thought I was being nice," Millie explained innocently as she moved past him in the hallway.

"I know, and you are. Why do you have to be so damn nice?" he groused comically as she picked up her purse with a giggle.

"Is it really as bad as all that? I didn't know you wanted me to stay," she flirtatiously whispered as he took her into his arms. "Last I heard, you were inviting a pretty young lady to stay in my room."

"*Your room*, huh?" he said softly repeating her words.

"I'm the only one that's ever slept in it," she said referring to the guest bedroom that she had used on occasion when the weather made driving too treacherous.

"Excellent point, worth remembering," he agreed with a sly smile. "Come on now, you know better than that. I was just being nice."

"*I know, and you are. Why do you have to be so damn nice?*" Millie teased sarcastically mimicking his earlier words.

"Now you're just playing dirty," he fired back playfully before he eased in for a long sweet kiss.

"I'm sorry, I wish I had known what to do, but this is all brand new," she explained.

"I know, I know, we'll figure it out. I just hate to see you go. I was looking forward to a nice long meeting with *you*," he moaned woefully.

"Well, you have a nice long meeting with Jake and Joe and miss me then," she said as his eyebrows sank.

"It won't be the same without you."

"And then tomorrow night, how about you pick me up and take me out on the town." Her words instantly made him perk up. It hadn't occurred to him that this was the New World and that anything was suddenly possible.

"Yeah?" he asked gleefully.

"Yeah," she confirmed as she put her hand behind his neck and kissed him again.

"I can do that!" he declared.

"All right then, you call me tomorrow afternoon and let me know where you're taking me and what time you're coming," she instructed. "That way, I can know what to wear and when to be ready. That's how it works."

"Yes ma'am!" he replied with exaggerated obedience which made Millie snicker.

"Ok, I better get going, Anne is out there waiting," she said in a more serious tone. Millie reached up and gave Henry a final gentle kiss and then hurriedly headed off. As she reached the doorway, she stopped and looked back at Henry, who was ogling her. The look in his eyes made her stomach do a backflip. She couldn't remember the last time any man had looked at her that way. With a decidedly provocative southern accent, she called back to him. "All right then Henry Engel, *I'll see you again*."

CHAPTER 15

Clean Living

THOUGH THIS SATURDAY was to prove to be quite different from the norm, the morning started out typically enough for Henry. By 7:45 a.m., his navy blue Ford Explorer was headed down County Road 27 and rolling toward town. The sky was dotted with puffy white clouds, but ample sunshine poured through to the landscape below. Henry enjoyed the scenery along the way and hummed to the country song playing on the radio in the background. Just after 8:00 a.m., he made his normal first stop at the Lewis Bank & Trust to handle the week's financial affairs. His dealings there went smoothly and soon he was seated in his customary booth at The Eager Beaver Diner and sipping on coffee.

Henry was in extremely high spirits and eagerly anticipating the day. He was excited about his date that evening with Millie and also anxious to pop-in on Anne and see how she had fared during her initial night in the Stewart house. For the next ninety minutes, he perused the morning's editions of the *Lewis Gazette* and *St. Louis Post-Dispatch* and enjoyed a robust breakfast. Occasionally, fellow patrons stopped by his table to say hello or exchange words with him. Henry received all comers with a smile and a kind word and genuinely enjoyed the exchanges. His good mood was contagious, and everyone that came into contact with him noticed it.

As he stepped to the cash register to pay his bill, Suzy Grainger, the owner, couldn't help but comment on Henry's demeanor.

"Somebody sure looks to be on top of the world! You look like you're having a really good morning, Henry," she observed as she accepted his ticket and a twenty-dollar bill from him.

"It shows? Yes, ma'am, I most certainly am," he confirmed with a broad smile and a chuckle that Suzy then matched.

"Well, I'm really glad of that! You deserve it, Henry," she said as she handed him his change.

"Thank you, Suzy! It's nice of you to think so. You have a great day now; I'll see you next time," he said as he turned and walked out. Suzy had known Henry for years, and he had been to the diner on hundreds, if not thousands of occasions. In all of that time, she could not recall an instance when he had seemed happier, and it tickled her.

Henry decided to delay his usual Saturday shopping trip and head straight to Anne's house. He was hoping to catch her at home, and if he did, she might need something from the store as well. If he missed her, he reasoned that he could proceed on and get the things on his list before swinging back by. Either way, he was anxious to see how she was getting along. Also, he had an idea to surprise Millie at home rather than call her to arrange their date later that evening. Since her house was just two blocks over from Anne's, he figured he could conveniently drop in on one and then the other.

In short order, Henry was turning onto State Street and approaching Anne's house. He was looking forward to surprising her and then Millie in succession, but he was the one that was startled. Not only did he see Anne's vehicle in the driveway, but Millie's sedan was also parked along the curb out front.

"Well, I'll be damned," he said aloud as he eased the truck to a halt immediately behind Millie's car. "I should have known," he mumbled as he shook his head with a smirk. *They were thick as thieves when I got home yesterday. Probably in there plotting against me right now,* he joked to himself as he exited the Explorer and walked up to the front door. In truth, he wasn't remotely upset to find Millie there. It was more a mild aggravation with himself that he hadn't seen it coming. He liked to think he could stay a step ahead of her, but that was more delusion than reality. Knowing Millie's nature, he should have realized that there was no way she would let a stranger move into town, much less a new friend, without offering to help her get settled in.

"Hello there, Henry!" came an elated greeting through the screen door as he approached. Anne had seen him pull up and was joyfully coming outside to welcome him. Henry noticed that the front door and all of the windows were open though it wasn't a particularly warm May morning. As he stepped onto the porch, she burst outside and gave him a friendly embrace and a kiss on his cheek.

"Such a nice surprise. What brings you over here?" she asked. Her hair was pulled back in a ponytail and she wore a sweatshirt, jeans, and sneakers much the same as Millie preferred when she cleaned house. Judging by the smudges of dirt on her clothing, Henry surmised that's what had been going on prior to his arrival.

"I came to see how you were doing in your new place," he explained.

"Aren't you just a dear! Please, do come inside. Millie's here too!" she proclaimed excitedly as she turned to lead him in.

"Yeah, I just saw her car." Henry followed her into the house and could instantly understand why Millie was there. She was without a doubt *The Queen of Cleaning,* and this clearly was no job for an author.

Upon passing through the doorway, one was greeted by a dank, musty smell that permeated the air. The carpet on the floor of the front room, which had served as Molly's parlor, was filthy and in need of replacement. In addition, the walls looked as if they could use a fresh coat of paint. It had been a while since Henry had been inside, and he was disgusted to see that it had fallen into such disrepair.

"Is the whole place like this?" he asked.

"Pretty much," she confirmed.

"Boy oh boy, Molly must be rolling in her grave."

"Poor dear. I suppose at the end she simply couldn't keep up with it all."

"I guess there at the last, it had been a while since I had made it by. I remember it was getting a little rugged in here but not quite this bad," Henry offered.

"Nothing a little bleach and elbow grease can't fix," Anne declared optimistically.

"Hey Anne, did you move the bucket?" Millie called from upstairs.

"Yes Millie, sorry, it's in the bathroom down here." She suddenly got an idea and brought her right index finger to her lips, motioning for Henry to remain silent.

"Shall I bring it up to you?"

"Nah, you stay put. I'll come down for it," Millie replied.

Anne motioned for Henry to move to the wall along the side

of the entry. That way, Millie wouldn't be able to see him down the hallway as she descended the staircase from the second floor. Henry was now on to Anne's meaning and realized that he was possibly going to get his surprise after all. He could hear the steps creaking as Millie approached and knew based on his previous knowledge of the floor plan that the bathroom she was headed to was in the opposite direction of the parlor. He was considering how to sneak up on her from behind when Anne flashed another glimpse of her mischievous side.

"Say, Millie, come quick please!" she shouted to her with urgency.

"Whatcha got? Another one of those big cockroaches like we've been seeing?" Millie answered as her voice rapidly drew closer.

"Yeah, something like that. But this is a *really big one!*"

"Where's he at?" Millie shrieked as she rushed into the room with her mop at the ready.

"Right here!" Henry exclaimed with evil glee.

"Ahhh!" Millie shrieked and threw her mop into the air before realizing it was only Henry. "Oh, good Lord!" she muttered in shock as Anne and Henry burst into laughter at the sight. She was not expecting to find such a tall bug in the room, and the joke was less than amusing to her.

"What in the world are you doing here?" she asked Henry angrily as she tried to catch her breath. "And you, you're just as bad as he is! I'd have thought you'd have more sense, being from England and all," she scolded Anne. Henry and Anne were uncertain what the connection was between practical jokes and heritage but regardless were totally unfazed. Despite Millie's rebuke, the pair of pranksters couldn't contain themselves or control their juvenile celebration. Their giddiness was contagious and in a moment Millie forgot that she was mad and instead felt happy to see Henry.

"So, what are you doing here? I thought on Saturdays you went to the bank and ran errands?" Millie asked, genuinely interested in his intentions.

"I do. I just finished eating over at The Beaver and thought I'd swing by to see how Anne was holding out," Henry explained.

"Thought you had more important things to do than running all over town. You know, like calling somebody about making some plans for tonight?" Millie added just for fun.

"Yes, I hear someone has a big date for tonight!" Anne chimed in, very much to Henry's surprise.

"How do you know about that?" a startled Henry asked Anne before turning to Millie. "You told her about us?"

Both women grinned impishly.

"I think it's fantastic!" Anne declared. "It's exactly the kind of love story that my readers go crazy about."

"That's great, but this isn't one of your books," he warned her.

"Oh, you're no fun," she playfully countered as she left the room to head back to her cleaning. After she walked out, Millie quickly moved to feel Henry out on the topic.

"You're not mad about me telling her, are you?" she asked quietly so that Anne couldn't hear as she poked his ribs with her hands.

"No, I guess not. I mean, of course not. It's just..."

"Kinda weird right?" she said with a smile.

"Yeah, I guess so. No, I don't want it to be a secret. I want the whole world to know," he said as he bent and kissed her tenderly. Millie's knees buckled slightly as he expressed how much he approved of their relationship. Once their lips had parted, he remembered that he still didn't know why she had come to help Anne even though he had a pretty good idea.

"Now, you know why *I'm* here, but why are *you* here? And how did you guys get talking about us?" he asked.

"Well, as we were driving in last night I got to thinking about how this poor girl has a lot to deal with. She's all worn out and doesn't know anyone in town and all. So, I asked if she'd like some help. You know me and cleaning." Henry shook his head. He was well aware of Millie's fondness for disinfectants and scouring pads.

"Anyway, I came over this morning about eight and jumped in," she explained.

Noticing her mussed-up hair, Henry took his right hand and pushed it away from her face. Millie had a heart of gold, and it was the size of Missouri. The explanation he had just received pretty well matched what he had suspected. It just left one thing missing.

"And the thing about us?" he pressed.

"She asked me! Said she could tell yesterday at the house that there was something going on between us. *She's good, Henry.*"

"I'll say!" he agreed.

"By the way, when exactly were you going to call me about tonight?" Millie quizzed him with a look of scorn.

"Well, considering you aren't home and don't own an answering machine, it doesn't matter a whole helluva lot, now does it?" he asked with great satisfaction at finally catching her off guard. After an exaggerated pause where all she did was look at him and bat her eyes, she conceded defeat.

"Yep, I got nothing. I walked right into that one, didn't I?"

"You certainly did," he said with complete satisfaction.

"So, what are we doing tonight?" she asked attempting to move past her blunder.

"I don't know. I guess we'll just figure it out," he said without any anxiety. "Now, as long as I'm here, how can I pitch in and help?"

Millie gave Henry an enthusiastic hug. She loved that he was unflappable and caring. She knew that as long as he was around, everything always seemed to be all right, and it made her feel safe, secure, and happy. Henry wasn't precisely certain what had caused this latest display of affection from Millie, but he enjoyed it nonetheless.

"Now then you two, get a room," Anne razzed as she passed through the parlor and out the front door with a rug that needed to be shaken out.

"Not a bad idea!" Henry whispered to Millie with a squeeze.

"Oh now, you stop that," she whispered back as she blithely pushed him away.

"What time is it?" Millie asked. She wasn't wearing a watch, and there were no clocks on the wall, but her stomach was complaining that it was approaching midday.

"Getting on toward eleven, why?" he responded after checking the time for her.

"I know you just finished breakfast, but I haven't had a bite to eat so far today. I'm guessing she hasn't either. Would you wanna run and pick up some sandwiches or something so I could stay with this?" she requested.

"Sure, what do you guys want?"

"Great, thanks. Hold on, let me ask her," Millie said as she walked to the front porch to find Anne. Before she could make it outside, the author was already coming back in.

"What gives?" Anne asked upon seeing them both looking at her.

"Henry's gonna run and pick us up some lunch. What sounds good to you?" Millie asked.

"Really? Oh excellent! I confess I'm famished. Um, I don't know. What sounds good to you two? Burgers maybe? It's my treat," she said as she started toward the kitchen to retrieve her purse.

"No, I've got this," Henry told her.

"I could eat a cheeseburger," Millie interjected.

"Don't be silly, you're helping me out. I need to..." Anne protested as Henry just shook his head.

"It's no use, trust me; you're gonna lose," Millie advised, knowing that Henry always paid for everything no matter how much she argued with him. Seeing that she was destined to go down in defeat, Anne could only laugh.

"You're really quite hardheaded, aren't you?" she joked to Henry.

"You have no idea," Millie jabbed before Henry could respond, causing him to turn to her.

"Hey!" he said defensively.

"What? You know I'm right."

"It's true," Henry admitted as he looked back at Anne.

"And you two are just now getting together? You banter back and forth like an old married couple!"

Anne was stating the obvious, but her accurate assessment brought a laugh from Henry and Millie. They were starting to see that the romantic aspect to their relationship was somewhat belated, all things considered.

Henry fetched lunch for the duo as the cleaning marathon marched on. Upon his return, the women took a break and gratefully devoured cheeseburgers and fries while they all sat around an old kitchen table. It was one of the few remaining relics from the previous household. Henry recalled that following Molly's death some distant relations had blown through town and hurriedly organized an estate sale. The haphazard affair had quickly cast a lifetime of accumulation to the four winds, and the aforementioned heirs had left town with the proceeds as fast as they had come. It made him slightly sad to think how little Molly's life's work meant to these people. All they had seen was a windfall from her death, not the generations of children she had impacted during her life. Henry himself was one of those kids. He wondered where he would be and how he might have turned out if he had never known her. He realized sitting there that it isn't the material possessions one has that define the person, it's the legacy they leave behind them when they go. He already believed this and was attempting to live his life in an honorable manner. However, on this day, sitting in Molly's kitchen around her table, the concept really hit home, and he resolved that he would be making some additional changes to his life.

By mid-afternoon, following a trip to the store for supplies, he was busily scraping old cracked paint off of the pantry door. Henry enjoyed working with his hands and being there with Anne and Millie made the whole experience that much more enjoyable. Like busy birds constructing a spring nest, they were hustling around the house cleaning and repairing things as needed all the while chirping merrily. Millie was busy catching Anne up on the latest town gossip, and Anne was eating it up with a spoon. Henry occasionally dropped in some seasoning here and there when the occasion called for it, but for the most part simply listened and savored the back and forth exchanges.

The afternoon evaporated and soon the sun was beginning

to ease toward the horizon. The air inside the house was growing cooler now and necessitated the closing of the windows. However, with the infusion of fresh breezes all afternoon, there had been a marked improvement in the quality of the air. The overall condition of the place had taken a turn for the better as well. Thanks to their persistent work, a hefty dent had been made in the list of chores required to get the home back into shape. Seeing that it had gotten later than expected and knowing that Henry and Millie were planning a night on the town, Anne called a halt to the overhaul.

"All right, you two, I'm throwing you out!" she said with a tired grin. "I just don't know how I can ever thank you both for all of your kindness."

"No thanks are necessary," Henry assured her.

"We're happy to be able to help," Millie agreed. "I sure had fun today. I love to clean; just ask Henry. This place is like paradise for a gal like me." Anne laughed and nodded, recollecting how awful things were in the morning when they started and acknowledging how much there still was to do.

"What time do you want us here tomorrow?" Henry asked without a hint of humor.

"Seriously? Oh no, Henry, I wouldn't dream of it. You've both done far too much as it is. I can handle it from here, really I can." Henry took one good look around and could see inestimable hours of cleaning and painting yet to be done.

"Nonsense. You have anything going tomorrow?" he asked while turning to Millie.

"Nothing better than this," she answered on cue.

"It's settled then. Are we starting early or are you sleeping in?" he asked Anne, now speaking for the both of them.

"No Henry, now I mean it, you've both done enough. I won't have it. It's just not…"

"Sweetie, you're gonna lose again," Millie interrupted as she picked up her purse. Henry smiled and nodded. The debate was over.

"All right then, if you both insist. What time do you want to get back at it?" Anne could see that there was no point in fighting them further. She was flustered but very grateful for their assistance and companionship.

"How about ten?" Henry proposed. "Is everybody good with that?"

"Works for me," Millie agreed easily.

"Me too," Anne concurred.

"All right, we'll see you then," Henry said as he and Millie moved toward the door.

"I just don't know what in the world to say to you both," Anne bemoaned, overcome with gratitude.

"Try 'see you in the morning,'" Henry joked as Millie chuckled.

"Ugh! You're a tough nut to crack, Henry Engel!" she called from the doorway as the couple stepped off of her porch and headed to their vehicles. The reference made Millie cackle, which in turn caused Henry to shake his head in amused disbelief.

"All right then, I'll see you in the morning!" Anne hollered. She had just learned firsthand that when Henry Engel made up his mind about something, there was no sense arguing about it.

CHAPTER 16

Love and Pizza

"I EXPECT IT'S GOT to be getting time to see Jake, isn't it?" Millie asked as they walked together to the street in front of Anne's house.

"Over a half hour past," Henry confirmed after checking his watch. "It's no big deal. I was figuring on a later get together for tonight anyway." He was referring to the fact that they were planning to have their first-ever Saturday night date.

"Yeah, I've been thinking about that, and I don't know, Henry. Did you still want to try and go out somewhere?" she asked as they reached the rear of her car.

"Well yeah, of course, I do. What do you mean?" he asked, a bit confused by her question.

"You know I want to, but what I mean is just look at us. I'm filthy from cleaning all day and could use a good long hot shower. You're a little mussed up too and probably could use one yourself," she said, noting the dirt on his pants and shirt sleeves. "By the time I get cleaned up, and you run home and do the same and then come back, it's gonna be getting late to go somewhere, isn't it? Besides, right now all I really want to do is sit down and relax for a little bit."

"So what are you saying?" Henry asked growing irritated by what he perceived as her negativism about their date. She could see that he didn't follow her line of reasoning, and she attempted to clarify things for him.

"What I'm saying is that maybe we could just stay home," Millie said as she took his hand.

"You mean just go home and not see each other tonight? Hell no, Millie, I don't want to do that," Henry declared, rejecting what he thought she was suggesting.

"No, Henry, me neither. What I'm saying is why don't we just pick up a pizza or something and go have a talk with Jake. We're both tired so how about we just watch a movie or something out at Oak Forest. If you don't care, I'll just get cleaned up out there, and we can lounge around. All I really want to do is be with you anyway. You can take me out some other night. We've got the rest of our lives for that."

Instantly, Henry's mood changed as he now understood what she had been saying. He was thrilled by Millie's proposal. In truth, his back and legs were barking from a lot of up and down movement all day. Having to rush home, shower, change clothes, rush back, and then drive back yet again to the estate later when he was more tired suddenly sounded like a really bad idea.

"Works great for me if you're sure it's ok with you. Do you want to throw some things in a bag and stay out there tonight then? I don't think either of us ought to be driving later."

"That's what I was thinking too, if it's ok with you," Millie agreed. "I've got the bag I always carry in my trunk with some sweats in it but if you don't mind, maybe we could drop the car off at my house and I could get something a little nicer to wear."

"No, I don't mind at all."

"Then you could bring me back in the morning before we come here. That way, my car won't sit here on the street all night and get people talking."

Henry sneered. He couldn't imagine that anyone cared much about his or Millie's social life, but he respected her wishes and gladly assented to follow her to her house. He had been extremely excited about their date when it first came up but now he was almost giddy. It was shaping up to be a night they'd never forget.

Henry thought that Millie's idea about pizza and a movie was brilliant. While she put together her overnight bag, he called ahead to Lou's Tavern and placed an order for an extra-large supreme. When it came to pizza, Lewis had several options to choose from including two national chains. However, Lou's Tavern had been around for decades, and the old-timers preferred their thin crust old-school Italian pies to most anything else.

By the time Henry hung up the phone, Millie was already waiting to go with a large bag with long handles draped over her shoulder. He had no idea what she had in there, but he was highly impressed with the speed and efficiency she had shown in packing it.

"Good girl. Man, that was fast!" he praised her as they walked out to his Explorer. "I thought the gal always made the guy wait on a date?" he jested as he closed the door behind her before walking to the driver's side and getting in himself. She waited for him to shut the door completely before she answered.

"Well, I'm no goofy teenage girl trying to make a boy suffer. I'm a tired old woman who's hungry for pizza and wants a drink, so I hustled!"

Henry burst into laughter as he started the truck and backed into the street. There were certainly some negatives to getting older, and he was feeling some of them as he'd begun to stiffen up from the day's labor. However, one of the positives to being a *mature* man was that he did not have to play the same games and endure the same frustrations as men a fraction of his age did when it came to the pursuit of the opposite sex. Henry was glad that he and Millie were older. He was glad that they could talk plainly and be straightforward with each other about their feelings. Henry reached across the console and took her hand. He knew that he was with the right *tired old woman* and it made him very happy.

As they drove across town toward the tavern, they discussed their possible movie choices for the evening. Henry was firmly in favor of viewing one of his many John Wayne VHS tapes for the umpteenth time. While Millie did not dislike "The Duke," she asserted that she was in the mood for something a little softer and more appropriate for a date. Henry argued unsuccessfully that a John Wayne movie was indeed romantic and in short order the Explorer was parked in the lot of Lewis' newest video rental store. Henry waited in the SUV as Millie vied inside with a bevy of hormonal teenagers for one of the meager selections still available at 6:30 p.m. on Saturday night. To her credit, she emerged rather quickly with two videos in her hands and looking no worse for wear. Once again, Henry thought, it proved that he'd rather be with this *old woman* than anyone else half her age.

"All right, *let's roll*," she said as she climbed in the truck.

"Let's roll?" Henry repeated.

"Yeah, let's go get the pizza. Sorry, I guess I'm a little amped up from being around all of those kids. *They're crazy!*"

Henry laughed as they pulled out of the parking lot and proceeded down the street.

"So what'd you get?" he asked.

"A comedy and a romance; I'll let you pick," she answered.

"Well, what are they about?"

"One's about a guy who loses his leg in WWII and then falls in love with his nurse. The other is about a girl who gets hit by a car and marries the guy who ran over her."

"Holy cow! So which one is the comedy?"

"Whichever one you think sounds funny," she dryly replied.

Henry shook his head in amazement. When he least expected it, Millie always seemed to catch him off guard.

"Slim pickings, eh?" Henry observed.

"I had to wrestle two cheerleaders just to get these," Millie cracked as they both chuckled.

Following a last brief stop to pick up their Saturday night feast, they were finally cruising down the county road as the sun hastened toward the horizon. The aroma of the pizza was overwhelming, and Henry convinced Millie that they should each eat a slice on the way to tide them over. Both Henry and Millie had eaten untold numbers of pizzas in their lives before that day, but neither could recall a time when it had ever tasted better.

Henry unlocked the door and then moved aside to allow Millie to enter first. As she stepped into the kitchen and put her purse and bag on the island, Joe scampered down the staircase to welcome Henry home.

"Hey, baby!" Millie greeted the little cat warmly. Joe didn't expect to find anyone other than Henry and stopped next to the kitchen table to study her with a clearly distinguishable look of befuddlement. "Bet you weren't expecting me."

"Hi, Joe!" Henry addressed his pal as he entered the room and set the pizza box and movies next to Millie's things.

Joe let out a series of small cries to acknowledge that she was indeed happy to see them both, even though she was still unsure about what was going on.

Millie stepped over and scooped her up as Henry walked past and gave Joe a quick pat on the head. He energetically darted around the kitchen and family room flipping on lights to combat the early evening darkness that was overtaking the house.

"All right, who wants to talk to Jake?" Henry asked, already knowing the answer.

"Count me in!" Millie declared jubilantly. "I've got lots to tell him," she said as she pulled a chair from the kitchen table and sat down with Joe still in her arms.

Henry poured the drinks and then grabbed the pizza on his way to join Millie and Joe at the table.

"Thank you, sir!" Millie said as Henry put a glass in front of her. "Gonna have to put you down for a little bit," she explained to Joe as she gently released the cat onto the floor.

Joe decided that it would be a good idea to retire to her cardboard box and sauntered over to it. Once there, she hopped inside and nestled into a comfortable position that allowed her to keep an eye on things.

"To a great night!" Henry toasted as he held his tumbler aloft and tapped it against hers.

"I'll certainly drink to that," she said with an amorous smile while bringing her glass to her lips.

The couple ardently dove headlong into the meal and savored ample quantities of food and drink. All the while, they talked and delighted in one another's company as Joe leisurely looked on. For Henry and Millie, this was more than just an ordinary "meeting" with Jake and Joe. It was a *celebration*.

With his appetite now fully satisfied, Henry's attention

turned to the matter of getting himself cleaned up and getting the evening moving along.

"Well, that was excellent!" he announced, noticing that it was now fully dark outside.

"It sure was."

"We better get ourselves cleaned up and get to that fabulous double-feature you lined up for us," he joked as he stood and carried the near empty box to the stove.

"You wanna go first, or do you just want to jump in the shower *together* to save time?" he asked with a straight face.

Millie nearly spit her drink. She wasn't offended, but she hadn't expected Henry to be so forward. For his part, Henry wasn't actually suggesting that they bathe together; he was simply attempting to bring his game up to her speed.

"Tell you what, sailor, let's shower *together*," she replied sassily without missing a beat, "it'll be fun and save time."

Henry's face flushed slightly. His joke had backfired. He was still a little nervous about pursuing a physical relationship with Millie, and this latest overture was a leap ahead that he wasn't sure if he was ready to make. Millie knew what he was up to and was simply toying with him. Before he passed out, she let him off the hook.

"You jump in your shower, and I'll use the one in the spare bathroom and meet you back here," she explained while grabbing her bag and heading toward the stairs.

Now that he was able to breathe once more, Henry recovered his wits and realized that she had gotten him again. Over the years, he had always believed that he had the upper hand in their relationship, but suddenly he was starting to wonder if that was truly reality or just what she had wanted him to think. With his tail momentarily between his legs, he followed her lead and headed for his bathroom to rinse off and regroup.

Henry had been highly impressed earlier by Millie's speed and efficiency in packing her overnight bag and also when it came to quickly procuring videos. However, he was now learning that when it came to hygiene she apparently fit more within the guidelines of the popular stereotype associated with women. Long after he had showered, shaved, combed his hair, and dressed, he was still waiting for her to come downstairs and join him. As he sat in his chair watching some sort of documentary on television to pass the time, he sipped on a drink and contemplated what might be taking her so long. Occasionally, he glanced at his watch or the clock as the minutes seemed to crawl ever so slowly by. Finally, he could hear the wood of the steps creaking and correctly assumed it was Millie finally coming to join him.

"I thought maybe you went home," he called out to her.

"Oh, now you stop. Was it really as bad as all that? I wanted to look nice for you," she said as she breezed into the room.

Before she passed by him, Henry was preparing a clever and crushing reply but once he saw her, he was rendered totally speechless. Whatever time it had taken her to get ready for their "movie night," it was time very well spent, in his opinion. Millie looked refreshed and relaxed and wore a well-fitting pair of long-sleeved, button-down navy blue satin pajamas with matching slippers. Her hair was pulled back, and she had small diamond studs in her ears that sparkled like her light brown eyes. Her face was perfectly accented with just the right touches of makeup and her lips glistened in the light. Henry had long known that Millie was a true natural beauty. However, he thought to himself that he had never seen her look more beautiful, and he had never felt more attracted to her.

"Holy smokes! Those are some fine-looking pj's you've got there," he complimented her with obvious excitement.

"I figured I might as well get comfy. You like them?" she asked playfully. She turned and modeled for Henry, allowing him a complete look at both her attire as well as her curvy figure. It had been a long time since she had dressed to woo a man, and his reaction was fun for her.

"Man, I'll say! I'm sorry I overdressed. If I'd have known it was a pajama party I'd have showed up in my boxers," he said, humorously referencing his own attire, which consisted of a dress shirt and pants.

"Never know, the night's still young," she flirted as she stepped to the television where Henry had put the rented movies. *Indeed it is*, Henry thought to himself.

"Do you want a drink?" Henry asked as he stood from his chair with his empty glass. Typically, he stopped after two talks with Jake but on special occasions or at social gatherings he was at times inclined to carry the conversation with his friend further. On this night, he was both nervous and excited, and a lengthy speech from Jake might not have been enough to settle his increasingly frazzled nerves.

"I'd love one, thank you," Millie replied as Henry headed to the kitchen. While he was gone, she studied the backs of the movie boxes to determine which of the two films might be a better choice.

"Which one of these classics do you want to watch?" she called to him.

"Makes no difference to me; put in the comedy," he joked

referring to the fact that apparently neither was a comedy despite Millie's original sales pitch.

"Very funny!" Millie laughed in approval. "Ok, wise guy, we'll watch this one." She slid one of the tapes into the VCR and picked up the remote control before moving over to the couch. Henry walked back into the room with a water pitcher, two glasses, an ice bucket, and a nearly full bottle of whiskey.

"Somebody's having a party!"

"Yeah, we are! You want popcorn?" he asked as he put the items down on the coffee table in front of Millie.

"Ok, that sounds good, I'll make it," she said as she hopped up instinctively.

"Hey, you're not on the clock. I've got it," he protested as he put his hand on her arm gently and tried to stop her.

"I know, that doesn't mean I can't help out," she said as she gave him a peck on the lips and slipped by. "Give me three and a half minutes and I'll be back. How about you fix me up with Jake while I'm gone?"

"Right on, it's a deal."

Henry poured a pair of highballs and took one for himself before slumping into his chair. He listened as Millie hummed while popcorn kernels exploded in the microwave oven. The two different sounds combined to make an interesting and pleasant melody, and it amused him. Meanwhile, Joe was awakened by the commotion and climbed from her box to investigate.

"Hey, darling!" Millie called to the sleepy cat who was leisurely stretching her stiff muscles.

"Yes, dear?" Henry called back tentatively, not understanding that Millie wasn't talking to him. The nicknames sounded awkward and weird to both of them, but neither told the other for fear of causing hurt feelings.

"Not you, Henry, I was talking to Joe," Millie explained as the popping slowed, indicating that her wait was nearly complete.

"Ahh, I understand," Henry hollered back before muttering softly, "That makes a lot more sense."

"What?" Millie asked. She was standing next to his chair and had heard the first part of his reply but couldn't make out the other. Her immediate presence startled Henry, who thought that she was still in the kitchen.

"Hey there, I didn't realize you were back. Are we ready to start the movie?" he asked, attempting to change the subject.

"Don't try to change the subject; what did you just say? I couldn't hear it."

"Oh, it was nothing."

"No, it wasn't. It was something; please tell me what you said," she pressed. Seeing that he was caught and unwilling to lie about it, he laid his cards on the table.

"When I thought you'd called me darling, and I answered back 'yes dear', it felt weird. That's all. I was just saying that you calling Joe darling made more sense than you calling me that. That's all it was." Millie laughed.

"Oh, that? Yeah, I was thinking the same thing. After all of these years, it might take a while before we can talk all lovey-dovey to each other. It'll come natural someday," she cackled as she moved to the couch and took a seat.

"Really? Ok, good. I'm sorry, I just didn't want to kill the mood we've got going."

Millie smiled and took a handful of popcorn from the steaming bag. "Not a chance," she assured him.

"What did you think I'd said?"

"I was wondering if maybe you thought I looked fat in these

jammies and were saying I didn't need any popcorn," she confessed. Henry chuckled and shook his head.

"Hell no, darling, you look *perfect*." Henry's sincere compliment embarrassed her a little but the way he said it and the nickname he used was anything but awkward.

"Wouldn't you like to come over here and sit by me?" she asked, coyly patting the cushion to her right.

"I certainly would." Henry switched off the lamp next to his chair and then stood with his glass in hand. On the way to join Millie, he stopped and switched off a second light leaving only the glow of the television in the room.

"There. Now it's more like a theater," he said as he sat down next to her and put his left arm around her shoulders.

Millie picked up the remote control and hit the "play" button to start the movie. She eased forward to put the device on the table and picked up her drink and the bag of popcorn. When she leaned back, she moved her body much closer to his. Henry welcomed the contact and embraced her more firmly.

"So which one did you end up picking?" he asked.

"You don't care, do you?"

"Nope. I'm more worried about what time my parents are going to be home," he whispered.

Millie couldn't help but giggle. His joke was funny but had a morsel of validity. It felt almost like they were a couple of love-starved kids, and they were doing something forbidden. It was exhilarating, but it also brought with it a strange sense of uneasiness.

"Henry, can I tell you something?" she asked gently.

"Of course, you can tell me anything."

"You know my past and all, right?"

Henry nodded. He guessed that she was referring to her

illegitimate son and the reason she had left Georgia so many years before.

"That was a real long time ago, and I haven't been with a man since then."

Henry turned from watching the movie previews and looked at Millie. Her eyes were sad and almost scared as she gazed back at him.

"That's all right. Why are you telling me all of this?" he asked tenderly.

"It's just that, I know I want to be with you... I just promised God a long time ago that I wouldn't ever be like that again unless it was with my husband. Now, I have all of these feelings and I just... I just don't want to disappoint you is all."

Henry now fully understood what Millie was explaining and why she felt afraid. He recalled that she had told him about being left at the altar in her youth and then going on a "wild" spree, which resulted in the child she ultimately gave up for adoption. She was ashamed of her choices and the promiscuous period of her life and to this day was still paying for it. He now realized that she had taken a self-imposed vow of chastity at that time as a form of penance for her sins. Her angst stemmed from the fact that she feared Henry might not understand or might be unwilling to tolerate her commitment. She hadn't expected things with him to go so smoothly or quickly, and it left her feeling very unsteady.

"Hey, I completely understand," he whispered as he kissed her forehead. "I'm not a kid. There's nothing that can't wait."

"I'm just confused," she explained as a tear streamed down her cheek from her left eye. "I know what I want more than anything, but I just can't." Henry smiled and wiped her cheek.

"You're forgetting, I'm a traditional guy, and this isn't some one night stand in the red light district. I'm pretty sure it'll be ok. Somebody keeps telling me to relax and just let everything happen naturally. You might want to listen to your own advice."

Millie smiled at his kindness.

"You know what I want to do more than anything tonight?" he asked her. She shook her head.

"I want to sit on this couch, talk to Jake, watch a funny movie about a girl who got hit by a car or a guy who lost his leg, and hold my best girl. Sound good to you?"

Millie broke into a grin that went from ear to ear. As the popcorn bag rolled onto the floor, she put her arms around Henry and kissed him passionately while the opening scene of the movie played on the television.

Many people grow to love another over time as the result of small actions or kindnesses shown. For others, it is a lightning strike that comes out of the blue without warning. In Millie's case, it didn't matter how or when it happened, all she knew from that moment forward was that she loved Henry and wanted to spend the rest of her life with him.

CHAPTER 17

"The Zone"

JUST AFTER 7:00 a.m., Henry started to stir and immediately began to feel the stiffness that had settled into his muscles overnight. He was disoriented for a few seconds before he realized that Millie's head was resting peacefully on his chest. They had fallen asleep during the movie and spent the night together in an exhausted and uncomfortable contortion on the couch. He laid there for a while, enjoying the warmth of her body and listening to her deep breaths. It had been a very long time since he had woken up next to a woman, and he liked the feeling of security it brought him. Even though the sleeping arrangements were cramped and considerably less than ideal, he made no move to wake her. Rather, he noticed the small pool of saliva that had dripped onto his shirt from her mouth as she snored softly, and it amused him. Joe had nosed her way into a tiny spot beneath his ribs on a sliver of the cushion, and he gently stroked her as he laid there and relished the experience.

For decades, Henry had slept alone comfortably in his bed where he had all the room in the world to stretch out and relax. After Joe came along, he gained the companionship of a sleeping buddy and it made him happy to share his bed with someone again. However, on this morning he discovered that his happiest night in years had been spent sleeping on a crowded couch with someone drooling on him.

"Oh Lord, did we doze off down here?" Millie mumbled as she began to stir. Seeing that she was now awake, Henry gently kissed her forehead.

"Yep, I missed the end of the movie. Now, I'll never know if that girl walks down the aisle or has to be wheeled," he quipped. Millie chuckled as she began to sit up carefully and stretch her arms into the air.

"Well, I never even got past the accident, and I was out like a light."

"I at least got that far. You missed it, funny as hell," he tossed in recalling that she had billed the film as a comedy.

"Hmm, yeah I bet."

Now that she had moved off of his chest, Henry was able to pivot his feet to the floor. However, his attempt to do so without disturbing Joe ended in failure.

"Sorry kid," he apologized as Joe was unceremoniously dumped onto the carpet. She was still in a stupor as she slid through spilled popcorn to safety underneath the coffee table.

"Say Joe, you slept down here too, huh?" Millie said addressing the little cat.

"Yeah, when I woke up, you guys were sawing them off pretty good." Henry pointed to a silver dollar-sized wet spot on his dress shirt as evidence.

"Oh goodness, is that from me? I'm sorry about that," she apologized as she attempted to straighten her twisted pajama shirt into a more comfortable position. Henry smiled.

"It's ok. I haven't had a good-looking woman drool on me in a long time."

He stood and stretched his back with a groan that was somewhere between a grizzly bear and Big Foot in tone and volume. The boisterous display caught Millie off guard, and she let out a yelp because it startled her.

"Good Lord! What on earth was that?" Millie exclaimed.

"Just busting off some rust," Henry crowed with pleasure as he walked with a mild limp out of the room.

"Heaven's sakes, it's too early for that nonsense. You're gonna stop my heart one of these days!"

"If I stop your heart, you can be damn sure it won't be from yelling," he jabbed back as he ambled stiffly upstairs toward his bathroom. The hidden meaning of his comment wasn't lost on her as she happily recalled the events of the past few days. *I believe you,* she thought.

After Millie had shaken off the cobwebs, she immediately headed to the kitchen and started a pot of coffee. While it brewed, she scooted upstairs to the spare bathroom to brush her teeth and assess the wear and tear a night with Henry on the couch had done to her. She was pleased to discover that she had come through it all relatively unscathed, and after washing her face, she brushed her hair and applied a few light touch-ups before changing into a clean set of work clothes. By the time she returned to the kitchen, she found Henry standing next to the counter enjoying a cup of coffee and looking equally fresh and ready to go.

"The coffee smells good," she said as she hit the bottom step.

"Here, let me pour you some," Henry offered as he pulled the pot from the warmer and proceeded to fill a cup he had waiting for her.

"Thanks!"

"You're welcome," he acknowledged.

"How's your back feeling?" she asked as she added some cream to her cup from a pitcher Henry had left for her on the island.

"I'll live. I took a couple of ibuprofen, and it's already starting to loosen up. It's not bad, though, just was a little stiff from all of the ups and downs at Anne's and then our slumber party."

"I'm sorry," she apologized. "I didn't expect to pass out like that. I guess a belly full of pizza, a couple of talks with Jake, and all of your kisses after a long day of cleaning did me in."

"What are you talking about? I had one helluva good time. I might have picked a better place for us to sleep," he said, stretching his back, "but I wouldn't trade last night for the world."

Millie knew that he meant every word, and she was touched by his sincerity. She leaned over and gave him a series of small kisses capped by one that was longer and filled with more emotion.

"What was all that for?" Henry asked softly after she had pulled away.

Millie looked lovingly into his eyes and paused for a second before answering. She knew what she wanted to say but decided to alter her words slightly for now. "Just for being you, sweetie. That's all, just for being you."

Henry and Millie took their time sipping on coffee and talking around the kitchen table. They were thoroughly enamored with their newly established intimacy and not in any particular hurry to change the venue and thereby the mood of the moment. Neither was particularly hungry anyway so they opted to forgo breakfast at The Eager Beaver for a thermos of coffee and a box of donuts they could bring with them to Anne's house. After all, Millie suggested, it was likely that Anne would not have eaten much either yet due to the state of affairs in her disheveled household. While this was certainly a distinct possibility, the truth of the matter was that they simply didn't want to be around other people right now. They were engrossed in discussing the past and the future, and it was a chance for them to explore a new facet of their relationship. Soon, it was time to get on the road if they were to arrive at Anne's on schedule. Once Millie had gathered her things, and Henry loaded a few tools he wanted to bring along in the back of the Explorer, they were off. It was an overcast morning that put a gloomy pall over the landscape, but their moods could not have possibly been brighter or more unaffected.

"What would you think about bringing some of your things out here?" Henry asked as they turned out of the driveway and sped down the road toward Lewis.

"Well, I don't know. Are you serious? Would you want me to do that?" she asked. She was surprised by his question but excited about the possibilities.

"Yeah, I mean why not? You could set up the spare bedroom as yours if you want to. Hell, nobody else is ever going to use it. I just thought that maybe now you'd want to stay out here with me sometimes."

Millie was stunned by his proposal. With all that had happened in such a short time, she was caught off guard but yet very receptive to the idea. She gave it a moment to roll it over in her mind and then made her decision.

"Ok, I think that'd be really nice, Henry. Are you sure? I mean, you want to do this so soon?" she questioned him, not wanting to do anything to damage the momentum that was building between them.

Henry couldn't help but laugh. He understood what she was

hinting at but, on the other hand, they weren't a couple just completing a first blind date.

"You know, it's not like we just met," he teased. "I kind of have an idea about who you are and you sure as heck know all about me. Come on now, you've been doing my laundry for twenty-five years; I think the secrets are out the window."

Millie couldn't help but chuckle. Henry had a way of cutting right to the heart of the matter that was hard to argue with.

"True," she conceded. "It would be nice to eat dinner together and not have to always worry about running home if it's getting late," she observed aloud.

"Exactly. I'm sick and tired of always spending my evenings and weekends alone. I'm not saying we ought to run out and get married tomorrow, but let's at least really try this thing on all the way and see if it fits."

There it was. Unwittingly Henry had crossed into a new territory that hadn't been traversed between them ever before. Both he and Millie immediately recognized what he had said, and they quietly reflected on what it meant. Silence overtook the cabin of the truck broken only by the sound of the tires on the pavement and the hum of the motor as they drove along. They suddenly were caught in a game, each waiting for the other to speak first. Sensing this, Henry finally moved to break up the logjam.

"Don't you agree that it makes sense? I'm not saying you ought to move in tonight and stay forever, but don't you at least want to stay with me sometimes and find out if we like living that way?" he asked wholeheartedly.

Millie could see how Henry had evolved from the cold and distant man who was once only an employer into the caring and sensitive man with her now. Her heart leaped, and she felt compelled to lessen the seriousness of the moment.

"You're only saying that because I said I wouldn't be with you unless you were my husband," she stated in the most dead-pan tone she could muster. "You're just trying to work me into your bed, that's all. I can see you coming a mile away, Henry Engel."

Henry digested her answer for a moment before he slowly began to chuckle and then ultimately erupted with laughter. "You're sassing me again," he declared jovially. "I hate to admit it, but I love when you do that."

"I know you do," Millie agreed. "I'm just trying to keep you on your toes."

"So what do you say? It's a plan then?"

"Oh yeah, it's a plan," she confirmed as they turned onto Main Street and drew closer to Anne's house.

Looking at the time, they decided to go past Millie's place and pick up her car later rather than before going to Anne's. After all, it now seemed likely that they would be going back to Oak Forest together that night. Instead, Henry drove to a small donut shop that was on the way, and they picked up a dozen assorted pastries to share with the author as they worked.

As they stepped onto Anne's porch, everything had a different texture than it had just one day before. It now felt to them as if they were a "couple" arriving at the home of their niece or daughter rather than two friends coming to the aid of another. It wasn't a strange or odd feeling, though, which was perhaps the most surprising thing of all. Rather, it felt as comfortable as slipping one's feet into a favorite pair of shoes. The fit was perfect.

From the very first that Anne saw them that day, she could tell that something had changed. There was an easiness between them that she had not witnessed before. She wondered what had passed between them in the night and noted that they had returned in a single vehicle rather than separately as before. The whole thing was almost as thrilling to her as the box of donuts that Henry carried. *Almost.* As Millie had suspected, Anne had neglected to eat and, in fact, had nearly forgotten to sleep. However, she looked well and was in especially high spirits as the trio sat around Molly Stewart's kitchen table munching on chocolate Long Johns and drinking coffee.

"I just knew this house was going to be spectacular!" Anne exclaimed through a mouthful of donut before catching her own lack of manners. "Sorry, I haven't eaten since yesterday."

"So you stayed up nearly all night?" Henry asked, attempting to clarify a previous statement she'd made about only getting an hour or two of sleep.

"Sure did. I get like this sometimes, almost obsessed. I've got this book that is almost writing itself right now, and I hate to sleep or do anything else until I get it all down on paper."

"Wow, that's something. This is the one that brought you here to talk to me, right?" he said as he took a drink of coffee.

"Actually no; it's another one that just sort of fell in my lap. That other one is good and all but it's on hold for now. This new one is solid gold, and I'm running with it as far as it takes me." Though she was tired and hungry, her words were inspired and passionate.

"How about that?" Millie commented with admiration. "Is it always like that when you write a book?"

Anne shook her head with a grin as she reached for another donut. "Not hardly. Mostly it's just filthy low-down work grinding out the pages. But sometimes, it's like magic almost. I know the story from start to end before I begin, but I don't know what the words will be until my fingers strike the keys. When it's like that, I lose hours and hours like they were minutes. It's an amazing feeling. I call it being in *the zone*."

"I guess it's a good thing then, right?" Millie asked, trying to understand.

"Oh yes, *it's the very best!* Each time it's happened before I've written a bestseller. My agent loves it! He always asks me why I don't always get that way, but he doesn't understand. I don't have any control over when it comes or goes, unfortunately."

"Ok, I kind of get what you're saying," Henry stated, starting to comprehend what she was feeling. "It's like a day on the golf course when you can't miss a shot or when you're suddenly hitting every fastball out of the park, but you can't explain why?"

"Exactly!" Anne exclaimed relating to his sports references. "It's surreal!"

"I had an experience like that one time golfing with Reagan."

His offhanded reference to one of our nation's most popular presidents and the former most powerful man in the free world stopped both women in their tracks.

"Excuse me?" Millie jumped in, catching the name Henry had just dropped without any hint of importance.

"Yeah, you know, Ronald Reagan? Except he wasn't the President of the United States then, he was the Governor of California," he added matter-of-factly without any special emphasis as if he was referring to the local butcher.

"You must be kidding!" Anne bellowed. "That's extraordinary!"

"Ronnie was pretty good, and we played a few times over the years before I came back here to Lewis but one day I just ate his lunch. I couldn't miss a shot. It was the damnedest thing. He just laughed and laughed and said he was going to tell Nancy he beat me. I never played like that before or after but that one day I could've beaten anybody on the tour, and I still have no idea how the hell I did it."

"*You were in the zone,*" Anne declared.

"Unbelievable," Millie muttered wondering what other former presidents Henry knew. "Do you ever still talk to him?" she asked with awe.

"Oh no, we weren't best pals or anything like that. I was involved in some of the same things that he was over the years, and I got to know him and Nancy a little bit. I saw that he and I were like-minded on a lot of issues, so I supported his campaigns, and we stayed in touch. It's been quite a while since he wrote me a letter."

"Oh, I see," Millie said as she shook her head and looked at Anne with exaggerated eyes. "Come to think of it, I haven't had a letter from Lincoln lately either."

Anne laughed at Millie's harassment of Henry as he made a move to stand and get to work. He didn't like braggarts and the intimation that he was dropping names offended him.

"Now, don't get all hurt, I'm just teasing you," Millie apologized. "I just never heard about any of this before. Makes me wonder what else I don't know."

"Lots and lots," Henry fired back with vigor as Millie giggled.

Indeed, Anne thought privately. *I am so completely in the zone! This just gets better and better.*

CHAPTER 18

Change

THE DAY THAT followed was filled with hard work, lively conversation, and a boatload of good stories. As a way to become better acquainted and pass the time while they toiled, Anne proposed that each of them take turns entertaining the others with tales from his or her past. Henry and Millie agreed that it was a good idea, and they got busy. Whenever it was Anne's turn, she talked about her wide travels throughout the world and her many adventures that had later led to some of her bestselling books. Millie didn't have a vast globe-trotting resume to recount, so on her turns she shared memories of her grandmother and her childhood in Georgia. Much of what she said was new to Henry, and he was delighted to learn more about her younger days in the Deep South. As for him, when it was Henry's opportunity to speak, he regaled the women with anecdotes about famous people he knew or exotic places that he had been to. Millie was amused by his antics and shook her head often, surprised by how much she didn't know about him though she had been in his household during much of the timeframe he spoke about. Anne, on the other hand, couldn't resist the temptation to ask plenty of questions and feed her author's curiosity. Along the way, she discreetly made detailed mental notes with plans to utilize them in a storyline that would enchant her readers.

Henry dutifully applied a coat of yellow paint to the dreary kitchen and by the afternoon had it looking fresh and crisp. Meanwhile, Anne scrubbed the hardwood floors on her hands and knees as Millie wiped down nearly every wall and surface in the house with disinfectant. By the time they were done, the home was greatly improved from the state that it was in just forty-eight hours before, and they were feeling good about their efforts.

"What do you say, gang? I think it's time for a chat with Jake!" Anne declared joyfully as she stood in the hallway next to the stairs and admired her handiwork.

"Is he here?" Henry asked from the kitchen where he was cleaning his paintbrushes.

"Sure is; I went out last night after you two left and picked him up," she confirmed.

"Hot dog!" Millie exclaimed as she came down the stairs. "That sounds pretty good to me right now." She was hot and tired and ready to sit down for a bit.

Anne stepped to the sink and filled a teakettle with water from the tap.

"I thought you were going to have a talk with Jake?" Henry asked.

"Oh, I am. I told you before that I thought he would enjoy a cup of tea, and I'm going to give it a try. Are you game?"

"Not me," Henry said, shaking his head while waving his right hand in her direction. "I like him just the way he's always been."

Anne shook her head in disapproval but didn't push the matter. Just then, Millie entered the room as Henry was taking a seat at the kitchen table. She heard the remarks that had just been exchanged and saw the blue flames from the gas stove licking at the base of the copper kettle.

"How about you, Millie? Are you braver than Mr. Engel? I've got some fine Earl Grey here that I think will mix ever so nicely with our friend."

"You've got Earl who?" Millie asked as Anne chuckled.

"It's Earl Grey; it's a type of black tea. It's blended with oil from an orange, and it has a delicious citrus flavor. Smells scrumptious too. It was named for British Prime Minister Charles Grey, 2nd Earl of Grey dating back to the 1830s."

Millie had been widely impressed by Anne and Henry's tales from their world travels, and now, the opportunity to try something different and exotic appealed to her.

"I think I'll try some of that Earl's tea," she said. "Count me in."

"Hooray!" Anne exclaimed. "That's the spirit; you won't regret it!"

Henry patiently sat and waited for Anne to retrieve Jake from the cabinet along with one glass and two cups. She placed a box of tea bags on the table next to the bottle as she took Henry's tumbler to the refrigerator for ice. When she returned, she put it in front of him but kept her hand on it for an exaggerated pause, which caused Henry to look up at her.

"Are you quite certain you wouldn't rather have a cup?" she asked playfully.

"Quite," he confirmed in his best English accent, which brought a smile to both Anne and Millie.

"So stubborn," Anne lamented softly.

"Boy, you don't know the half of it," Millie added as Henry poured a portion of whiskey into his glass and stepped to the sink for water to top it off.

"I don't need to change now. Jake and I have gotten along just swell all these years just the way things are."

As Anne waited for the water to come to a full boil, she put a tea bag into each cup. She then collected a small pitcher of milk from the refrigerator and a bowl of sugar from a cabinet. She told a brief story about how her father's mother had taught her to love tea the way that she preferred it, and she was about to show Millie the family's secret formula.

When the moment had arrived and the water was at a rolling boil, she filled each cup three-quarters full. She then explained that they must allow the tea to stand for a couple of minutes so that it could steep. Once she was confident that the flavor had been released from the bags, she removed them and added sugar along with a splash of milk to each cup.

"There we are, that's lovely! Now, we just need to wait a couple more minutes to let it cool. Then we can introduce Jake to his first cups of tea," she announced as she inspected the color of the liquid to ensure that she had mixed in just the right amount of milk.

Henry watched with amusement as he sipped on his nice cold drink. He wondered why anyone would go to such lengths when clearly the best way to enjoy a conversation with Jake had been established long ago. Millie, on the other hand, was filled with anticipation. The aroma from the tea was taunting her, and she was anxious to give it a try. Finally, Anne determined that the proper moment had arrived, and she carefully flavored each cup with a dose of the guest of honor. After a stir from their spoons, the ladies were ready to begin high tea.

"To your health," Anne toasted.

"To yours as well," Millie reciprocated before bringing the cup to her lips. She tested it slowly to make sure that it was cool enough to drink. Once she was certain that it wasn't too hot, she took a large sip and gently swirled it in her mouth before swallowing.

"Oh my word!" she declared with a grin as she looked toward Anne.

"You see? I told you it was going to be spectacular."

"You were sure right!" Millie agreed before taking another drink. "Henry, you have to try this."

"I'm over seventy years old; I don't *have* to do anything," he protested.

"Oh, come on now, just take a sip," she encouraged him and handed the cup his way.

Reluctantly, Henry cautiously brought her cup to his lips and took a small sample from it. Immediately, he made a wild grimace and a grunt akin to one made by a bull moose on the move.

"Really? As bad as all that?" Anne questioned after watching his reaction.

Henry broke into a smile and took another small sip. "Nah, I'm just fooling around. It's not terrible," he said as he handed the cup back to Millie.

"Well, I think it's fantastic!" Millie proclaimed. "I'll have to get some of that Earl's tea for Oak Forest. From now on, when I talk to Jake, I'm gonna do it like Anne's grandma did."

Henry shot her a skeptical look, but she nodded her head with conviction.

"After all, we've got a teakettle now. Might as well put it to use," she said as Anne grinned in support.

We've got a teakettle. Henry liked the way it sounded. He was reminded of all that had happened in just a few days' time, and he was very happy. As they sat and talked with Jake and each other, he relished the path he now found himself on. If it included tea, perhaps Jake would understand. As far as Henry was concerned, it now didn't seem like such a bad idea.

The meeting went on for a while and by the time Henry and Millie got back to her house, they both were exhausted from the long weekend. It was mutually determined that Millie should stay in town and get a good night's rest while Henry went back to the estate alone to do the same. He suggested that she should take time the next day to get things in order and gather some belongings to move to Oak Forest. Whenever she had accomplished what needed to be done, she could join him and then be able to stay for as long as she liked.

*

The following afternoon as Henry returned from the mailbox, his eyes were drawn to a large thick manila envelope that was amongst the day's delivery. The return address indicated that it was from a firm called Johnston Investigations. Henry concluded that it was the information he had sought from Carl Johnston pertaining to Millie's son and waited to reach his desk before cracking the seal. He closely studied the detailed report and the associated supporting documents that Carl had assembled. It was a tragic tale of a young man's life gone awry, and it saddened him to read it. He had expected it to be a negative report. However, the actual accounting of Edward's life was truly depressing. There was no doubt whatsoever in Henry's mind that this poor soul had been destined almost from birth for a life of pain. It was not a narrative that Henry intended to share with Millie, and he was reminded that she had asked him to help her discover this very thing. Fortunately, there was time to figure out how to divert her from the pursuit, but at that moment he was perplexed as to how he would be able to do it.

Henry took pen in hand and was writing out a check to cover Carl's fee as Millie came in through the kitchen.

"Hi Henry, it's just me," she called out to him.

"Hey there!" he shouted back as he nervously scrambled to push the file and envelope beneath some other papers on his desk. He quickly moved to head her off in the kitchen, both because he was eager to see her and because he did not want her to discover what he had been doing.

"I'm happy to see you!" he said as he approached and kissed her softly.

"Me too!" she replied excitedly. "I'm sorry I took so long. Are you mad that I'm later than I thought I'd be? I had some bills to pay and then I needed to clean up a little too. I hate to leave knowing it's a mess behind me. You know me and cleaning." Her words were rapid and excited. It was clear that she was enthusiastic about the move.

Henry understood just what she meant and assured her that he was in no way agitated by her late afternoon arrival. He was very happy to see her. He knew privately that any discord she was sensing was due to the extremely unpleasant report he had just read. Also, he was feeling guilty and uncomfortable about having pursued the matter without her knowledge. Now that it had come to such a negative conclusion, it was hard for him to recall why he had believed it was a reasonable idea in the first place.

Millie and Henry unloaded her car and carried several bags and boxes upstairs. She had brought necessary items to establish a foothold in the spare bedroom and bathroom and spent the remainder of the afternoon unpacking. As Millie gleefully worked, Joe frolicked about jumping from one bag or box to another and playing among her things. Henry retreated to the outdoors and spent his time doing some much-needed maintenance on the yard.

Later, Millie broke in the teakettle, and they enjoyed a fine meeting with Jake and Joe. Despite her newfound affinity for Anne's version of Jake, Henry opted to stick with tradition.

Following a good dinner consisting of fried chicken, mashed potatoes and gravy, green beans, and sweet corn, the couple spent the evening watching television in the family room. Joe slept fitfully next to Henry in his favorite chair as Millie stretched out on the couch. Though they had rarely spent such time together, they chatted about a wide variety of things and the time flowed by naturally. The most important topic that they discussed, however, was saved for last. They had each lived and slept alone for a majority of their lives and to suddenly entertain a different way of life left both of them slightly uncertain about how to proceed. After considering and debating all of the options available to them, they decided that for now it was best to move forward as they had. They agreed that it would be best to simply allow things to happen naturally when, and if, they did. After some fond goodnight kisses, each retired to separate bedrooms for a pleasant night's sleep. Joe was somewhat confused by the strange happenings but finally settled into her typical place at Henry's side. Though they were not all sleeping in the same bed, they were under the same roof, and it felt very warm and cozy.

Tuesday began with Henry's realization that he wanted to get a new filter for his lawnmower. The grass was growing more aggressively now in the early May sunshine, and he hadn't yet changed out the oil from last season. He drank his coffee and read his newspapers before excusing himself and heading off to Lewis. Millie and Joe promised to hold down the fort until he returned and set about getting involved with some light cleaning.

As Henry drove to Lewis, he was blissfully ignorant of the storm he would be returning to.

While Millie dusted the family room, Joe was especially frisky. She was intensely focused on a small paper ball that she was batting and then chasing around the floor. It was quite a show to behold, and Millie frequently laughed and encouraged her as she pursued her prey. Clearly, Millie thought, Joe was as excited as she was that they were now staying there together on a more permanent basis. After a particularly aggressive swat of her paw, the ball shot into Henry's office, and Joe raced after it. Millie could hear her scrambling around but never knew what happened next. Apparently, something startled the little predator, and she jumped up onto Henry's desk in panic. What followed next was a large crash as a stack of his papers flew across the floor.

Millie heard the commotion and rushed to see what had happened. She was startled to find Joe now on the back of Henry's chair with every hair on her body on end. In addition, the floor of the office was littered with debris.

"Oh my heavens!" she exclaimed. "What on earth has gotten into you?" she asked the wild-eyed little cat who then dove off the chair and past her out of the room. Millie surveyed the war zone and sighed as she bent down to begin the cleanup. She reached for the various papers and envelopes that were scattered about and organized them into stacks as she crept along. Suddenly, something caught her attention that stopped her cold.

A folder with the name *Edward James* printed on the front of it was protruding from a large open manila envelope. Millie turned it over, and the return address revealed that it was from some sort of private detective agency. In all her years, she had never pried into Henry's private affairs or papers, but now the curiosity was utterly overwhelming. She guessed that he had hired someone to find her son for her, and her heart stopped. She was both excited and terrified by the possible outcome of an investigation. *But that's impossible, I just told him a few days ago that I wanted to find Edward. How could this get done so fast?* She slowly pulled the folder completely out of the envelope and began to read the report.

"I'm home!" Henry announced as he opened the side door. When he stepped into the kitchen, he could instantly tell that something was terribly amiss. Millie was sitting at the table in the chair nearest the French doors with her face in her hands.

"Millie, what's wrong?" he asked with alarm as he walked toward her. Spread across the table were papers, a folder, and the large envelope. The sight of these items left him speechless, and he halted next to the island. For several minutes, neither of them said a word. Finally, Millie removed her hands from her face to reveal tear-stained cheeks and swollen eyes that had been concealed beneath them.

"What do have to say for yourself?" she demanded.

"I…" He attempted to answer her but couldn't find the words. He imagined all of the emotions that she was feeling—hurt, despair, guilt, and betrayal. Henry reached for something to say to comfort her, or to explain himself, but nothing came. Millie stood and stepped to the front door to get her purse as Henry watched.

"Where are you going?" he asked meekly as she passed by him on her way to the door. His words brought her to a halt next to the refrigerator.

"Home. I don't belong here," she said softly without turning toward him.

The day was hard and long for Henry. He wished time and again that he had done something, said something, to stop Millie from leaving that morning. He had not. In his mind, he knew how terribly wrong he had been, and there was no way to justify his actions or the concealment of them. It was the second time in his life that he had broken the heart of someone he loved, and it was devastating to him. He didn't know what to do or how he could ever make this right. It seemed that just when he had been freed from his burden by one woman, he had repeated history and wronged another. By early evening, he was at his wit's end. In his sorrow, he turned to the one person that he thought might be able to help him navigate the troubled waters.

"Hi George, it's Henry. You got a minute?"

"Hi Henry, what's the matter?" George answered from the other end of the telephone with alarm. It was highly unusual for Henry to call him at this time of day, and the tone of his voice concerned George.

"I stepped in it something fierce today. Millie got ahold of the report from Carl, and all hell has broken loose." From there, Henry and George spoke for nearly two hours. George was stunned to learn all that had transpired just since the week before and felt a little hurt that Henry had left him out of it. However, now was not the time for bruised egos and he parked his at the door. Henry needed a friend and George tried to decipher what had happened and how best to advise him to mitigate the damage.

"Henry, it sure sounds to me like Millie is in love with you. If that's the case, I think if you talk to her and explain how this all happened, she'll forgive you. Hell, tell her it was my idea and I did it on my own." George was offering to sacrifice his own integrity to protect his friend. Henry, of course, would have nothing of it.

"Damn it, George, you know that's a lie. I was in on this all the way. It was just such a dumb thing to do. Why didn't I tell her about it?" he wondered aloud.

"I think the obvious answer is because you love her too, Henry."

Henry knew that George was right. He was in love with Millie and to fully realize it now that he might have lost her was heartbreaking. However, unlike so many years ago when he wouldn't let George get a word in edgewise, he was all ears today. They reasoned that the best thing to do right now was to let her cool off and to give her some time and space to think. After all, it wasn't only Henry's actions that were upsetting to her. It was certainly an even more crushing blow to learn that the son she had given up for adoption was dead after having led a most painful and unproductive life. Knowing Millie's kind heart, Henry was sure that she was suffering for a decision made by a scared and desperate teenager long ago.

Henry agreed with George that perhaps the best thing to do now was to wait for Millie to call him or to come back to Oak Forest. Then, when emotions had calmed a bit, he could offer his sincere apology and express his deep remorse while hoping for a chance to make things up to her. He was counting on the fact that their history together was too long and too vast to be destroyed by one wrong move made with the best of intentions.

It was to have been a jubilant day at Oak Forest marking the start of a new life together for Henry and Millie. Instead, there was no celebration with Jake and Joe. In fact, there was not even a meeting or dinner. After Henry had completed his call with George, he slumped into his chair in the family room and sat alone with Joe in the dark hoping that the telephone would ring.

CHAPTER 19

True Emotions

O N WEDNESDAY, HENRY waited impatiently all day for a call from Millie that never came. The telephone rang on several occasions, but each time it was only George checking in to see if she had called yet and to ask how Henry was faring. After a second grueling night with little sleep, Henry was through with the "waiting game" and was ready to mobilize additional resources in an attempt to repair the damage. He decided that he was going to talk to Anne and seek a woman's advice. After all, she and Millie seemed to have really hit it off, and he guessed that as a world-class author she understood people as well as anyone. However, since she had just moved into town, her telephone service had not been connected yet so he deemed that he would drop in and see her in person. If she agreed that it was a reasonable move, he was prepared to drive over to Millie's home from there and speak with her.

At just past 9:00 a.m., Henry grabbed his keys and urgently made for the door. Before he could reach for the knob, it turned and the door swung open, smacking him in the face.

"Good Lord! Are you all right?" Millie exclaimed in surprise as she saw that she had just plowed into Henry.

"What are you doing here?" Henry asked, more shocked to see her than she was to see him as he grabbed for his forehead.

"I work here, remember?" she fired back. "Are you ok? That looks nasty." She was referring to a lump that was quickly forming above his left eye.

"Yeah, I'll live," he said as he backed into the kitchen to allow her to come in.

"What were you doing standing right by the door?" she asked as she dropped her purse on the island and swiftly rushed to the sink for a kitchen towel.

"I was heading to see Anne, and then I was going to come find you."

Millie took the towel to the ice dispenser and caught a half-dozen cubes before wrapping it tightly.

"Here, you better put this on that bump," she directed, noting that it was starting to swell into a fairly good-sized black and blue egg at that point. He did as he was told and took the ice pack to the wound with his right hand while taking a seat.

"What are you doing here?" Henry asked again timidly, hoping that she wasn't there to collect the things she had just brought to Oak Forest on Monday.

Millie sighed and took a deep breath before she spoke. She looked at the floor to gather her thoughts because she wanted to say exactly what was in her heart without fumbling the speech that she had meditated on for two days.

"Henry, I'm so sorry," she began.

"You're sorry? Millie, I'm so damn sorry I can't sleep at night," he interrupted.

She placed her right hand on top of his left. "Please, let me get this all out. First off, it was so wrong of me to run out on you like that without letting you explain. I was just so hurt and confused that I wasn't seeing straight. Joe knocked all of those papers all over the place, and when I was cleaning up, I found that envelope with Edward's name on it. I had no business going into your mail, but I was so excited and scared that I just felt like I had to look. I couldn't imagine how you'd got all that done in a day or two because I had just asked you to help me find him. When I started seeing the dates that detective had written down that he'd been working on the case, I realized that you had done this on your own before I said it was ok. I got really mad and confused but then I started to read about my son and my heart just broke in two. All those terrible things that he went through and the rotten way he turned out in the end. I was just sick to my stomach that I had ever given him away. It made me feel like it was my fault. It felt like my worst nightmare had come true, you know?"

Henry nodded and then let her continue without interrupting.

"Right before you came home, I saw something that just tore me up. I realized that you had found the wrong man."

"*What?*" Henry asked incredulously as Millie nodded.

"This boy wasn't my son, Henry."

"But that's impossible," he argued, wondering if she was just deluding herself. "How can you be so sure?"

"I saw on the report that *this* Edward James was born in Atlanta."

"Exactly! He was the only Edward James born in Atlanta then."

"Henry, my son was born in *Athens*."

"But you told me you were staying with your grandmother in Atlanta when your son was born."

"I was. I was living with her but the couple that adopted my

239

baby was from Athens. We worked it out that I stayed over there at the very end so they could be right handy when he was born."

Athens? Oh my God, she's right: we've got the wrong man. Henry was greatly relieved to learn of the mistake he had made.

"Well, that's wonderful news! That means your son might still be out there and might have a terrific life going for him," Henry declared.

"That's what I thought too when I first realized you had the wrong guy. Then, I thought how could any mother ever think such a terrible thing. Some poor woman's child is dead, and I'm happy about it? What kind of monster does that make me? So, I was just sitting there crying and asking God to forgive me when you walked in."

Henry could see the tenderness of her heart displayed yet again.

"But Millie, you weren't happy about that. You were just happy that your son might be all right. Anyone would feel that way. Why didn't you tell me all of this the other day before you walked out? And why did you stay away and not call me?" he asked.

"You'd made me mad. You went behind my back and did all of that and then when I brought it up on our date Thursday you lied to me by not telling me you had already found him. I was really hurt, Henry. I needed some time to sort it all out. I needed to understand what had happened and why you did it. I also needed to know why I was happy that boy wasn't mine."

Her words struck a nerve, and he again felt terrible about what he had done.

"Millie, I am so sorry for…"

"Hush now, it's all right sweetie," she assured him as she patted his hand. "I had a good long talk with Anne yesterday, and she made me realize that sometimes people we love do the wrong thing for all the right reasons. You weren't trying to hurt me, Henry; I know that. You were just trying to protect me. I bet you figured that you would check him out first and if he was no good you'd hide it from me to keep me from all of that extra guilt and pain. Once you got that report, no way you were going to show me that. Is that about what happened?"

I'm going to have to read some of Anne's books; she's really good at figuring things out, Henry thought.

"Incredible. That is precisely what happened. Say, did you say something about 'sometimes people you love do the wrong thing'?" Henry questioned with a sly grin.

Millie's face matched his. "Yes, I did."

"So does that mean that you love me?" he pressed as he moved the ice bag off of the bump that had receded considerably.

"It sure does. I love you, Henry Engel," she said as she stared into his eyes. "I guess I've known it for a long time, just never let myself feel it all the way before."

Henry's face beamed. What had started as one of the worst days in his life had suddenly become one of the best. He gazed intently back at her and shared what was in his heart.

"I love you too, Millie James. I was so sad these past two days when I thought maybe I'd lost you. I never want to know another day without you in it."

His sweet sentiment touched her deeply, and she kissed him with all of the love in her heart. At one point, her head brushed against his, and he let out a cry.

"Oh dear, I'm sorry about that," she said as she lightly ran a finger across his bump.

"It's ok. I deserve that and a lot worse."

"You sure do!" she teased.

"You know, I hate to bring it up in the middle of all this, but we've got something else to consider now."

"What's that?" Millie asked still focusing on the latest kiss and how nice it felt to be back in Henry's arms.

"Well, you've got a son out there. The guy I hired to find him told me about a second Edward James that was born in Athens. Millie, we've already got a lead on him. Do you want me to call Carl and track him down?"

Millie recoiled a little at the proposal. She had just lived firsthand through the horror of learning a tragic outcome and was hesitant to commit to another spin of the wheel.

"I don't know, Henry. I'm not sure I could live with it if it was like this one. It was bad enough to feel that way for a few minutes. I can't imagine hauling that around your whole life."

"I understand. It's *your* decision. I promise I won't do anything unless you specifically give me the thumbs up. Deal?" he asked.

"Deal," she said with a smile. "Can you promise me something else?"

"Yes ma'am, anything."

"Would you promise to always tell me the truth about things no matter whether or not I'll get hurt? I'd rather know that stuff than to wonder if I can trust you," she explained.

"Honey, I can absolutely guarantee you that," Henry promised emphatically. He had clearly had enough of dabbling in deception and partial truths, and he vowed that he would never compromise his integrity again.

Though they had been through a crisis, now that it was resolved and their feelings were completely out in the open, they felt closer to each other than ever before. Because of this, Henry and Millie decided to publicly cement their status as a couple by hosting a dinner party. Millie loved to cook so the only questions now were to determine when it should be held and who would be on the guest list. After considering several combinations of attendees, they opted to instead make this first-ever event more intimate and to include only two key guests in addition to themselves and Jake and Joe, of course.

George was thrilled to get Henry's phone call later that afternoon with the news and the details of how everything had transpired. He was even happier to receive a dinner invitation for the following weekend. He had heard an awful lot about Millie's cooking and the chance to finally meet her *and* get a fabulous home-cooked meal sounded perfect to him.

The next day, Millie and Henry stopped in to see how Anne was doing. They were happy to discover that a load of her furniture had arrived from New York, and several movers were busy carrying things into her house. It was good to see her getting more and more established. Likewise, she was very pleased to hear that her favorite couple had worked through their differences.

"I'm tickled that you both look so happy!" she declared after Millie gave her the nod that everything had worked out.

"So are we," Henry agreed. "I understand you had a hand in that."

"Who me? No, not at all," Anne said, deflecting the credit modestly.

"Now, you know better than that. You really helped me to see things clearly, and I appreciate it," Millie thanked her.

"Looks like you only had to knock him on the head once, eh?" Anne teased in reference to the knot on Henry's forehead that was now a faded dark purple.

"Once was enough," Henry joked as Millie giggled.

"We'll have to wait and see; you never know with these old German men," she quipped. "They can be slow learners."

"While we're here, we want to invite you out to a little dinner party we're throwing together a week from tomorrow," Henry said, referring to the following Saturday night.

"Yes? I think that would fabulous! I'm off to New York on some business the Monday after that, but I'm definitely available that night. Thank you so much! I'll certainly look forward to it. What can I bring?" she asked enthusiastically.

"Yourself and your appetite," Millie replied decisively without hesitation.

"Very good then! What time should I arrive?"

"How about six for a talk with Jake and we'll go from there?" Henry responded.

"Sounds perfectly smashing to me!" Anne stated.

Seeing that she had her hands full with managing the proper placement of the furniture throughout the house, Henry and Millie said their goodbyes and headed home. They had spent the better part of the day running errands and had also made a brief stop at the grocery store for items that Millie felt they might need over the weekend. As they drove back to the estate, Henry wondered aloud about something that he had just realized.

"Say, it just occurred to me, today is Friday, right?"

"All day long," Millie confirmed.

"Well, pretty much since you first came to work for me Friday has always been *deep cleaning* day, hasn't it?"

"Yes, and what exactly is your point?"

"My point is that I'm not sure I'm getting full value for my dollar here. I mean, you don't work evenings or weekends. How am I going to get compensated for the lost time today?" he joked with a flirtatious tone.

"You'd like some compensation, would you?" she hissed in a sexy voice.

"I sure as heck would. You think we can work something out?"

"Oh yeah, I think I have just the thing to get you *all satisfied*." Henry was starting to enjoy the game even more now that she was playing along. "That sounds great to me. What do you have in mind?"

"I'm doing the deep cleaning tomorrow, you big dummy," she said with the vocal inflections of a high school math teacher. Since she expected to be a more permanent fixture at the estate, many of her regular daily duties would naturally be blended into a larger, and more open-ended schedule. She felt much more like a *homemaker* now than she did a housekeeper.

Damn, she got me again, Henry thought to himself. However, he was indeed very satisfied on this Friday night. Millie was with him and they were going home together. The sassy attitude that she flashed from time to time was just extra icing on the cake.

Henry and Millie returned home to the estate and spent the evening lounging around and just catching their breath. The past week had been a true whirlwind of action and emotion. From their picnic date to their reconciliation just a day before, events had transpired rapidly and unexpectedly, and they both felt physically and emotionally spent. The scene played out in many ways the same as had their movie night the previous Saturday with both of them dozing off on the couch while Joe snuggled up between them. They were at home together now, and all was well at Oak Forest.

CHAPTER 20

An Engaging Party

LIKE A LOT of other things these days at Oak Forest, Henry's Saturday morning routine was suddenly different. Rather than head off to Lewis for banking and breakfast, as he typically had done on most Saturdays over the years, Henry chose instead to eat at home with Millie and Joe. He preferred to remain in the company of his family and get a head start on a long day of grass mowing and gardening. Before heading out to begin his chores, Henry paused next to the island to give Millie a kiss. Not a word was said between them, but the love they shared for one another was obvious. The house was now becoming the home it had always been meant to be.

Millie eagerly dove into her *deep cleaning* with passion and vigor. She had certainly taken immense pride in her work and done her very best for Henry, but now it seemed that somehow it was all just a little bit different. She was no longer working just for him but instead felt like she was cleaning *their* home. It was a distinction that gave her great pride and made her very happy.

The next week was pleasant and uneventful as the couple settled into a new normal way of living. They slept in their separate bedrooms and congregated each morning for coffee and to catch up on the news by scanning the daily papers. Then they went about their business in much the same way that they had been for years. In the evening, they shared dinner and conversation before moving to the family room to read or watch television. Millie stayed every night at Oak Forest that week, but she and Henry occasionally dropped by her house to check on things or stopped off to visit Anne. On a couple of days, the British author took a break from her writing and came out to Oak Forest to pay them a visit and have a chat with Jake and Joe. Henry and Millie's daily life developed a natural rhythm that was both unexpected and truly satisfying. After so many years of close contact, they were clearly highly compatible. The emotional intimacy that naturally followed romance had only enriched their relationship, not threatened it.

On the day of the dinner party, the estate was buzzing with activity. Henry was flying around making sure that the grounds were manicured and in perfect order. Though no one besides him would care or possibly even notice, he was truly proud of his home and wanted it to look its very best. To him, it didn't matter if the effort was for two guests or for the president of the United States. Inside, Millie was intensely focused on preparing the evening's meal. As Henry entered the kitchen, she stood at the island assembling an entree in a large rectangular glass dish.

"Hey, white lasagna!" Henry announced with approval. "Man, I love that!"

"I know you do, that's why I'm making it," she explained as she carefully laid big flat strips of noodles on top of a layer of cream, cheese, and chicken.

"You didn't have to go to all that trouble," he said as he moved behind her and slipped his hands around her waist. He peeked over her shoulder to see her handiwork and then gave her a gentle hug and a kiss on the side of her cheek.

"Now, don't start up with all of that, I've got a lot to do still," she said as he released her and moved toward the family room to inspect the state of things.

"Ok, so what else is on the menu?" he asked.

"I'm making homemade rolls and going to put together a salad. For dessert, you get fresh baked apple pie with vanilla ice cream on top."

"Wow, we should've invited Anne and George over for dinner a long time ago. How come we don't always eat like that around here?" he teased.

"Because we'd both be as big as this house if we did," she shot back with pinpoint accuracy. Henry nodded with a smile.

"You know, Millie, I've been thinking about something."

"That's good, Henry; they say men in later years need to keep using their brains to stay sharp," she quipped.

"Ha ha, very funny," he acknowledged as he took his usual seat at the island. "No, wise guy, I mean I was wondering, just wondering mind you, about someday when we get married."

Millie's head snapped in his direction, and she dropped her noodle.

"You just said *when* we get married, not *if?*" she asked with caution.

"I did. Let's be honest, we both know where this is going, don't we? I mean, we're not kids here and everything this week has been so perfect. It just makes sense, doesn't it?"

Millie shook her head with a growing smile as she went back to her work.

"Besides, how else do I ever get you into my bedroom?" he

said with a straight face. Millie caught the joke and lobbed a noodle directly off of his forehead.

"Hey!" he protested.

"You deserved that!" she said pretending to be angry at his jest.

"At least you didn't use a door this time," he said as he rubbed the almost gone bruise above his eye.

"Not yet, anyway. But keep it up and we'll see," she warned.

"All right. Seriously though, I've been thinking about it. You know this whole living together thing is ok for some people, but I'm an old-fashioned guy. A man and woman sharing a house ought to be married as far as I'm concerned."

"I agree," Millie added.

"So, I've been wondering how I would ask you and how we'd get married, that's all. I was just curious if you've thought about it too."

"Of course I have, Henry," she said as she poured a final layer of cream and cheese on top of her creation.

"And?" he asked.

"Like you just said, we're not kids anymore, Henry. I used to dream about big romantic proposals and diamond rings and elaborate weddings and all that. You know, like little girls do? Then I got left at the altar. Now, I know that none of that means anything. What matters is who you love and being together with that person for the rest of your life. I don't want anything fancy, Henry. It wouldn't be us. Honestly, I think it would take away from what really counts. Sure, I'd like some kind of a ring of course but I want something plain and special, not big and expensive. You know, like a band? And *when* we get married," she declared with emphasis noting his choice of words, "I don't want a big fancy wedding, either. Just a private little ceremony with just us. None of that other stuff is important to me. All I really want now is to be with you."

Henry listened intently to every word she said without saying anything. He had correctly guessed that she might feel this way because he felt he knew her so well but needed confirmation before taking any sort of action. Based on all that she had just said, he was now more certain than ever that she was the right girl for him and was destined to be his wife.

"What can I say, Millie? I feel exactly the same way."

While he spoke, she opened the oven and placed the dish she had been working on inside.

"Come here," he directed. "I want to show you something."

Without hesitation, she stepped around the island to him as she calculated her next move to get dinner ready.

"I need to keep moving here, so you're going have to..."

"What do you say, how about we turn this into an engagement party?" he asked as he dropped to one knee and held out a simple yellow gold band with his right hand. Millie's face flushed, and she could feel the room begin to spin for just a brief instant. Gathering her wits, she held up her hand as tears began to pool in her eyes. Henry slid the ring onto her finger and stood.

"Yes! Oh yes, Henry!" she cried as she threw her arms around him.

Joe had been resting in her favorite box during the conversation, but Millie's excitement had disrupted her slumber. She stood, stretched, and then peeked over the side to see what the uproar was about. Realizing that it was just Millie hugging Henry, which was becoming a common occurrence these days, she laid down and went back to sleep.

The remainder of the afternoon was a blur of frenzied

preparation and joyous celebration. Before they knew it, it was nearly 6:00 p.m. and their guests would be arriving at any moment.

"How's the table look? Is it ok? Are we missing anything?" Millie frantically called to Henry. He was standing at the front door on the lookout for arrivals and took a few steps back toward her to perform the requested inspection. Joe was at his feet peering outside, but she did not follow him. She preferred to continue to wistfully study the outdoors that she missed roaming.

Looking to his right through the doorway to the dining room, he was very pleased. As usual, Millie wanted everything to be perfect, and she had succeeded. He wondered why she was so concerned about the appearance of the table but then realized that it was no different than his obsession with the exterior of the estate. They were perfectionists and perfectly matched to each other.

"Very elegant. You know, I still can't believe you've never eaten in there before," he said, repeating an earlier revelation that the new lady of the house had never enjoyed a meal at the antique mahogany table.

"Nope, never have. But I sure am looking forward to it," she thought aloud as she checked on the progress of the dinner rolls. Henry pondered the reasons why that was so, as he stood for a moment and admired the beautiful scene. The table was set for four with fine china positioned atop a snow-white cloth. All of the silver had been polished to a high sheen, and it glistened in the light provided by the antique chandelier suspended above it. Along the wall to the left of the entrance, Jake and all of the necessary accessories were waiting on top of a matching buffet.

"Did you fill the ice bucket?" Millie asked.

"Yes ma'am, just a minute ago."

"Is Jake in there? How about a pitcher of water for you and George?" she questioned.

"Got them both," he replied while looking at all of the items she was referring to.

"And your tumblers? Did you check to make sure they didn't have any water spots on them?"

"Yeah honey, everything is in place," he assured her. "You know, you're already starting to nag just like a regular wife," he called to the kitchen.

"Just practicing, is all," she cackled as Henry broke into a grin and shook his head. Just then, he thought he heard a car door close and turned to the front entrance. A second car door shut and he wondered if perhaps he was imagining things.

"I think somebody is here," he said as he looked at his watch on the way to find out what was going on. It was exactly 6:00 p.m. on the nose. When he reached the storm door, he saw Anne's Jeep parked directly in front of the house with George's silver Mercedes right behind. It struck him as slightly odd that they would both arrive at the same time. However, he chalked it up to a happy coincidence and let the thought go. What was of more interest was that they were standing between the two vehicles having an animated conversation. They looked like two people who had met before rather than a pair of total strangers.

"It's Anne and George all right; they're here," he called to Millie before stepping out onto the porch to greet them.

"Hi guys!" he called to his friends.

"Hello, Henry!" Anne replied blissfully.

"Hey there, Henry!" George chimed in as the pair walked up the sidewalk to meet him.

"Do you two know one another?" Henry asked with a curious look on his face.

"Us? No, of course not, just happened to pull in at the same time is all," Anne stated with a somewhat peculiar tone. "I guessed that he must be your friend George that you talk so much about."

"I just swung in right behind her and when she got out, I realized that it was Anne Francis Wagner, your author friend. I recognized her from her book covers," George explained. "How come you didn't tell me you'd invited her? I'd have brought some of my daughters' books for her to sign."

"Oh, you're very sweet, George. Not to worry, I'm sure we'll be seeing each other again, and I'll be happy to sign anything your daughters would like me to."

"Splendid! Thank you very much, Anne," George gratefully replied to her gesture of kindness.

Realizing that he was making something out of nothing, Henry pressed the issue no further and explained that he had purposely not told either of them about the guest list as a fun surprise. Though they didn't seem surprised, nonetheless all agreed that it was fun.

"Well come on in," Henry directed as he stepped aside and pulled open the storm door.

They moved by him and stepped into the house. As George passed, Henry slapped his pal on the back and whispered, "Man, do I have some really big news for you!"

"Oh yeah?" George asked. "What gives?"

Rather than reply Henry pointed for George to head for the kitchen where the women were saying "hello" and complimenting each other on their attire.

"Millie, this is George," Henry said as he introduced his best friend to his new fiancée. Millie's face broke into a broad smile as she held her hand out to greet him.

"It's just wonderful to finally meet you in person, George," Millie exclaimed.

"Boy, I couldn't agree more!" the older man declared. "I have heard such amazing things about you, and I can't begin to tell you how happy I am that you and Henry have gotten together."

"Thank you! That's very sweet of you to say."

"Wait a minute!" Anne shouted. "What is that on your finger?"

"Huh?" Millie teased holding up her right hand.

"Oh, no you don't, let's see the other!" Anne cried as she grabbed Millie's left hand with her own and thrust it into the air.

"What?" George shouted as he swung around to Henry. "Is that the big news?"

Henry smiled and nodded as George embraced him.

"My God, you old sly fox! You sure played things cool with me. I told you to take her out for dinner, not marry her," George proclaimed, completely overjoyed by his friend's good fortune.

"Excuse me?" Millie interrupted him, making everyone laugh.

"No, no, I didn't mean that the way it sounded," he apologized and then tried to explain. "I was giving him some trouble a few weeks back that he ought to ask you out. He's such a turtle that I never expected things to move like lightning. Turns out he fooled me, and he's actually a rabbit. Believe me, I couldn't be happier for the both of you."

"After we get married, I'll have to let you know about the turtle or rabbit thing," Millie quipped to everyone's delight which brought on another round of laughter.

"Well then, I'd say we've really got something special to celebrate tonight!" Anne said gleefully.

Henry was in complete agreement. "How about I get Jake and Joe and let's get this party started?"

Everyone agreed that it was a lovely spring evening, and they gathered on the front porch for their celebration. Henry moved a pair of chairs outside for Anne and George to complement the bench he shared with Millie. Several rounds of *conversation* with Jake took place as Joe looked on from the other side of the storm door.

"So, how goes your new book?" Henry asked Anne. "Are you still in *the zone*?"

"Good heavens, yes! I'm writing day and night like a woman possessed! I hate to sleep and sometimes even forget to eat."

"That sounds thrilling," George offered.

"Indeed it is. I hate to admit it, but it was hard for me to put things down and get ready to come here tonight. It's all just going so well and keeps getting better that I don't want to lose it," Anne confessed.

"What kind of book are we talking about?" George inquired.

"Sorry, top secret. But I can tell you, it's unlike anything else I've ever written before, and I think it could be my best work ever," she proclaimed.

"My, that is exciting!" Millie praised as the men agreed.

"It's a shame you're off to New York on Monday. I guess that will interrupt things for a bit," Henry lamented.

"Oh, that's right," George chimed in.

"Huh?" Henry said while shooting a curious look at George. "How did you know about that?"

"Umm... well, Anne just mentioned it while we were chatting out front when I first got here," George explained unconvincingly while looking weakly at Anne.

"I say, Joe sure is plumping up nicely," Anne interjected

out of nowhere referring to the little face looking back at her through the glass door.

"Yep, that's right," Millie jumped in immediately. "Just gonna be four or five more weeks and we'll have kittens!"

"Fantastic!" George declared. "I'm pretty excited about having a new friend at home. My grandkids are going to love it too."

Henry wasn't sure what had just happened, but he knew that something was going on. However, before he could carry the thought further, his mind became distracted by talk of Joe's motherhood and the new arrival of kittens.

Following their cocktail party, Millie served dinner, and all went off without a hitch. Everyone loved the meal and raved about Millie's white lasagna. Not to be left out of the fun, Joe was spoiled with an evening saucer of milk in the dining room and found it to be very satisfying. Long after the last morsel had been eaten, they sat and sipped coffee as Henry and George slipped back in time and entertained everyone with stories from their youth. Anne and Millie were captivated as the men spoke of similar evenings at the Schuetz's table with George's father and grandfather. They pulled their matching silver dollars from their pockets and remembered the night they had received them as gifts from Joe Schuetz. Henry then went on to explain how his coin and George's grandpa had combined to determine how he'd selected the name for a certain stray Siamese cat that was now part of the family. One story led to the next, and the festivities went deep into the night. In particular, Anne seemed to be having a superb time as she listened intently and probed for more and more details of Henry's past. It was a perfect dinner party highlighted by terrific company and engaging conversation.

Finally, realizing how late it had gotten, the guests gave their thanks and said their farewells. Henry and Millie attempted unsuccessfully to convince George to spend the night rather than drive all the way home to St. Louis. He assured them that since Claire's passing, he had become a bit of an insomniac. He liked to listen to talk radio late at night and was actually looking forward to the lengthy trip back. As Henry closed the door, Millie walked toward the kitchen to put a few things away.

"I sure feel sorry for George, having lost his wife, and now he's gotta go back to an empty house," she commented.

"Yeah, I know what you mean." They each had lived alone for a great portion of their lives and knew all of the aspects to it. One of the downsides was returning alone at night to an empty home and an empty bed knowing that no one would be there in the morning. It was a feeling of solitude unlike any other and very hard to grow accustomed to. For George, it was still a very new and unpleasant reality.

"But he seems like he's handling it as well as anyone could. That's just the way George is," Henry said as he sat down at the island. "He always lands on his feet. You know, while we're talking about him, I got the weirdest feeling all night that Anne and George have met somewhere before. I just can't put my finger on it, and they both denied it, but…"

"Nope, I didn't get that at all," she interrupted abruptly and then quickly changed the subject. "You know, that man lands on his feet because of you."

"Huh, what do you mean?" he asked as he watched her wipe the counter with a yellow and white dishcloth.

"Well, if you hadn't saved his life, he wouldn't even be here, and I think what you did gives him courage."

"Oh, that. Yeah, that was a long, long time ago. He's saved me more than once since then."

"He's a good man, isn't he?" she asked.

Henry smiled and nodded. He knew that George was the best kind of man and his very best friend, this side of Millie.

"He said something earlier when he helped me carry in the dishes from the other room that got me to thinking."

"Oh yeah, what's that?" Henry asked.

"He apologized for getting you involved in looking for my son and said he was sorry about all the trouble he'd made."

Typical George, Henry thought. *Always trying to help me out.*

"I told him that I understood but then he said something else that got me to thinking," she said as she stopped cleaning and turned to Henry. "He said that if he could, he would do anything to have just one more second with Claire. That part of his heart was missing, and he would give anything to find it."

Henry listened intently to try and follow where this was leading.

"He asked if maybe my heart was missing a piece too and if I could, would I still want to find my son and get to know him before it was too late."

Same old George, working his magic. Henry knew that George was only thinking about Millie's sense of guilt and loss and he remained silent to allow her to continue,

"I've been thinking, Henry; he's right. I won't ever feel totally at peace until I find my son. Let's find Edward."

CHAPTER 21

Building on a Strong Foundation

THE WEEK THAT followed was filled with notable events that were impactful for the residents of Oak Forest. First thing on Monday, Henry traveled to Lewis to do the banking that he had neglected over the weekend. In addition to his usual dealings, he spent nearly an hour in a closed-door meeting with the bank's president, Tom Donaldson. Both men emerged looking pleased with the meeting, and Henry walked out of the bank with particular vigor in his steps.

Later that same day, Anne left for New York to attend to her affairs there. She was uncertain exactly how long she would be gone but thought that it might be at least ten days or more before she would return. Henry was unclear as to why she did not have a better idea of when she would be back but gladly assured her that they would hold down the fort until whenever that was. Unbeknownst to him, in addition to gathering more of her belongings and meeting with her publisher, she had a private agenda to pursue. Regardless of the duration of her absence,

Henry and Millie offered to check on her house periodically and collect her daily mail.

Also on Monday, Henry called Carl Johnston and authorized him to follow up on the lead for the Edward James that was born in *Athens*, Georgia. Henry wanted to know anything and everything about this man, including his current whereabouts. Carl was very understanding of Henry's situation and apologetic about his role in the mishap. He agreed to devote his full attention to the location of this person and promised to report back to Henry as soon as possible.

On Tuesday, Joe made a visit to Dr. Miller's office to get a checkup and to see how her pregnancy was progressing. The veterinarian was extremely pleased with her appearance and weight gain and pledged that Joe was "right on schedule" to deliver her babies. Also, she could see no reason why the expectant mother would have trouble delivering her litter naturally.

"Any idea how many of the little scamps there are going to be?" Henry asked.

"Well, I felt around and I'm thinking you're looking at five. I might have missed one, though," Dr. Miller replied. "If you like, we can do an x-ray and see for sure."

"Isn't the radiation bad for those little ones?" Millie asked with concern.

"It shouldn't harm them to take just one if you are curious," she replied.

Shouldn't harm them?

"No thanks, we can wait to find out," Henry stated firmly. He had no intention of risking anyone's well-being over his own curiosity or impatience.

"All right then, Mom and Dad, I'd say you have a very healthy little momma here," the doctor declared as she gently petted Joe's neck and then handed her over to Millie.

"Are we still thinking sometime mid-June?" Henry inquired.

"Let's see," she said, looking at a calendar hanging on the wall of the examination room. "Today is May 12th, so based on her size and the way the kittens feel, I'm thinking we're looking at more like that first week in June."

The day of the kittens' arrival was nearing, and their excitement about becoming grandparents was growing. As they all drove back to Oak Forest, Henry and Millie speculated about what Joe's offspring might look like and how many there might actually be. It was a fun diversion, and they felt like doting parents who were proudly envisioning their daughter's future children. The sense of family that he was feeling reminded Henry of another matter that needed attention.

"One of these days, we need to figure out how and when we're going to get married."

"Any way you want to do it is ok by me," Millie offered.

"Well, I know you go to church and all, but that isn't really my thing. Were you expecting we'd get married at Calvary?" he asked, referring to the Lutheran church in Lewis, which had long been her parish of choice.

"I don't know, Henry. I mean it would be nice and all but I don't want you to be uncomfortable. Isn't that where you and Mary had your wedding?"

"It is."

"What would you say about getting married at Oak Forest?"

"I don't know," he wondered. "Would that be ok with you?"

"Of course! I think it would be just perfect. Most all of our best times have been there, and it's so pretty this time of year."

Henry considered her suggestion while weighing all of the

other possible choices to serve as a venue for their wedding. The only thing that exceeded his devotion to the beloved estate was his love for his family. He concluded that there was no place on earth better suited for the auspicious occasion.

"It's settled then. We'll get married at Oak Forest. When should we do it?"

"I'd kind of like Anne and George to be there, wouldn't you?" Millie asked.

"Yes, for sure. I think that would be really nice."

"Then we better wait until she gets back and talk to her and George before we decide when to do it. When we find out what works for them, we can set a date. Does that sound ok to you?"

"It sure does, honey." Henry was in complete agreement with her on the matter. It was worth it to delay the event in order to ensure that it would be a perfect ceremony.

On Wednesday, Henry spent the entire morning and most of the afternoon in his office. Millie was unsure about what he was up to, but she didn't disturb him. She had business of her own to deal with, and spying on him was not of interest to her. While he worked, she plotted and planned how to rearrange drawers, closets, and cabinets in the home to accommodate her things when they combined households. Henry made and received multiple phone calls and on two occasions closed the doors to the office for privacy. Though he intended to allow Millie the power to veto the plan he was constructing, he was not yet ready to unveil it to her. Just before 2:00 p.m. the whir of a motor and a rap on the front door announced the arrival of Lucy Dawson with the day's mail.

Millie was standing in front of the hall closet and called to Henry that she would receive the delivery. Once all was in hand

and Lucy was back on her way, she stepped into the office with a pile of correspondence and handed it to Henry.

"You're sure a busy bee in here. What are you up to, sweetie?" she asked with mild curiosity as she glanced at his desk. It was covered by a myriad of papers and files, and she couldn't make much sense of it.

"I'm cooking something up, but I'm not ready just yet to talk about it. Don't worry, you're going to hear all about it real soon. I've just about got the outline worked out."

"Is it something big or something little?" she asked, becoming considerably more interested.

"Big. Now scoot," he directed with a devious grin as he patted her behind and sent her out of the room.

With the knowledge that something "big" was in the works, Millie's curiosity now went into overdrive. She attempted to move around in the family room from time to time to eavesdrop. Unfortunately, Henry was through with telephone calls, and all she could hear was the occasional movement of papers or tear of an envelope being opened. She imagined that perhaps he was planning a surprise trip for them or had some new idea for the estate. She wondered if maybe he was thinking about adding on to the house but then quickly hoped that wasn't the case because she already had more than enough to clean. Soon, she abandoned her speculation and became occupied with thoughts of what to prepare for their dinner.

Henry emerged from the office just before 5:00 p.m. ready to conduct a very important meeting. He asked Millie if she'd like to sit on the porch, and she accepted. In moments, the pair were having a chat with Jake as Joe peered at them from the dining room window. Millie was expecting to hear all about Henry's day and what this secret plan was. However, what she heard was more shocking than anything she had expected him to say.

"I'm thinking about calling Bill," Henry opened the conversation.

"What? Your brother? Really?" Millie couldn't believe her ears. "That's wonderful, Henry, but why? I don't mean it in a bad way; I imagine he'd love to hear from you after sending all those letters. I just mean, why all of a sudden now?"

"That's just it. I got another letter today."

Millie was having a difficult time discerning how he was feeling. His face was calm and pleasant, and his demeanor was peaceful and almost emotionless.

"Well, come on now, what did it say?"

"It was a lot shorter than last time." Henry was referring to the most recent letter received prior to this one. In it, Bill had revealed his attempt to woo Mary from Henry's side. It had gone on to inform Henry about Bill's wife and his sons as well. "It just said he was really sorry that I had never answered any of his letters, and that he would never lose hope that I still might someday."

"That sounds kinda sad to me," Millie said as she took a sip from her drink and looked out at the horizon.

"You know something, for the first time ever, it kind of felt sad to me too to think about how he's tried for so long to make amends. I don't know, maybe it's time. I'll have to sleep on it some more."

Millie didn't speak and just let Henry's words float off into the air. She wanted him to absorb all of their meaning and to truly feel his emotions. She imagined that perhaps now that she was searching for her son, he might see the value in reconnecting with his brother.

"Anyway, that's not what I wanted to discuss with you," he said, breaking the silence.

"No? You've got something bigger than that to talk about? Well then, are you planning to give me a million dollars for a wedding present?" she asked with a laugh.

"Funny you'd say that. No, actually I'm thinking about *giving away a million dollars* and then maybe a few million more after that," he announced proudly.

"You what?" asked Millie stunned by the news.

"Don't worry, if you don't like my idea, we won't do it, but I'd like you to hear me out first before casting your vote."

Millie was caught off guard by the mention of such a sum of money. However, she was absolutely floored that he was actually asking her opinion about what he intended to do with it. It was not something she had given any thought to before this.

"All right Henry, but you certainly don't need my say so about what you do with *your* money."

"Honey, it's our money now and as my wife you absolutely get a vote," Henry explained. His words made her extremely proud. She was to become Millie Engel and apparently Henry was determined that meant she had an equal hand in all of their affairs.

"Ok then, what's this big idea you've got?" she asked, eager to hear every detail.

"It started the other week when we were sitting around at Anne's house. There we were, relaxing at Molly Stewart's table and all of a sudden it hit me. That dear woman had worked and sacrificed for a lifetime to better those around her. She touched generations of kids from Lewis. I mean every one of us practically had passed through her classroom. When someone didn't have a notebook or a pencil, Molly gave them one, paid for from her own pocket. She tutored kids at home for free and donated all of her time to any cause she could find. When she died, she didn't have two pennies to rub together. All she owned was a little bit of furniture and that house. What family she did have, came through and cashed out without ever having known her or how important her life had been to the people around here."

"That's sad," Millie thought aloud.

"Anyway, her generosity got me to thinking. I've been very blessed in my life, and I've always tried to help out when asked. But after sitting in Molly's house, I realize that isn't nearly enough. I've got millions of dollars, Millie, far more than we could ever spend in five lifetimes living the way we do. I don't want to die and leave a pile of money behind for someone else to carve up. and burn through on diamonds and trips. I'd like to see it really help people who need it while I'm still here to enjoy it." He paused to take a sip from his drink. Millie's chest swelled with pride at the sincere goodness of the man she was lucky enough to now call her own.

"I don't want a bunch of fanfare or congratulations, believe me. I've worked hard over the years to keep my name out of the headlines. I'll leave that stuff for guys like John Everett." She may not have known every charitable deed he did, but working for him for over two decades had afforded her hundreds of occasions to see firsthand how generous he was.

"So, I talked to Tom the other day at the bank and went over my accounts there. Today, I was talking with all of my brokers and other financial people to get a real handle on what we have. We've got *a lot* of money, my dear," he declared with a smile as he finished off his drink. Seeing the devilish look in his eyes, Millie started to feel slightly faint and guzzled the remainder of her drink as well to steady her nerves.

"Like how much is *a lot* of money?" she asked cautiously with a nervous smile.

Henry leaned over and whispered the approximate total into her ear.

"Holy Lord!" Millie shouted. "You have got to be kidding me, right?"

Henry shook his head; this was not one of his famous pranks.

"Five lifetimes? Henry, that'd pay for twenty!" she proclaimed in astonishment at the wealth he had accumulated.

Henry laughed. "I honestly had lost track. It's definitely more than I realized. How about we go inside and reload and I'll sketch out my plans for you?"

Millie followed Henry into the house and listened attentively as he went over his ideas. While he spoke, he refreshed their drinks and then joined her at the kitchen table. The proposed plan was to create a charitable foundation funded initially by a large pool of money they would donate from their personal fortune. Later, fundraising could be organized to perpetuate the endeavor.

To start, the work of the enterprise would be to assist children of families in dire need and to support causes that would benefit the people of Lewis and the surrounding area. To that end, Henry's first priority was to build the Molly Stewart House. He wanted it to be a place where impoverished and disadvantaged kids could turn for help.

Millie was overwhelmed with emotion. Tears began to well in her eyes as he finished his impromptu presentation. Henry misunderstood her display and moved to dispel her fears.

"Don't worry, sweetheart. I intend to keep enough to make sure that you are always well taken care of for the rest of your life long after I'm gone." Henry was acutely aware of their age difference and thought that her reaction was based on the fear that her money might run out without him around. In fact, nothing was further from the truth.

"Henry, I'm not crying because I'm worried about me. I'm crying because I'm proud. I'm proud of the man you are, and I'm proud that I'm going to be your wife. It's the most wonderful thing I've ever heard, and I am all for it."

Henry was thrilled to have her support. He had hoped that she would be understanding and in agreement with him but was prepared to scrap the idea if she dissented. With the issue now settled, there was another pressing matter to decide.

"Good! Now, we need to figure out what to call this thing. I don't want our name anywhere near it," he declared emphatically with genuine modesty.

They sat back and consulted Jake for a time as Joe sat on the staircase and watched. She had little to say but was there to offer her moral support. Suddenly, Millie lurched forward in her chair as if she had been struck by lightning.

"I've got it!" she cried.

"Yeah? Well, what is it?" Henry asked with excitement.

"*It's perfect!*"

"Come on, give! What is it?" he demanded.

"The Oak Forest Foundation!" she proclaimed.

Henry stood with his drink in his hand. *By God, she's right.* It was absolutely perfect. He raised his tumbler as Millie stood to join him and did the same. Henry proposed a toast and they touched their glasses. In that instant, the fortunes and futures of children and families they had yet to meet were altered for the better as The Oak Forest Foundation was born.

CHAPTER 22

A New World

A NNE CALLED ON Friday of the following week to let Henry and Millie know that she had returned home safely. She thanked them for keeping tabs on the house and for collecting her mail. Her Jeep Cherokee was loaded to the breaking point, and she was thoroughly exhausted, but she assured them that the trip had been well worth the effort. Not only had she accomplished everything she had set out to, but she had also even found the time to write a half-dozen more chapters for her latest book. Anne was still unwilling to reveal what it was about, but she said that she was steadily marching toward the conclusion and reiterated that she believed it was the best work of her life. At least, Anne said, she hoped that Henry and Millie would think so.

The world-famous author's homecoming was made extra special by the invitation to serve as Millie's maid of honor. She gleefully accepted and after a round of phone calls between Henry, Anne, and George, the newly appointed best man, it was determined that the couple would be married at 2:00 p.m. on Saturday, May 30. A reverend friend of George's had agreed to officiate, and all that remained now was to decide where on the grounds to hold the ceremony.

Henry and Millie spent Saturday walking around Oak Forest and surveying their options. Henry was fond of the island in front of the house due to the old and majestic trees that created a cathedral effect above it. He also astutely pointed out that it was conveniently located near the bathroom and the bar, should either need arise. Millie objected on the basis that she hadn't waited her entire life to get married only to finally do so next to a driveway. Instead, she favored a place alongside the pond at the foot of the hill. It was grassy and sloped and overlooked the glassy water, which reflected the sky and the nearby trees in the afternoon sun. Like any smart groom, Henry capitulated and acquiesced to her wishes. They would be married next to the pond.

Amidst all of their excitement, the couple remembered that they had forgotten a critical detail crucial to any wedding. As of yet, the bride and groom's attire had not been determined. Millie assured Henry that a yellow dress that she already had would be fine, but Henry put his foot down. He intended to wear one of his many tailored business suits but she would be wearing a brand new dress, and it would be white. He firmly insisted that she deserved at least that much for her first and only marriage. Despite Millie's protests to the contrary and her objections that there wouldn't be time to find something so quickly, Henry persisted. He placed an emergency phone call to Anne for support, and she fervently agreed that a used yellow dress was not good enough for the occasion. Anne assured Henry that writing was the only thing on earth superior to what she called her *retail proficiency*. She asked to speak to Millie and with a bit of coaxing, was able to get the bride to agree to go to St. Louis on Monday for a shopping spree. The plan called for Millie to come to Anne's house, and from there Anne would drive them to the Gateway City for a day of fun.

On Monday, once Millie had departed, Henry darted into his office and began to work the phone. He had much research to do and many arrangements to make before she returned that afternoon. The previous night, George had called to discuss the wedding plans and was somewhat surprised to find that there weren't really any plans to discuss. He lobbied Henry to consider that this was perhaps the most important day left in their lives and to make it as special as possible. During the course of the conversation, Henry had seen the light, and he now was determined to surprise Millie with a wedding day that she would never forget. It would certainly take a herculean effort to make it happen with just five days to work with. However, Henry possessed nearly unlimited financial resources, an indomitable spirit, and a best man named George. Between them, the fellows were convinced that they could pull it off and do so in record time.

The only real wild-card was whether or not Anne could come through and help Millie find a well-fitting, spectacular wedding dress on such short notice. *Come to think of it, I've actually never even read a word she's written. What if she's no good at writing or shopping?* Henry thought, recalling Anne's assurances. If Millie failed to find a special dress, Henry's best efforts to make her feel like the princess he believed her to be might be in vain. Nonetheless, it was beyond his control at that moment and worrying about it was senseless. He resolved to trust in his British accomplice to achieve her mission and focused on the task at hand.

By day's end, Henry learned that his anxiety had been all for naught. The issue was never in question. Anne took Millie to the premier bridal shop in St. Louis and by the end of the afternoon the ladies had departed with a magnificent dress, already perfectly altered to suit Millie. Being a man with no experience whatsoever in shopping for wedding dresses, Henry could not possibly fathom the miracle that Anne had pulled off. He simply accepted Millie's word that she was thrilled with the gown and checked it off his list. Truth be known, it had nearly required an act of God. If not for the fact that the owner of the shop had recognized Anne and identified herself as "Anne Francis Wagner's biggest fan," it would likely have never come to pass. As it was, Millie had found a lovely, simple dress on the rack that landed just at her knees and almost fit her perfectly from the beginning. A few signed books and a large check sealed the deal. In any event, Millie loved the dress and reluctantly agreed with Anne that it looked fabulous on her. She told Anne that as much as it embarrassed her to admit it, the dress made her feel like a princess. Mission accomplished.

On Wednesday, Henry was walking through the kitchen just as the telephone rang. He stepped to the counter and picked up the handset to accept the call.

"Hello?"

"Hello, Mr. Engel?" came a man's voice from the other end. "Yes, this is Henry Engel."

"Hello sir, this is Carl Johnston. We spoke the other day about Ms. James' son."

"Yes, of course. Do you have something for us?" Henry asked anxiously.

"I sure do. Are you sitting down?" Carl asked as Millie descended the steps.

"No, not at the moment. Do you think I need to?" Henry replied with trepidation while making eye contact with her.

Millie's heart skipped a beat as she sensed that this call might be related to her son.

"I've got him, Mr. Engel. We've run a full bio and background check on him. This guy is alive and well and the polar opposite of the other Edward James we found. This man is a solid citizen with a good job and a family. Heck, he was even an Eagle Scout." Henry had been unconsciously holding his breath and let out a huge sigh of relief at the news. Millie had moved to the corner of the island just steps from him and was hanging on his every word and movement.

"What is it, Henry?" she pleaded.

"Carl found him. He's alive, and he says he's a good man."

"Thank you, Lord!" Millie lifted her voice to the ceiling above her.

"I just thought I would call and let you both know. Unfortunately, I'm traveling this afternoon on another case, but I'll be back in the office next Tuesday. I'm going to get all of this information compiled into a report like the last one when I return. I'll get it out to you as soon as I can."

"Thanks a million, Carl, we really appreciate your prompt help on this. I'll keep an eye out for the package and fire a check off to you right after I have your bill. We really appreciate it; goodbye now," he said as he hung up the phone.

"How about that?" Henry shouted as Millie leaped into his arms. It was an enormous load lifted off of her and the best gift she could have imagined. For her entire adult life, she had been burdened by the guilt that the baby she had given up for adoption had somehow been tragically destined for ruin by her decision. To learn that at least her son was alive and well and apparently prospering was a huge relief. There were certainly many difficult hurdles ahead on the road to some sort of reconciliation with him. However, on this day it was more than enough just to know that he was all right.

*

The morning of the wedding, Millie awoke early and lay for a while beneath the sheets gazing out of her bedroom windows. She could see daybreak casting light onto the leaves of the forest, and it was a serene and glorious sight. The forecast called for a perfect spring day, and it looked as though that was exactly what they were going to be blessed with. Her mind drifted through her life and all of the events that had transpired to bring her to this moment in time. She closed her eyes and prayed for a bit, thanking God for all that she had and all that she was receiving. She asked that He would bless their marriage with many years of health and happiness. As she rose, the pleasant thought struck her that she would never spend another night in that bed again. Tonight and forevermore, she would be sleeping with her husband.

The bride and groom met in the kitchen for coffee and relaxed in one another's company for a time. Henry browsed the newspaper as if it was just any other Saturday while Millie sat at the kitchen table affectionately cuddling with Joe. Abruptly, Henry said something that got Millie's attention.

"Oh, and by the way, I need for you to close all of the blinds on the front of the house."

"You what?" Millie asked without understanding why.

"Yes, close the blinds. You also need to promise me that no matter what happens, no matter how curious you get, you won't look out front until it's time for the ceremony," he said, adding another stipulation.

Millie was beginning to smell a rat. "I thought we decided to

276

keep this thing simple, Henry? What are you up to, you rascal?" she inquired impishly.

"*You'll see!*" he responded in his comically high-pitched voice with a devious grin. It was the same tactic he had used the day he had taken her to the spring for their first date.

"Uh-oh," Millie reacted with a laugh.

"I need you to promise me, Millie. No peeking."

"I can't promise that, Henry, you know me," she said with a giggle.

"No kidding, promise me. I really mean it. I need you to do this," he said again. This time, he looked more serious. Millie could see that it was important to him.

"Ok honey, I promise," she agreed reluctantly.

Anne arrived mid-morning to help Millie get ready. The women had made plans for a manicure, pedicure, and hair-styling session.

"Did you see Henry?" Millie asked as Anne entered the kitchen with both arms full.

"Yes, he's down by the pond," Anne answered innocently as she sat her bags on the island.

"What's he up to?" Millie pried, hoping to find out what was going on.

"Oh no, I'm sworn to secrecy!" Anne said as she snapped a single finger in front of her lips. "And you know I'm good at keeping secrets," she added slyly with a wink.

"So, you're in on it too?" Millie knew that it was no use and laughed as she abandoned the attempt to uncover his plan. Nevertheless, the sound of banging and movement outside was gnawing at her. It took all of her strength to keep her promise to Henry, but she kept her word. As much as she was dying to see what was going on, she was determined not to begin their marriage together by betraying his trust.

Around 1:00 p.m., Millie could hear George and Henry talking in the kitchen. She and Anne were flying between the spare bathroom and the bedroom busily getting ready, and she couldn't hear what they were saying. She noted, though, that the sounds outside had stopped.

"Do you fellas need a sandwich or something? I can fix some lunch," she called down from the railing on the second floor.

"No!" came a unified and resounding reply from the two men in the kitchen *and* the maid of honor from the bathroom. They weren't surprised that on her biggest day, just an hour before the wedding, she was concerned with everyone else. However, there was no way that they were going to let the bride interrupt her all-important preparations to make lunch.

"Well excuse me! I was just asking," she cackled as they all broke into laughter.

"Hey you!" Henry called upstairs.

"Yes sir," Millie replied.

"We'll be down at the pond, but I'll send for you and Anne when it's time," Henry informed her.

"All right sweetie, we'll be ready." She wondered what he meant but thought better of questioning him. He obviously had gone to a great deal of trouble to put together whatever was waiting for her. She decided that the best way to thank him was to simply enjoy it and not attempt to spoil the surprise with more questions.

Millie and Anne anxiously stood in the kitchen as the clock edged toward 2:00 p.m.

"Are you nervous?" Anne asked, trying to contain her own excitement.

"Nope," Millie replied with complete composure. "I've been ready for this day my entire life."

Anne was struck by Millie's calm countenance and extreme beauty. The snugly fitting knee-length dress that they had selected was satin with a lace overlay delicately accented with tiny rhinestones and pearls. The neckline of the gown scooped toward her bust, and she wore an intricate pearl necklace with a large teardrop rhinestone and matching earrings. Her hair was pulled up and held by a comb, also adorned with the aforementioned embellishments. Finally, she completed the ensemble with a simple pair of pearl white patent leather heels.

"You look simply gorgeous, Millie!" Anne exclaimed, taking her hands into her own. "I've never seen a more brilliant-looking bride in my entire life!"

Millie was touched by Anne's generous compliment. It was high praise coming from perhaps the most beautiful woman Millie had ever seen. The maid of honor had selected a similarly cut dark green dress for the occasion, and it almost made her eyes glow. Before she could tell Anne how lovely she thought she looked, a knock on the door interrupted them.

"Oh my! It's time!" Anne announced as she hurried Millie to the entrance.

Millie had imagined what she might find on the other side of the door. However, nothing in her wildest dreams could have prepared her for this. Just as Anne began to turn the knob, Millie stopped her suddenly.

"Hold it!" Millie shouted.

"What? What's wrong?" Anne cried with a look of concern. "You're not getting cold feet are you?" she asked with genuine anxiety.

"Huh?" Millie replied looking around in a daze before

comprehending what Anne was implying. "Oh, goodness sakes no!" she blurted out with a laugh. "I just want to say goodbye to Joe! Next time I see her, I'll be her real Momma!"

Anne exhaled a large sigh. She was glad to hear it was not something else that was wrong.

"I don't know, Millie, I haven't seen her all morning," Anne declared, frantically walking past her back toward the kitchen.

Just then, there was another knock on the door indicating that it was past time to leave.

"Oh, that's all right. I'll find her later. She's probably sleeping somewhere. We better get going. I don't want to make Henry wait; he might change his mind," Millie said jokingly as she opened the door. On the other side, the *new world* was waiting for her. She stepped through the doorway as Millie James but would soon return home as Millie Engel.

CHAPTER 23

The Biggest Day of All

MILLIE'S EYES WIDENED as a dashing young man in his late twenties held the storm door open for her. He was sharply dressed in a black tuxedo complete with white gloves, top hat, and tails.

"Ms. James?" he greeted her.

"Yes?" she replied in shock.

"Ma'am, Mr. Engel has directed me to escort you to your wedding. If you'll just come with me." He reached and took her hand and led her across the porch. Waiting for her at the end of the sidewalk was a spotless white carriage pulled by two magnificent white horses. She froze and stood for a moment as her eyes scanned the scene.

"Oh my God!" Millie cried with delight. She had never seen such a sight before. Along the route to the pond, two continuous hedges of white carnations had been erected. Above each of the flower pots, a single white balloon had been tethered with a satin ribbon. There were hundreds of them, and it created two white walls to outline the driveway. Also, the asphalt had been literally blurred out by a blizzard of white rose petals. It was the most spectacular thing Millie had ever seen.

"Oh my God!" Anne cried reiterating Millie's exact words as she pulled the front door closed behind her.

"It's unbelievable, Anne!"

"It most certainly is!" the author agreed as she stepped next to Millie. Just then, the horse nearest them whinnied, anxious to get to work.

"You can say that again, big fella!" Millie chuckled.

"Ladies, if you please, the gentlemen are waiting," said the young man as he led Millie by the hand to the open door of the carriage. Once they were both inside, he climbed aboard and signaled for the team to begin the journey.

In her entire life, Millie had never ridden in as much as a horse-drawn wagon. Sitting on luxurious leather seats in the open air as the hooves of the horses clippety-clopped along was truly a surreal experience. She was astounded as they slowly rolled past the seemingly endless display of flowers and balloons. For a moment, she became lost in the magic of it all and forgot that she was a bride on her way to be married. Instead, Millie felt like a princess on her way to a ball. She craned her head forward to see what was coming as the forest gave way to the edge of the pond and the meadow below. The driver slowed the horses and the carriage eased to a gentle halt at the bottom of the hill. The best man and a lovely young woman with two bouquets of flowers in her hands were waiting there to receive them.

"Thank you kind sir," Millie said as the driver helped her down from the carriage.

"You're very welcome ma'am," he responded as he reached for Anne's hand to assist her as well.

"Hey there, George!" Millie called to the best man.

"My Lord, Millie, you are a vision!" he proclaimed as he embraced her.

"You look awfully handsome yourself in that fine tuxedo! Thought you and Henry were going to wear your suits?"

"To *your* wedding? Not a chance my dear."

Millie smiled and winked at George as she straightened his boutonniere, which had been jostled by their hug.

"Here you are ma'am, these are for you," greeted the young woman as she handed Millie her wedding bouquet. It was a gorgeous assortment of miniature white roses accented with baby's breath.

"On my, isn't that lovely!" Millie accepted the bouquet and brought it to her nose to indulge in the fragrance. "They smell so wonderful too!"

The florist complimented Millie on her dress and wished her all the best on her special day before moving on to Anne. The author accepted a smaller bouquet of roses from the woman, which had been accented with daisies and greens. It complemented her dress and eyes perfectly.

"Ladies, shall we?" George asked as he held out his right arm for Millie to take. A long, pale and narrow runner with white rose petals scattered atop it had been laid across the meadow grass. It led off into the distance up the gentle slope just above the pond. From where they were standing, they could see that a small archway and canopy had been erected. There was no sign of Henry or the reverend, but Millie felt confident that they were close by.

"I'm ready if you two are," Millie said eagerly as she stepped to his side.

"All right then, let's go!" he said as he shepherded Anne to take the lead before them. The carriage driver remained with the horses, but the florist followed behind at a distance. As they strolled along, George directed their eyes to the pond on their left. It was partly to distract them, but also partly to bring their attention to the eight white swans that were attending the wedding that day.

Millie was awestruck by the scene that she claimed looked *just like a photograph from a magazine.* They floated peacefully near one another at the center of the mirrored water and looked back at those on shore with keen interest.

Soon, George indicated that it was time to proceed. When the ladies turned, they noticed that the scene had changed dramatically. Two violinists in formal attire now stood just a few yards ahead on either side of the "aisle" and began to play *Here Comes the Bride.* Millie's eyes began to well up as she could see Henry along with the preacher now positioned at the archway. Another woman was off to the side with a large camera anxiously taking pictures.

Millie began to cry and realized she hadn't planned for that possibility by bringing a tissue or handkerchief along. George was on the job, however, and had an ample supply at the ready. Having given away two daughters at the altar made him a veteran, and he had foreseen the inevitable. He handed one handkerchief to Millie and another to Anne, who also had joined in the weeping at this point. Because all of it was so overwhelming and such a surprise, it took Millie a few seconds to realize that Henry was holding something. She couldn't quite figure out what it was yet but as she drew closer, she was shaken by the biggest surprise of all.

In his arms, Henry held the official flower girl and ring bearer for the wedding. It was none other than the feline officially named Hobo Josephine Engel, now simply known to friends and family as Joe. She looked plump and a wee bit uncomfortable but contented to be in Henry's arms. Around her neck, a white satin ribbon had been loosely tied with two wedding rings dangling from it.

"Oh my Lord! It's Joe!" Millie cried as she rushed to Henry's side to the utter delight of all in attendance.

"You're crazy, you know that?" Millie joyfully stammered to Henry while she nuzzled the little cat into her chest.

"I know I'm crazy about you," Henry said as he put his hands on her waist. "Man that is some kind of dress! You look like a million bucks." He leaned to kiss her before he was reminded by the best man that he was getting a little ahead of himself.

"Excuse me, if you two want to get a room, you first have to say *I do*," he teased.

"Fair enough. Let's get this going then," Henry fired back, which brought more laughter from all.

"I just can't believe you brought her down here!" Millie whispered to Henry with amazement.

"Would you have had it any other way?" he whispered back.

It was true. This was a day that Joe had to be a part of. Following her mysterious arrival at the estate the previous spring, Henry, Millie, and Oak Forest had changed forever.

Anne stepped over and took Joe so that Millie would be able to give her undivided attention to her groom. The little feline was starting to wonder if perhaps they thought she was a football or a hot potato. However, she liked everyone that she had been handed to so far, so she opted not to complain. After all, it was her first wedding, and she guessed that maybe passing the pregnant cat was some sort of weird marital custom. Still, if they tried to pawn her off on the photographer, whom she thought looked a little sketchy, she intended to speak up.

With Joe now taken care of, the reverend gathered everyone together and began the ceremony. The proceedings were relatively brief, but they were very moving. Henry and Millie exchanged vows they had written for each other, and even George needed a handkerchief afterward. When it came time for the exchange of rings, Millie was stunned to see that Henry had pulled another surprise from his bag of tricks. She hadn't noticed that one of the rings that Joe had carried around her neck featured a large diamond with several smaller ones mounted on either side. Conversely, Henry's was a simple band akin to the engagement ring he had given to Millie. It had been Henry's plan all along. The jeweler who had crafted the set for Millie had designed it to allow them to be fused together at a later date. Henry had correctly guessed that it would be a fun surprise. Millie loved the ring and loved the man who had thought of it.

"That diamond would take care of a lot of kids, Henry," she said in protest, thinking of their new charitable venture. He smiled and laughed but assured her that they could afford both. Henry insisted that it was deserved because she had always taken care of him and everyone else around her.

When all else had been said and done, the reverend pronounced them man and wife and then blessed them. Henry took the newly anointed Mrs. Engel into his arms and gave her the kiss of her life while everyone clapped and cheered. The two violinists broke into a jovial tune as the photographer snapped countless pictures. To top off the occasion, the florist had slipped to the side of the archway and now opened a large box releasing scores of doves into the air.

"They're beautiful, Henry!" Anne shouted with glee as the graceful birds flew up into the sky.

"We had to do it," Henry declared as George looked on in approval. Millie was also in complete accord. She knew exactly what he was referring to. Henry had explained to her what doves had meant to Mary. Millie also understood what they had come to mean to him. In Henry's mind, they were symbols of redemption, renewal, and forgiveness. Millie knew that if it hadn't been for Henry's visit to the cemetery and the mysterious appearance of a dove, he would have never been able to love again. She was grateful for Mary's absolution of Henry and thought that the gesture was the perfect way to honor her memory.

Following the ceremony, the wedding party boarded the carriage and were promptly taken up to the house so that Joe could be safely deposited indoors to rest. While they were there, Henry directed everyone to refresh themselves as needed and then reconvene out front for a ride through the countryside. When they returned to the carriage, it had been decorated with balloons, crepe paper, and a traditional "Just Married" sign that had been affixed to the rear. A tub of ice with bottles of champagne and glasses at the ready was also waiting for them.

Henry explained that since it was their wedding day, he'd expected Millie to want something to drink that was fancier than the usual. Instead, she protested that though champagne was the drink of tradition for a wedding party, it would have to wait.

"We're Engels, and Engels don't celebrate with champagne. We're the kind of folks who talk about important things with a guy named Jake," she proclaimed proudly. All were in agreement, and soon the tub of champagne was replaced by a bucket of ice, several bottles of water, a couple of glasses, and their old friend. The women preferred to do their toasting differently and boiled some water for tea. After all the preparations had been concluded, they were off.

The wedding party's sojourn through the surrounding back roads lasted for more than an hour, and Jake was quite talkative along the way. By the time they pulled back into the estate, everyone was feeling quite relaxed and happy but they were getting just a tad hungry.

"When we get up to the house, I'll fix something for us all to eat," Millie announced as they headed up the hill.

"No, you won't," Henry objected.

"What are you talking about? Of course I will," Millie countered. "That's what I do."

"It's your wedding day, my dear; you aren't cooking. I've got it all taken care of. There's a snack waiting at home, and then we're off to dinner." George and Henry looked at one another and smiled as the ladies were left to wonder what was coming next. The men had conspired to create a final adventure that they were hoping would leave the bride speechless.

Upon their return to the house, Millie was surprised that the others had gone. She felt badly that she hadn't said goodbye or thanked them for their wonderful efforts to make the day so special. She also noticed that George's car was missing and urgently informed him that someone must have stolen it. He assured her it was nothing to worry about, and they went inside to find a supreme pizza from Lou's Tavern waiting on the island.

Anne and George were happy to see the snack but didn't quite understand the significance of it. So, Henry relayed the story of their movie night date and explained how much they had enjoyed their first Saturday night pizza together. He also decided that it was time to open at least one of the bottles of champagne for a toast. Millie was thrilled by his romantic gestures, and all savored the delicious treat that he had arranged.

"Do you know where we're having dinner?" Millie asked Anne as she finished up her slice of pizza.

"No, no idea," Anne answered honestly.

Overhearing them from across the room, Henry stepped in. "It's top secret, girls," he said cryptically.

"You're just full of surprises today!" Millie declared as she put her arms around her husband. Henry smiled with satisfaction as George patted him on the back. Thus far, it was a perfect day, and Henry was saving one of the best surprises for last. Just before 6:00 p.m., he announced that they would be leaving in fifteen minutes and that they should get ready accordingly.

Millie was stepping out of the bathroom when she first heard the sound of the aircraft passing overhead. It was unusual to hear such a thing these days at Oak Forest. However, once upon a time, Henry had occasionally commuted this way to business meetings. It didn't register at first that the helicopter was arriving to pick them up, but she soon realized what was happening when it landed in the meadow below the house.

Soon, all were safely buckled in and on their way to dinner. Because of their careers, George and Henry had each traveled via helicopter many times over the years. Likewise, Anne frequently had occasion to fly this way in the various parts of the world where jets and airplanes were impractical or impossible to utilize. But for Millie, this was a first, and she was awed by the experience. The others chatted during the flight, but the bride was utterly mesmerized by the view. She sat at the window and stared at the passing landscape below as they flew toward their mystery destination.

When they arrived at Spirit of St. Louis Airport, Millie was sorry to see the exciting ride come to an end. Nonetheless, she quickly regained her exuberance when Henry mentioned that they would be returning to Oak Forest the same way they had come. A black stretch limousine was waiting for them to land and promptly swept them away to the restaurant. Henry and

George remained tight-lipped about where they were going until at last the limo stopped in front of one of the premier steak-houses in the entire city.

"The Ranch," Millie read aloud as she stepped out of the vehicle and onto the sidewalk. The large neon sign above the door was turned off, and the windows were blacked out by heavy curtains. The parking lot to the right looked to be mostly empty, but there were some cars parked toward the back including a Mercedes just like George's.

"Henry, I think this place is closed. Are you sure this is where we're supposed to be?" she asked worriedly.

"It's not closed to us," Henry assured her as Millie noticed that the air smelled awfully good for a vacant restaurant.

He led her by the hand to the front door as George escorted Anne closely behind. Upon arriving at the entrance, Henry executed a series of knocks that seemed to Millie like some form of Morse code. Almost immediately, they could hear locks clicking, and the door swung open. A heavyset man opened the door and greeted the wedding party warmly. He was quite affable and after shaking Henry and George's hands, he explained to the ladies that he was the proprietor of the establishment.

"My given name is Benjamin Franklin," he said to their amusement, "but for obvious reasons I prefer that my friends call me *Blimpy*. I guess I get my sense of humor from my parents, huh?" His words made them laugh, and he then invited them inside. Millie was astonished yet again by what Henry had orchestrated for their special day. He had bought out the entire restaurant for the night so that they could dine in privacy.

The center of the dining room had been cleared and a lone, beautifully appointed table was all that remained. As they entered the room, the violinists from that afternoon began to play soft sweet music to welcome them. All around the restaurant, various flower arrangements had been strategically positioned to create a festive setting. The young woman who had been taking photographs that afternoon was also in attendance and was working feverishly to capture the moment. Standing off in the corner, under a spotlight, a glorious three-tiered wedding cake stood majestically on a small table. With all in place, the complete staff stood at attention at their stations throughout The Ranch and waited to go to work.

Before seating them, the owner made an announcement that temporarily halted the music. "Can I have your attention everyone? It is my great honor to present for the first time, Mr. and Mrs. Henry Engel." The room erupted into polite applause as the wedding party made their way to their table.

Henry and Millie's reception was an unmitigated success. They enjoyed a fantastic meal that was amongst the best they had ever eaten. Millie wasn't sure how Blimpy was able to get a steak to taste that good, but afterward she milked him for his secrets. The music was pleasing, and the atmosphere was cozy and romantic. After dinner, the bride and groom shared their first dance as husband and wife while everyone looked on. It was a touching scene and even Blimpy teared up slightly at the sight of true love. Following that, Henry and Millie invited everyone in attendance to join them for cake and coffee. From the owner to the dishwasher, all came and sat in the dining room with the wedding party. As it turned out, it was one of the best moments of the day. While the excess of the once-in-a-lifetime occasion was certainly enjoyable and unforgettable, Henry and Millie truly preferred just sitting around talking with good people to opulence.

Following their farewell and thanks to those inside, they

stepped out to the limo. For George, it was also time to say goodnight. He explained to Millie that one of the violinists had driven his car into the city so that he wouldn't have a long trek home from Lewis after the full day. Everyone agreed it was a wise plan but was sorry to see him go. Anne and Millie said goodbye and got into the limo leaving George and Henry alone on the sidewalk.

"What a day!" George exclaimed as he put his hand on Henry's right shoulder.

"Best day of my life," Henry agreed.

"You really pulled it off, pal! She's a wonderful gal. I am so happy for you."

"I couldn't have done any of this without you, George."

"Are you kidding? You did almost all of it by yourself. I got the preacher and made a couple calls, but you did the rest pal."

"Hey, it was your idea that I bring Millie to dinner here, remember?" Henry said, reminding George of the conversation they had during the weekend of the coin show that spring before Henry had ever approached Millie. George shook his head.

"But that's not what I'm talking about. I didn't mean just today. I meant everything since we ran into each other again. If it wasn't for you, I'd have never gone to see Mary and we wouldn't be here right now."

George now understood what his friend was saying, and he was deeply touched.

"Henry, everything I have in life I owe to you. If you hadn't pulled me out of the pond that day, I wouldn't have had my life with Claire, my kids, or my grandkids. All I've ever wanted to do is be worthy of what you did for me that day and to find a way to pay you back."

Henry was moved by George's sentiments but didn't see things that way. "Let's finally call it even, ok?"

"I promise I'll try," George said as he embraced his friend. "I love you, pal."

"I love you too, buddy. Thanks again for everything."

*

Just before 11:30 p.m. the newlyweds were finally back home and alone together for the first time. They had asked Anne to sleep over rather than drive back to town, but she insisted that it would be bad form to intrude on the wedding night and that she couldn't wait to get busy writing. After the long and eventful day, that seemed crazy to Millie, but Henry knew what it was like to be obsessed by business and could relate to her passion.

"I'm ready to ditch this penguin suit," Henry declared while pulling at his collar button.

"I hear you; these heels have got to go. I won't be able to walk for a week," she said, observing her swollen feet. "It sure was worth it, though."`

"Can I interest you in a nightcap? We haven't had a chance to be alone and talk all day. It just sounds good to me right now."

"Yeah, that would be really nice. Can you get Jake ready? I'll be right back. I want to find Joe," she said as she ascended the stairs.

Henry began preparing their drinks as Joe lazily wobbled into the room to see what was going on. She was nearing the bursting point and was stiff from an all-evening nap.

"Hey honey, here's Joe down here," Henry called as he topped off the highballs with water.

"Oh ok, I'll be right down," she called back.

Henry sat the drinks down on the island and scooped Joe

up while he waited. She liked his affection and began to purr as a means to hopefully encourage him to continue rubbing her ears and neck. Millie seemed to be taking longer than expected, but Henry was distracted by Joe and didn't mind. Jake was also patiently waiting for the return of Mrs. Engel and said nothing.

Finally, Henry heard Millie coming down the stairs. He was about to ask what had been delaying her when he saw the reason for himself. The wedding dress was no more and had now been replaced by a racy black satin negligee.

"Holy moly! Where in the world did you get that?" Henry blurted out with excitement as he started to sweat slightly.

"I bought it the day I was shopping with Anne. Do you like it, Mr. Engel?"

"Do I like it?" he repeated as he took an enormous gulp from his glass.

"I'm going to send you shopping with her more often!" he declared while admiring her beautiful figure. His compliment made Millie blush, but she appreciated it very much.

"I just figured I should look nice for my first celebration with Jake and Joe as Mrs. Engel. After all, a girl only gets one chance at her wedding night with her husband, right?" she asked as she took a sip from her drink.

Indeed, thought Henry. *Indeed!*

CHAPTER 24

D-Day

HENRY AWOKE ON Sunday feeling on top of the world. He felt alive and rejuvenated. Waking up next to his wife in a bed for the first time proved to be much more to his liking than the couch in the family room. Millie agreed that it was preferable to sleeping alone, and the marriage was off to a rousing start. For the next couple of days, Millie and Henry kept to themselves and enjoyed all of the benefits of being man and wife. Neither had much interest in taking a trip with Joe so close to motherhood, so they turned the time into their own private honeymoon at Oak Forest. They watched and waited as the little cat continued to progress toward her expected due date and puttered around the estate doing things they enjoyed. Mostly, they just spent time with each other being in love.

On Wednesday, they decided that they would go to Millie's house for a while to begin the process of sorting through which things were coming with her and which others she didn't want or need. Once Henry's SUV was loaded to the hilt, Millie suggested that perhaps they could stop in and say "hello" to Anne on their way home. They hadn't spoken to her since the day of the wedding, and Millie was anxious to find out how the author was getting along. It was late afternoon but not yet time to see Jake, so Henry consented and they drove past her house for a brief visit.

"Well, look at you two!" Anne exclaimed excitedly as she answered the front door. "You look so happy!"

"I guess marriage agrees with us," Millie confirmed. Anne was pleased to hear that and invited them inside.

"So, what gives? Just passing through the neighborhood?"

"Nah, Millie was curious to find out how the secret book is going," Henry said as he pointed to his wife.

"Oh, stop your teasing," she told him. "Truth is, we were over at my house getting started on the move and I thought we'd check to make sure you weren't working too hard. Have you been getting some rest and remembering to eat?" she asked the author as a mother might check on her daughter away at school.

Anne looked slightly fatigued but said that she had never felt better. Just that morning, she had been working on her new novel and had been planning to surprise them with a visit to Oak Forest that evening to discuss it.

"I've got just a bit more to do and then I'll be ready to write the ending," she explained. "That's where you two come in. I was hoping that you would read the manuscript and help me decide how I should end the story. I'm not sure how you're going to react to it, but I think it is simply the very best work of my life."

Henry and Millie were excited to be honored with the privilege of being the first to see a book written by the renowned author. It wasn't something either of them had sought or expected to happen. However, to be asked to offer an opinion on how to conclude the story seemed beyond their expertise.

"I don't think either one of us is in a position to help you write, Anne," Henry countered.

"Honey, I'm good at a lot of things, but I'm no author," Millie added as reinforcement to her husband's statement.

"Just trust me on this one," Anne requested. "It will all make sense after you read what I have so far."

Millie and Henry excused themselves and drove home filled with curiosity. They discussed what Anne's book might be about and wondered why she had added the disclaimer *I'm not sure how you're going to react to it* to her request that they be the first to read it. Henry suggested that perhaps it was some sort of erotic thriller, but Millie quickly dismissed that notion. She was convinced that Anne was not that sort and suggested that it might be a mystery of some type. For a second, Henry even entertained the thought that Anne might have written a book about him, but he didn't mention it to Millie. He trusted Anne and had been assured from the beginning that she would not use him as a subject.

The afternoon passed slowly as they anxiously anticipated her arrival, but at last her Jeep made the turn into Oak Forest, and the wait was over. She was just in time for their meeting with Jake, and Henry prepared three drinks before joining the women at the kitchen table. She had brought along a medium-sized cardboard box that presumably contained the manuscript she wanted them to read.

"All right guys, here it is," she said, patting the top of the closed container with her hand.

"I'm still not sure how we're going to be able to help you, but we're happy to try," Henry said as he took a swallow from his glass.

Anne slid the box over to him and held her breath. He opened the flaps to find a large stack of typed pages inside.

"It's separated into individual chapters so that you can each read parts of it at the same time," she explained.

Henry removed the first chapter from the box and slid the container over to Millie. He glanced briefly over the text of the first page, but his heart stopped when he saw the title of the new book. He could feel the blood rush to his face as his anger rose.

"How in the hell could you do this?" he said sharply with growing rage.

"Henry! Don't talk to Anne like that," Millie scolded him. "What is it?"

He slapped the chapter down in front of Millie so that she could see the title.

"Oh honey, what have you done?" she whispered with disappointment toward Anne.

On the table, the first chapter of Anne Francis Wagner's latest novel Chats with Jake and Joe sat between them.

"Please let me explain before you get angry," Anne pleaded.

"I'm afraid it's a little late for that," Henry informed her, attempting to control his emotions.

"It's not at all what either of you must be thinking. I would never betray your trust. Your name isn't anywhere in the book; it's all written as fiction. I created a small town like Lewis as the setting and borrowed some ideas from the stories you've told me, but I promise, the characters are not any of you. The only names that are the same are Jake and Joe. I really like the way that sounds but if you don't approve, I'll change that too."

Starting to calm down just a little, Henry questioned why Anne had written such a book in the first place. He had been under the impression the entire time that all she'd cared about when she came to Lewis was Henry's African adventure.

"Yes, of course, that is absolutely true. I wanted to know

about the hunt to use it for a character in a book I was working on. But then, when I met you, Henry, I got an overwhelming feeling I've never had before. I suddenly had a million ideas for a book about a man with a cat named Joe. He had a rich life and traveled the world and in his later years he'd tell stories to Joe and his friend Jake," she said, holding up her glass. "It's an extraordinary concept for a novel. I promise that if you just read it, you'll find that though I borrowed some of your experiences, the book is definitely not about you. The only problem I have now is that I don't know how to end it."

"It wouldn't hurt for us to read it, Henry," Millie suggested, attempting to broker peace.

"It's the finest book I've ever written; I'm sure of it. It's different than anything I've ever done. I wasn't looking to do this, but it found me. I tried to ignore it, really I did, but something persisted and insisted that I write this story. With that said, I make two promises to both of you here and now. First, I pledge that unless you both agree that it is one hundred percent ok with you, I will not publish the work. I'll destroy it and never reproduce it. Second, if you do allow me to publish it, any and all royalties will be donated to any charity you choose."

"Why would you do that?" Millie wondered.

"I don't need the money. I've already got a lot more than I will ever spend. I just would love to reward my loyal fans and readers with this marvelous story. If I can generate lots of sales and do some good for others at the same time, I'd love to do so," the author explained.

"Sounds kind of familiar, doesn't it, honey?" Millie asked her husband.

Henry regretted that he'd allowed himself to become upset

before he had heard Anne out on the matter. He was a little ashamed that he had so easily doubted her integrity.

"So, you're willing to let us read this and if either of us has a problem with it, you'll scrap it?"

"Yes Henry, I give you my solemn word. I truly hope that you'll both approve of what I've written but if you don't, it will never see the light of day. I respect and care for you both and would never do anything to hurt either of you. You've become like family to me and you can trust me completely."

Based on those terms, Henry and Millie agreed to read Anne's manuscript. He had always been an extremely private man but if the names and details in the book had been altered, he reasoned that it probably was not an egregious intrusion into his personal affairs. After all, unbeknownst to Anne, the Engels had a new charitable foundation to support. If the book was as good as Anne believed that it was, it would sell well. The possibility for a new and potentially vibrant source of funding for their venture was music to his ears.

Millie decided that Henry should read the book in its entirety first before she did. If there was something in it that he disapproved of or did not want her to know, he could veto it on his own. Henry appreciated her sensitivity and agreed that it was a good idea. Over the next two and a half days, he was consumed with reading Anne's manuscript. In his opinion, she hadn't remotely overestimated its quality. He sat for hours in his recliner in the family room and devoured the chapters, unable to break away from the story. Henry was intrigued by the masterful way Anne had woven some stories about his life with her own fictional places and events. He was surprised by the inclusion of several anecdotes from his childhood and adolescence because he could not recall ever telling her about them. It seemed to be more than just coincidence, but he guessed that maybe George had a hand in it.

However, there was one aspect to the story that was of particular interest to him. The main character, around whom the whole book revolved, had betrayed his only brother in a business deal and the two had not spoken for over fifty years. He had lived with extreme guilt and had attempted to repair the relationship by writing letters to his brother several times per year for decades. However, the brother who had been wronged never replied. The protagonist moved on, marrying and having a family. He was now an older man and nearing the last season of his life. His burden had only grown more cumbersome with time, and it affected him deeply. He was certain that his eternal destiny was to be determined by whether or not he received forgiveness for the transgression committed so many years before.

On Saturday morning, the sixth of June, Henry turned the final page of the final chapter but was left hanging. There were no more words beyond that for him to read. He was anxious to know how the story ended but realized that from there it was entirely up to him what happened next. Clearly, the main character of Chats with Jake and Joe was his brother Bill and the business deal gone wrong was really a reference to Mary. Anne had cleverly altered the facts to assure that no one would ever guess that it related in any way to Henry, but the point had been made. While reading the chapters, he had empathized with the protagonist and rooted for a reconciliation between the brothers. It was the first time Henry had ever put himself in Bill's place, and it made him truly understand how he must feel. Just then, Millie passed into the room to join him and took a seat on the couch.

"Did you finish reading Anne's book? Is it good?" she asked as she opened the cover of a magazine she had brought with her.

"It's terrific, but I guess you already know that, right?" he said sarcastically.

"What's that supposed to mean?" Millie replied without answering his question.

"Come on, Millie, you're in on this. I get it," he said with mild annoyance. After reading the manuscript, he now guessed that it was simply an elaborate scheme to get him to contact his brother. He wasn't exactly certain who all of the co-conspirators were but figured Millie was in on the plan. The most unbelievable part of it, in his mind, was that Anne had fabricated a bogus novel about his brother's life just to make a point.

"I'm certain I have no idea what you're talking about Henry," Millie responded convincingly. "And I don't appreciate your tone, either."

"I'm talking about this fake book about me and Bill," he said holding up a few of the chapters.

"Good Lord Henry, did she really write about you and Bill in there? I am so sorry, baby." Henry was confused now. Millie seemed genuinely shocked and apologetic. She was either a much better actress than he had ever known or was truly in the dark about it all.

"Well, not exactly: it's about two brothers and one cheats the other out of a huge boatload of money. They don't talk for over fifty years after that even though the bad guy keeps writing letters to the other one trying to fix it. Sound familiar?" Henry asked with eyebrows raised.

"I'm so sorry, honey, I had absolutely no idea whatsoever that was what this book was about. I guess it's my fault. The day Anne first came to Oak Forest we had a good long chat and talked about all sorts of things. Somehow we got to talking about you and Bill, and then I had a dumb idea. I told her how I wanted to help fix things and asked her to call George because he would know where Bill was in New York. Since Anne was from there too, I wondered if maybe she could get in touch with him and try to figure something out to help get you two together."

Henry listened intently and waited to pass judgment until he had heard the entire tale. Anne had indeed called George and then determined how to get in touch with his brother. When she traveled to New York to attend to her own affairs, she also paid Bill a visit to get his side of the story. In addition, she let him know that there were allies in Lewis attempting to help him mend his relationship with Henry. Millie further explained that neither she nor George had known anything about the new novel or its contents.

"So, you're telling me this isn't a fake book? She really does want to publish it?" Henry asked, trying to be certain that he fully understood the situation.

"Yes, I'm afraid so. I guess you're going to tell her no now, huh?"

"You know what? I'm going to tell her to run with it. I tell you something, it's one helluva good book! Millie, I couldn't put the damn thing down. I think it's going to be a bestseller, and we're going to raise all kinds of money for the foundation." Henry went on to detail the entire plot to her. He shared some excerpts about real events that were included in the novel and compared them to how he remembered things to actually have happened. Henry now knew where Anne had gotten her inside information. It was fun for him to relive memories of certain events but through Bill's eyes. For the first time in fifty-plus years, he missed his brother just a little.

"So, are you mad at me for going behind your back?" Millie asked sheepishly. Henry weighed his options. He could chastise her and be angry or understand that she was merely acting in a manner that she believed was in his best interests. Her heart was in the right place even if she had made a mistake. Once upon a time long ago, he had driven a woman he loved from his life over a botched attempt to get him back together with his brother. Now, Henry had learned from his past and handled things differently.

"No sweetheart, of course not. I know why you did it, and I love you for it. *Just don't ever do it again*," he added with a wink that made her smile with relief.

"So, do you know how you want Anne to finish the story?" Millie asked.

"Yes, I know what happens next," he said with conviction.

Henry stood and walked into his office. From where she was seated on the far end of the couch, Millie couldn't see what he was doing, but she heard the weight of his body gently descend into the desk chair. Next, she heard a drawer and then the sound of an envelope being opened. She listened as Henry removed a letter from it and unfolded it. There was silence for a time after that and then a long deep sigh followed by the sound of Henry picking up the telephone and dialing. Millie heard the chair squeak just a tad from the load of his shifting weight as he leaned back. She wondered if perhaps he was calling George to harass him about his role in their conspiracy to reunite him with Bill. It seemed like a long delay but then she heard words that she had never dreamed she would.

"Hello Bill, this is your brother Henry."

"*Dear God, Henry, is that really you?*" cried an older but still familiar voice from the other end of the line. "You finally called me; I can't believe it!" Bill exclaimed with immense relief as he began to weep.

"Well of course; after all, it's D-Day, Bill," Henry said, dryly referring to the fact that this day was the 54th anniversary of the invasion of Normandy by Allied forces. "I always call a World War II veteran on D-Day. It just took fifty-four years for your number to come up."

The joke broke the ice and relieved some of the tension of the moment. With her fingers crossed, Millie stayed put and eavesdropped for a while to see how things would unfold. She didn't know if the call would be short and to the point or long and emotional. To her relief, it was the latter. Henry and Bill exchanged heartfelt sentiments that culminated in Bill's sincere apology for his past wrongdoing and Henry's apology for withholding his forgiveness of the same. With that business finally behind them, the conversation turned to lighter topics, and Millie left the room to give her husband his privacy. The brothers talked for nearly two hours and shared the details of their lives. Before finishing their call, they agreed to speak again early in the coming week to formulate a plan for Bill and his family to come to Lewis for a visit. It would truly be an Engel family reunion as most of the participants had never met one another before.

Millie was seated at the island when Henry finally emerged from the office and made his way into the kitchen to find her. His face looked relaxed and completely at peace as he approached. As he neared, without saying a word, he extended his arms and gently placed his hands on her cheeks before giving her a lengthy and very sweet kiss.

"What's that for?" she asked softly after their lips had parted.

"Just because I love you Millie Engel. No other reason, just because I love you."

"I'm guessing the phone call went pretty well," she said

before he smiled and kissed her even more vehemently this time. Millie's toes began to tingle, and her stomach did a flip as butterflies danced about inside her. "You tell Bill he needs to call her all the time from now on," she joked as she leaned in for another round from Henry.

While they embraced, a low guttural sound emerged from somewhere in the corner of the breakfast room.

"What on earth was that?" asked Henry as he broke away from her and swung around to see what was dying. After a short delay, a second moan emanated from the corner but this time they could tell it was coming from the cardboard box that Joe had claimed as her safe haven.

"Uh-oh, I think I know what that is," Millie said with alarm as she rushed across the room. As she had suspected, the little mother-to-be was in the final hours of her pregnancy. "Yep, I thought so! Henry, it's time!" she cried.

CHAPTER 25

Boiling Water

"WHAT DO WE do?" Henry asked with nervous excitement. "Doc Miller explained all about what to expect and how things will go. It's going to be just fine sweetie." Millie could sense his anxiety and knew that he had never been a party to the birth of anything before in his entire life. Being a mother herself, she had delivered a child and was far better suited to handle the stress of the affair than he was. Joe's initiation into the sorority of motherhood would likely take hours to proceed to its fruition. Millie quickly determined that Henry was going to need some distractions in order to survive the ordeal.

"How about you boil some water?" she asked.

"Water? Ok, I can do that," he replied as he rushed to the stove. The teakettle Anne had given him now resided permanently on the back left burner, and he took it in hand.

"How much do we need?" he asked innocently.

"Oh, you better go ahead and fill it up," she directed, knowing that a full kettle was slower to boil and, therefore, would keep his attention longer. After all, the request for hot water had nothing to do with Joe. Millie simply wanted a cup of tea while she waited for the kittens to arrive.

"We're going to need towels, right? I better go and gather up some," Henry exclaimed anxiously as he fired up the burner and placed the kettle atop the blue flames.

Towels? What on earth is he talking about? Millie wondered. She assumed it was something he had seen in one of the old movies that he loved to watch. Though there was no practical reason for it, she opted to take advantage of the opportunity to keep him busy.

"Oh yeah baby, we're gonna need lots and lots of towels. How about you run and get me some," she encouraged him as she took a seat at the end of the kitchen table.

"Ok, I can take care of that. You keep an eye on Joe and the water on the stove, and I'll be right back. If you need something else, just holler," he said as he rushed up the stairs. Millie was undecided about what she found more interesting, waiting with Joe for the birth of her litter or watching Henry run around the house in a panic. She could see that it was going to be a long afternoon and evening and moved to bring in some reinforcements.

"Say, Henry?" she called to him.

"Coming honey!" he shouted as he flew down the staircase with urgency. It was all that Millie could do to contain her laughter as she caught sight of him. In his arms, Henry carried an enormous stack of towels representing Oak Forest's entire inventory. He dropped them on the kitchen table in front of her like a cat laying a prize at the feet of its owner.

"I got the towels," he exclaimed, nearly out of breath.

"You sure did," Millie said while attempting to keep a straight face.

"Are there any kittens yet? Did you need something? Is Joe all right?"

"She's fine sweetheart; nothing has happened yet. Hey, I was just thinking, how about you give Anne a call? If she's not busy, I bet she'd like to be here, and she could help me out."

"Anne? Yeah, that's a great idea," he agreed as he hustled over to the telephone. "I'm going to call George too. He's got three kids and seven grandkids; he can help for sure," Henry added as he dialed the author's number.

"Good idea honey, you do that," Millie encouraged her husband. She thought that it was a brilliant suggestion and was disappointed that she hadn't thought of it first. Unlike Henry, she had no reason to think that George's experiences as a father and grandfather would help Joe safely deliver her kittens. Millie knew that one had little or nothing to do with the other. She did, however, think that George could play a key role in assuring that all would go smoothly. He would be the ideal babysitter for Henry.

Upon receiving the news that Joe was in labor, both Anne and George were equally glad to be invited to Oak Forest for the festivities. It just so happened that neither of them had anything particular going for the night. Therefore, each was willing to scurry out to the estate to wait with Henry and Millie for the arrival of the babies. Besides, since they were first and second on the list of prospective parents to adopt one of Joe's kittens, it was an exciting proposition to be on hand as they were born.

Being considerably closer, Anne was the first to arrive on the scene. At just past 4:00 p.m., Millie answered the front door with a broad smile and a warm greeting and invited their friend inside. Henry was upstairs, so the two women had a chance to speak privately as they walked into the kitchen.

"How's Joe doing? Anything happening yet?" Anne inquired.

Millie motioned for Anne to step over to the box where Joe

was resting. "Nope, nothing just yet but I think we're getting real close. It'll be any time now."

Anne kneeled and greeted Joe while gently giving her some affection. "How's Henry handling things?"

"About like any first-time daddy I guess. He's a nervous wreck," Millie said softly with a laugh so that he couldn't hear her. "He's been busy boiling water and gathering up all the towels in the county," she added as she pointed to the kitchen table.

"Is that what that is about? I thought perhaps you were folding laundry to pass the time while you waited," Anne confessed quietly while shaking her head in amusement. "He sounded quite out of sorts when he called me. Poor fellow, where is he?" Anne wondered as she stood.

"He's upstairs; got a little bit of a nervous stomach over all of this," Millie explained.

"Hi, Anne! Thank goodness you're here," Henry declared as he made his way down the staircase.

"Henry! How are you holding up?" Anne asked, acting as if she had no idea how things were going.

"Who me? I'm doing fine. Millie's been looking after Joe, but I've been keeping a close eye on both of them. So far, I'd say they're hanging in there pretty well." Henry spoke without a hint of comedy in his voice as he put his arm around Millie's shoulder.

"What can I say, Anne? He's my rock," Millie declared with a wink and a grin that Henry couldn't see.

They stood and chatted for a few minutes about Joe before deciding to move to the comfort of the family room. Once there, it occurred to Henry that he had an important matter to discuss with Anne that wasn't related to cats or kittens.

"With all that's going on, I forgot to tell you that I finished reading your book." His face was expressionless when he spoke, and Anne was left feeling a little uneasy.

"Are you angry with me?" she asked cautiously.

"Let's just say, I'm very disappointed," he said with a stern look.

"But Henry..." Millie interrupted.

"Millie please, this is between Anne and me," he said with firm conviction.

"Henry, I'm truly sorry you feel I let you down. I certainly did not intentionally try to hurt you. I just followed the inspiration that came to me and wrote the story I felt in my heart."

"Well, that's really not the problem at all," he said shaking his head. "No, the reason I'm disappointed is that you wrote such a great book and it turns out my brother gets top billing? Come on now, you even gave him Jake and Joe and I'm just a guy who gets cheated out of his money. Doesn't seem very fair considering most of the good stories in there came from me." Henry was smiling as he finished his mock "rebuke" of Anne, and she was vastly relieved.

"If you would rather, I could rewrite things and make you a star," she offered in jest.

"Don't even think about it," he warned her playfully. Anne threw her hands up in surrender to indicate that she was only joking.

"All right then, what would you like me to do? Shall I submit it for publishing or scrap it?"

"Without a doubt you need to publish it. It's really terrific. I don't read a lot of novels but kiddo, you had me from the first page."

Anne's face beamed. She was an affluent bestselling author

and had been praised for her work at the highest levels, but no review ever left her feeling prouder.

"I'm very humbled that you would say that, Henry. Thank you."

"You're welcome. I meant every word. I expect we're going to raise a terrific amount of money for our new foundation, too," he added, now thinking about the reason for indirectly exposing his life to the world. This was the first Anne had heard of the Oak Forest Foundation, and she was delighted as Henry and Millie offered their vision for it. She not only reaffirmed her original pledge to donate all royalties from the new book to the charity of their choice but also promised to make a personal donation as well. Also, she was very interested in becoming directly involved in the project. Henry and Millie welcomed the idea. They continued to chat about it all as Millie periodically checked on Joe, but things remained in limbo. As of yet, no kittens had arrived.

"If we're going to sell lots of books to fund the foundation, we're going need a really top-shelf ending. Any ideas where I should go from here?" the author asked the others.

"Oh gosh, with all that's going on, Henry, you still haven't told her the big news!" Millie exclaimed.

"That's right, I guess I haven't," he said as Anne's eyes widened with curiosity.

"What news?" she asked enthusiastically trying to read his expression.

"Let's just say I think I have the ending for your book figured out. Thanks to you, Millie, and George that is," he answered with satisfaction.

Henry went on to share a bit of the content from his conversation earlier that day with Bill and to tell her that his brother and family would be coming to Lewis at some point for a visit.

Anne was thrilled beyond words that their secret alliance had contributed to this breakthrough and was genuinely moved by his sentiments. Before the discussion could go further, a knock on the front door announced the arrival of George.

Henry was glad to see his friend's face and quickly noted that it was a few minutes past the normal time for the arrival of another old pal. In light of the festive occasion, all agreed that a celebration with Jake was fitting and the preparations began. Now becoming an expert, Henry reheated the water in the kettle as George and the women conversed about Joe and cats in general. At one point, Henry thought he heard George whisper something about towels but Millie and Anne laughed so he assumed that it must have instead been a joke that he missed. Soon, Henry had again proved his skill with the stove and the contents of the teakettle were back at a rolling boil. In short order, two highballs and two cups of tea each flavored with just the right touch of Jake's personality were being held aloft for a toast.

"To Joe!" Henry proclaimed as all chimed in. They tapped each other's drinks and took a sip in her honor. Perhaps sensing the dramatic moment or maybe just wishing to remind them that *she* ought to be the center of attention, the little Siamese cat once again stole the show. Everyone looked on in amazement as the first kitten arrived without complication. Anne and Millie were awed by the creation of a new life and cried as the tiny kitten took its first breaths. However, Henry and George were slightly less impressed. They decided that witnessing the birth of one kitten was more than enough for them, and they retreated to the safety of the front porch.

Once outside, Henry paced back and forth like a father in the waiting room of a hospital anxiously hoping for news. He was relieved that the first kitten looked to be healthy and normal, but he knew they were not out of the woods yet. There was a long way to go, and he was still very concerned about Joe's health and well-being in addition to that of her offspring. In contrast, George was considerably more composed than Henry. He had never been inside the delivery room before during the action but had been on hand for scores of births over the years. Therefore, he was better prepared for the rigors of sweating it out and tried to engage Henry in conversation to distract him from his anxiety.

"Helluva nice day today," he observed.

"Huh? Oh yeah, it's just like last Saturday," Henry responded, comparing the two days in his mind.

"I sure hope it stays like this all summer, not too hot and no humidity."

"You're dreaming, George; it's the Midwest. It's not going to happen."

George chuckled and took a swallow from his glass as Henry moved to sit beside him. The simple mention of the weather had been enough to begin to settle Henry's nerves and it was time to move on to more significant topics.

"A little bird told me you had a very big phone call today," George tossed out casually.

"How in the hell could you know about that?" Henry asked with surprise.

"I heard a rumor. So, how was it talking to your big brother after all of these years?"

Henry couldn't fathom how George already knew about his phone conversation with Bill. Anne had just found out about it upon her arrival, and Millie certainly had not had an opportunity to speak with him privately either. That left only one possible source.

"You tell me," Henry said dryly as he took a drink from his glass. "Apparently, you must talk to him more than I do."

"I heard it went very well," George answered, confirming Henry's suspicion.

"That's two!" came an exuberant shout from the kitchen. "So far, so good, fellas!"

Both men smiled at the news and then returned to their sparring.

"First, I find out you stayed in touch with Mary through the years after I left. Then, I find out her daughter calls you *Uncle George*, which of course you neglected to mention to me. Now, you're telling me that you've been talking to Bill too. These are kind of big secrets you're keeping pal, don't you think?" he sarcastically jabbed his friend.

"They weren't secrets, Henry. I've never lied to you about anything in our whole lives. You just never asked me the right questions, that's all. You just never asked me the right questions," he repeated with a mischievous grin.

Henry had to laugh. Leave it to George to get himself out of hot water on a technicality. *Oh well, what does it matter now? All's well that ends well,* he thought. Henry was far too happy and had changed far too much to let such a thing make him angry now. The men sat and discussed Henry's phone call with Bill as they finished their drinks. Once the newly christened grandfather returned with round two and the news that kitten number three had arrived safely, they continued.

George assured Henry that there had not been a sinister conspiracy behind his back as it might have first appeared. He explained to him, in great detail, how the events of the last month had transpired. It all began with Millie innocently mentioning Bill in a conversation the day she and Anne first met. That was what had gotten the ball rolling. Anne's curiosity and deep admiration for Henry had been the impetus for her desire to see if she could somehow lend a hand in arranging a reconciliation with his brother. Millie had given George's telephone number to Anne and contact was made. At her request, George tracked Bill down and gave him a call to broker a meeting. Prior to that, he and Bill had last spoken in 1953 after Henry stormed out of St. Louis and out of their lives.

Fortunately, though they hadn't spoken in decades, Bill was very receptive to George's overture and agreed to a meeting with Anne. He was desperate for any and all assistance in his quest to repair his damaged relationship with his brother. George and Millie understood the plan to be that the author was going to New York on business and then was to visit Bill while she was there. The goal was to figure a way to get Henry and Bill together. Neither of them had any idea that at the same time Anne had already begun feverishly writing a new novel that just happened to be centered around a character loosely based on Henry's life and experiences. George's account of the events mirrored Millie's and filled in the gaps so that Henry now felt certain he knew the whole story.

"Good Lord George, is there anyone you don't talk to?"

"Bill Clinton," George answered immediately without hesitation. "Not a fan of President Clinton."

Henry shook his head and again laughed at the complex and witty man that he called his best friend but loved like a brother.

"Four!" cried Millie from inside. "We've got four, Henry! And Joe is doing great!" she shouted.

"Hot damn!" Henry said with glee while slapping George's

knee. He looked at his watch and calculated that the births were coming approximately every fifteen to twenty minutes like clockwork. He was relieved that all was going so well, and he wondered just how many more kittens there might be.

The mood was temporarily dampened as the next kitten was stillborn. However, following a short wait, the appearance of a beautiful sixth and final kitty quickly helped spirits to rebound. The realization that Joe had come through it all safely and given birth to a litter of five perfectly healthy kittens was cause enough for jubilation. George retrieved cigars from his car and passed them around. The traditional gesture brought laughter and smiles but since none of them smoked, not even George, the cigars went unused. Following a brief clean up utilizing a couple of the controversial towels, each of the tiny creations was weighed using Henry's vegetable scale and recorded as Dr. Miller had directed. That way, their growth could be charted and tracked to assure their proper health and development. Joe was spent from her efforts and rested in her box as the newborns nursed for the first time from their mother.

Everyone gathered at the kitchen table to watch and to admire the little family. The runt of the litter was white and appeared to be the only true Siamese kitten amongst them. Henry immediately staked claim to it, and Millie approved wholeheartedly. It was the same kitten that she had instantly fallen for as well. The other four were marked with varying patterns of white and black blotches giving some clue as to what their father looked like. George fell for one that had a completely black head while Anne said that she was fond of another that sported a black tail and one black paw. The two that remained unclaimed were equally adorable. It would be at least eight weeks before any of them could be separated from Joe, so there was ample time to figure out who was going where. In the meantime, Henry called Dr. Miller to inform her of the happy news. Though she was sorry to hear about the loss of one baby, she was glad to learn that Joe had done so well and offered to pay a visit the following afternoon to Oak Forest. She wanted to examine the mother and newborns as well as to see if she could tell Henry and Millie the gender of each kitten. Henry was grateful that she would sacrifice part of her Sunday afternoon for them and gladly accepted.

Meanwhile, Millie threw together an impromptu meal. They all sat around eating and chatting about a variety of topics including Bill's upcoming visit to Lewis, Millie's search for her son, Anne's latest novel, and the new charitable foundation that the Engels were forming. Joe spent the time switching between resting and grooming her litter while Henry looked on proudly as any father would. His world had changed dramatically over the past year and a half, and there was no slowdown in sight. Over the weeks and months to come, there would be new joys and sorrows, victories and defeats. However, along the way, he would be surrounded by an ever-increasing circle of family and friends and would enjoy all of the richness that life's imperfect journey has to offer.

Just over a year before, Henry Engel was a single man living contentedly alone in a world of his own with no idea what he was missing. Now, he was a husband, father, and a grandfather. Henry was surrounded by those he loved and those who loved him. Soon, he would see his long-lost brother and meet his nephews and their families for the first time. He would help Millie reconcile with her past and introduce her to the son she had given up for adoption. Henry would use his riches to help the less fortunate and change lives. He would watch as Anne fell in love in the unlikeliest of romances and take a husband. Finally, Henry would be forced to say goodbye to a lifelong friend. Laughter and tears awaited him, *but he was truly living now and flourishing.* Henry never in his life felt happier or more alive, and he awoke each morning with a sense of deep gratitude to embrace the day.

From solitary man to family man. The evolution was now complete. The little stray Siamese cat that mysteriously appeared and then refused to leave had changed it all. After that day, there were far fewer *meetings* held at Oak Forest. From then on, most of life's twists and turns were marked by *Celebrations with Jake and Joe.*

EPILOGUE

Improbable Romance,

Love, and Family.

From solitary man to family man,

the story continues…

About the Author

Roger W. Buenger is an author and entrepreneur who was born and raised in St. Louis, MO. He is an avid numismatist, historian, movie aficionado, and sports fan. These diverse interests serve him well when he is crafting tales and pursuing his passion for writing historical fiction. He is the creator of the *Jake and Joe* series and his debut novel, *Meetings with Jake and Joe*, was published in May, 2014. Mr. Buenger resides in St. Louis with his family.

www.rogerwbuenger.com

Facebook– Roger W. Buenger - Author

Twitter- @RogerWBuenger